T0152591

VERMILION JUSTICE

Visit us at www.boldstrokesbooks.com

By the Author

Crimson Vengeance

Burgundy Betrayal

Scarlet Revenge

Vermilion Justice

VERMILION JUSTICE

by

Sheri Lewis Wohl

2014

VERMILION JUSTICE
© 2014 By Sheri Lewis Wohl. All Rights Reserved.

ISBN 13: 978-1-62639-067-6

This Trade Paperback Original Is Published By
Bold Strokes Books, Inc.
P.O. Box 249
Valley Falls, NY 12185

First Edition: June 2014

THIS IS A WORK OF FICTION. NAMES, CHARACTERS, PLACES, AND INCIDENTS ARE THE PRODUCT OF THE AUTHOR'S IMAGINATION OR ARE USED FICTITIOUSLY. ANY RESEMBLANCE TO ACTUAL PERSONS, LIVING OR DEAD, BUSINESS ESTABLISHMENTS, EVENTS, OR LOCALES IS ENTIRELY COINCIDENTAL.

THIS BOOK, OR PARTS THEREOF, MAY NOT BE REPRODUCED IN ANY FORM WITHOUT PERMISSION.

CREDITS
Editor: Shelley Thrasher
Production Design: Susan Ramundo
Cover Design By Sheri (graphicartist2020@hotmail.com)

Acknowledgments

To Radclyffe, you took a chance on me and invited me to be a part of the incredible BSB family. Thank you, thank you, thank you.

To Shelley Thrasher, you are the best editor in the world, and working with you is a true joy. Thank you, thank you, thank you.

To the entire BSB family, thank you for your help, your advice, and most of all, your friendship.

ex sanguine Draculae

You will come to know the truth,
And the truth will set you free

John 8:32
New Jerusalem Bible

PROLOGUE

Wallachia, Romania
1476

If God would grant her one wish at this moment, she would wish the man she served dead.

Nicoletta bowed deeply, keeping her eyes on the floor as she backed out of the chamber. The fire roared, sending heat flowing into every corner of the room. The food was rich and plentiful. He lolled back against the bountiful pillows, a goblet of wine in his hand. He smiled, though the sight did not reassure her. Instead it sent ice into her entire being.

The servants had washed the blood from his body and brought clean clothing, covering him from head to toe in soft, vibrant fabrics fit for those of royal birth. Still, warmed water and clean cloth could not wash away the stench of death. She could barely keep herself from retching at his newly washed feet. She dare not do such a thing. Not in this chamber. Anyone with even the slightest bit of sense knew better than to bring attention upon themselves.

Moving about the chamber, she tried to keep calm as she helped him into the princely garments and combed his thick black hair. All the while, she hoped her silence would be his wish. *Dear God, let him be pleased.*

Outside, the torches, hundreds of them, burned so brightly it was as if daylight lingered, unwilling to extinguish what spread out for all to see. Except nothing was bright in the flickering firelight. The corpses hung on tall stakes that surrounded the city, a grisly reminder of the price extracted from those who dared to cross the Prince. No one could escape his influence. It hung before their eyes. It was in the air they breathed. It seeped into the very water they drank.

It was in the light that reflected off the solid gold cup perched on the fountain ledge at the center of the square. All drank from it. None dared to steal it, even in the face of their family's starvation. Not a single person had even tried.

So many of her people hailed him as their savior—the prince who'd returned from imprisonment by their sworn enemy to save them. They all said he came to free the land from the invasion of the Ottoman Turks. So many believed it was the will of God. She did not. Nicoletta did not feel free.

Here, far from the horror outside, firelight reflected like stars in the black sky in his eyes. Some might find it alluring. It did not comfort Nicoletta. She could only meet his eyes for a moment before she turned her gaze away. More than the chill it sent into her heart, it was not wise to look the Prince in the eye.

The powerful son of the dragon and hailed as their rightful leader, he was strong, virile, handsome. But something was not right with this man, and it seemed that Nicoletta was the only one who knew it. She felt it in his touch and saw it in his face.

Despite the macabre ring of corpses, their mouths still open in silent screams, outside, the people of the city celebrated. He had returned and set them free once more. No matter that twice before his rule had been snatched away. Each time he returned to reclaim his throne. His name rose in the night sky on the glorified shouts of her friends and neighbors. She wanted to scream at them to open their eyes, to see the truth. It would do no good. They would not believe, for they could not see that which she did.

Servants of the castle bustled about, readying for the celebration of the nobles. Nicoletta wanted to join in and to embrace the feeling of hope. Instead, she stood trembling in the shadows, her eyes downcast and staring at the bowl filled with bloody water, wondering when it would be her blood washed from Vlad Dracula's hands.

CHAPTER ONE

Bucharest, Romania
Present Day

Outside the car window, it was as if she'd been carried back in time, and how she wished that were true. Lura Tappe had boarded a connecting flight in Seattle many hours earlier and stepped off the plane into a country light years away from her home in Washington State. She actually had a passable grasp of the language, courtesy of Sofia, her Romanian nanny oh so many years ago, but even so, Lura couldn't shake the feeling she was as out of place here as a tuxedo at a baseball game. Perhaps exhaustion left her disoriented, or maybe the whole reason she'd come here in the first place made her feel so strange.

It didn't really matter one way or the other. She was here and she'd do what she had to. She owed him that much. At the moment, though, she really wanted to get to her hotel and grab a little rest, impossible as that was probably going to be. Tomorrow promised to be another long and even more stressful day. No rest for the wicked…literally.

By this time tomorrow, she and Alexandru Vizulea would be on the drive to Tirgoviste. She'd meet him for a breakfast she doubted she'd be able to stomach and then leave the city behind. Time didn't allow for jet lag, sightseeing, or any other tourist luxury. Then again, she wasn't exactly a tourist and didn't plan to spend one minute more here than necessary. Though the country was rich in culture and history, she couldn't put her heart into appreciating what Romania had to offer right now. Instead, she simply wanted to do what she came here to do and then run home and hide in her work.

On the phone last week Alexandru's voice had been gentle and his words kind. Bearing bad news was never fair, especially to an innocent, but he'd delivered his news with incredible grace and compassion. She'd looked forward to putting a face to the voice, even if their meeting was the result of tragedy. She'd wanted to thank him in person for all he'd done.

When Alexandru had telephoned and offered to accompany her to Tirgoviste, his generosity had surprised her. He'd already done more than he should have had to. Across the thousands of miles between them, Lura had tried to make him understand. She could make the journey alone; he didn't need to take any more of his time on her account. He'd insisted.

If she was truthful, she'd admit her argument against his accompanying her didn't last long and wasn't very strenuous. Deep down she was more rattled than she'd ever admit out loud. Her attention span was right on par with a severe case of ADHD, and frankly, his offer to go with was her was a huge comfort. It didn't matter that they'd never met. What did matter is that she wouldn't be alone. She had the rest of her life for that.

So far, everything about this trip was tinged with the surreal, like it was happening to someone else, a 3-D movie that had snapped her up only to toss her aside. Even as she stood here now, nothing seemed real. With all her heart, she wanted to believe it was a terrible mistake. Any minute the phone would ring to tell her they'd made a horrible error and offer her a heartfelt apology.

The phone didn't ring. No mistake. No heartfelt apology. This was as real as it got. Tomorrow, she'd take a journey with a stranger in a strange land, and she would pay for her sins with the passage of each mile.

At least she wouldn't have to make the journey alone. Hearing his deep voice and thickly accented English, she somehow believed she'd be safe with Alexandru, that nothing more could hurt her. She needed that right now, desperately. Alexandru was her safe harbor in the eye of a really bad storm. Poor guy, he had no idea about the train wreck he was picking up in the morning. An honorable woman wouldn't burden a stranger. Her accepting his help said a lot about her.

The drive from the airport to the tiny hotel on the outskirts of the city had been interesting, even as exhausted as she was. Seeing the Sulu Palace, the Parliament Palace, and even the Old Court Citadel brought the flavor of Romania into clear view. The old and the new, the taste of Ceausescu's grandiose vision and the rich legacy of a distinctive culture were apparent in those buildings. So much damage had been wreaked upon this ancient country filled with a history rich in tradition and legends. Yet even the wars and strife, the years of struggle and economic dishevelment, couldn't dampen its natural beauty. Under different circumstances, it would be almost magical.

Sofia's stories of her homeland came to life as the driver maneuvered the small dark sedan through the narrow, winding streets. Vic's mother, Sofia always spoke warmly of Romania, her wonderfully accented voice wistful when she recounted stories of her own youth. As a child Lura had imagined this place as Sofia's words, often spoken in her native tongue, lulled her to sleep night after night. But her stories didn't do justice to the old-world charm that passed outside the smudged window of the cab. She wanted to stop, reach out, and touch this place that had brought Sofia into her life.

Her already aching heart pounded even harder as she tried not to fall apart. Suddenly all she could think about was Vic, his tall athletic frame, his slightly too-long black hair, his lively brown eyes. Through Sofia they'd met as children, and when reunited years later while attending college, their shared childhood brought them close. She'd been adrift in those days, unsure of her future, feeling as though something was missing and not knowing what it was. Her understanding parents never pushed her, yet she was never quite able to free herself of that sense of being out of sync. Vic was her anchor during that time, and somewhere along the line she interpreted that as love. When he'd asked her to marry him, it seemed the natural thing to do. What did she know about love?

Medical-school years and even into the early days of their respective practices, Vic always spoke with great wistfulness of the desire to visit his mother's birthplace. In her mind, she could picture him at long last realizing his dream and riding in a cab like this, filled with excitement at the start of his great adventure. Knowing Vic, he'd hit the ground at a dead run. How wrong for her to have to be here now under these unthinkable circumstances.

Tears trickled down her cheeks as she pressed her face against the window and watched the city flash by. To let him come to this place alone had been dishonest on her part. They should have come together.

Walked down these streets, hand in hand, finding the places that Sofia had made vivid in their minds. Together they should have walked the pathways of Vic's mother and ancestors, soaking in the culture and the richness of the old country. There was so much they should have done together as husband and wife, as partners in life, if only she'd tried a little harder.

Now it was too late for anything. Too late for the walks, too late for sharing, and far too late for apologies. The amends she owed him would never come. Lura had made many mistakes in her life, but nothing topped this one.

❖

"Fucking A!"

Riah Preston rounded the corner and walked into the study just in time to see her beautiful partner Adriana James jumping up and down while clapping her hands like a child who'd just discovered some new and wondrous thing. She whirled and caught sight of Riah, a huge smile lighting up her face.

"Did you see it, Riah? Did you see what I did? It was fucking awesome."

Riah felt like a heel. Frankly, she hadn't seen a thing except a gorgeous black woman hopping around in the study. Caught up in her own thoughts, she'd been oblivious to anyone else.

She wanted to tell Adriana she'd seen whatever had her so jacked up. She didn't. If she'd learned one thing in her five hundred years, it was that the truth usually worked best. Saved a lot of problems in the long run, and she had every intention of making a long run with Adriana. "No, babe, I didn't see a thing."

A crestfallen look crossed her face. "You really didn't?"

Riah smiled and touched her cheek. "All I saw when I walked in was you bouncing around like you were about twelve."

"God, don't I wish." Her grin was devilish before she grimaced. "Oh wait, hell no. Twelve sucked. Boobs just starting to sprout, boys eyeing me, and my dad acting like a maximum-security prison warden. No, I'll stay right where I'm at, thank you. Wrinkles and all."

That made her laugh. Like a single wrinkle dared make an appearance on Adriana's beautiful face. Even if it did, it wouldn't matter. Riah loved her, and how old Adriana was or wasn't could never change how she felt.

"So what did I miss?" Riah dropped to an oxblood leather sofa and pulled her feet up. In the large home of the Spiritus Group, this was undoubtedly the most comfortable room. They all seemed to gravitate here.

Located in Spokane, Washington, the monster estate was originally the whim of a local wealthy eccentric. It fell into disarray before it was finished and ultimately abandoned, once the owner lost interest. His bad luck. Her good luck. Riah bought it years later for a song and it became their home base.

Though the Spiritus Group had started informally with Riah and Adriana, friend and fellow vampire, Ivy Hernandez, and her other half, former vampire hunter, Colin Jamison, the *family* had grown. The estate was also home to yet another vampire and former vampire hunter turned lay minister. After a rather bloody battle in Washington D.C., Tory Grey and Naomi Rand had accepted the Spiritus Group's invitation to join them in the never-ending battle against evil. The large estate boasted plenty of room for the now-three vampires and three humans who lived here full time.

On occasion, they were also joined by witch Kara Lynch, who they'd saved from a rogue werewolf intent on destroying her so she would fail to lift the curse from his family, and her wife, shape-shifter Camille "Cam" Black Wolf. All in all it was a pretty awesome group of folks, so far removed from the solitary existence Riah had embraced for centuries that it still boggled her mind. In a good way, that is. She wouldn't trade this life for anything.

Even given all that, the biggest surprise of all had been the appearance of Adriana in her world. Riah had completely given up on any hope for love. Believed it had died five hundred years ago on that gloomy and stormy night when her life forever changed. Then Adriana made her see the truth and the beauty in opening her heart. She'd never been happier.

Adriana's face lit up once again. "Okay, so remember when I went home to New Haven and met my aunt from Tigeran and we stopped a wizard from opening a doorway between this world and Tigeran and…"

Riah's smile grew as she listened. Adriana was usually quite articulate, but tonight her words tumbled out in an enthusiastic rush. Riah remembered all too well Adriana's trip to her childhood home.

At the time, she'd been the only one of the Spiritus Group who didn't possess any special skills or powers. Ivy and Riah were vampires who brought all sorts of preternatural skills to the table. Colin was a vampire hunter without equal. Trained since a teenager, he'd been a threat to all who called the night home. At least until he'd met Ivy and Riah. Now, he was a threat to any and all, human or preternatural, who chose evil to guide their existence.

After Adriana came home from New Haven, the game had changed. It turned out that her black beauty wasn't even of this world but from a parallel dimension. Brought here by her magical parents to keep her safe, she was the sorceress destined to save both this world and Tigeran.

She did, of course, and rather than return to the land of her birth after she'd made sure they were all free from harm, she came back to Riah. Since her return, she was even more focused than ever, and that was saying a lot. Her main mission appeared to include discovering the full width and breadth of her powers. It seemed that every day she encountered something new and exciting in her ever-expanding range of magic. The delight it gave Adriana warmed Riah's heart.

"I remember," Riah said. She had never seen Adriana quite this wound up. Something interesting must have happened.

"Yeah, well, if you remember, in the cemetery that night I had to use the dagger with the precious stones to open the veil between here and Tigeran. A mad skill, if I do say so." Her words were a breathless rush of pure energy.

A mad skill was an understatement. Riah had been on the other side of the country on that horrible night, although she'd been able to sense the danger that confronted the woman she loved with all her heart. Adriana had been under incredible pressure and yet, even in the face of almost certain death, managed to save herself and all of them as well. "Right, and your aunt took the dagger back to Tigeran."

"Why, yes, she did, and I figured that was the end of that. Not so, my pretty. Now, with these—" she waved her hands in the air and wiggled her fingers, "I just managed to open a righteous doorway."

"To Tigeran?" If she wasn't impressed enough before, Riah certainly was now. She loved watching Adriana progressively embrace her potential and was even more awed by the sheer power packed into one tiny body. Why she'd resisted the love that grew between them for such a long time was a mystery to her these days. Usually she was a little brighter than that.

Adriana shook her head. "No, not the motherland. Different. More like I peeled away layers and opened up a window to the past. I was here but it wasn't the same, if you catch my drift. I wish I could describe it better because it was incredible. Pretty sweet."

"Time travel?" A tingle flickered up Riah's spine. The idea was both intriguing and alluring. Through the years she'd heard whispers that some had the ability to walk between worlds, to open portals or wormholes and move from time to time. Until now, she hadn't given the rumors much credence. Now she wondered if she should have listened a little closer to those whispers. What if she could go back… say five hundred years before a certain Rodolphe showed up in her life? How great would that be?

Then again, if that happened, she'd lose Adriana and the chance to know the kind of love that made everything worthwhile. Going back would change everything, bad and good. As much as she hated Rodolphe, she guessed she'd stay right here. The advantages weren't worth the risk.

Adriana shook her head. "No, not like that. It didn't feel like time travel, more like opening a door that was already here, and all it took was a little presto-chango magic for me to see it. Whatever it was, let me just say it was righteous." Waving her hands out in a wide arc, she said, "If I can do that, who knows what else I can make happen. Yeah, I rock."

Riah took one of Adriana's hands and pulled her down to the sofa. She captured her face between her palms and kissed her. She loved the feel of her lips against hers, the soft, sweet touch. If she lived a thousand years, she'd never tire of her. "Yes, you most certainly rock and are the most amazing woman I've ever known."

Adriana's smile was slow and sexy. She winked. "You just say that 'cause you're hot for my body."

Those chocolate eyes staring into hers made her breath quicken and pulse race. "I say it because it's true. On the other hand, no doubt about it, I'm absolutely hot for your body." And she proceeded to show her exactly how hot.

❖

The cab driver pulled up in front of a three-story white hotel with tidy red shutters dusted with the finest trace of snow. The paint was just beginning to peel here and there, the front steps chipped at the edges. Not exactly the Davenport Hotel back home with its gold-covered entrance and gleaming front façade. Or the gorgeous luxury hotel with its baroque style in downtown Bucharest. Charming nonetheless. She'd like to care but didn't. It was a place to sleep, that's all.

As far as she'd been concerned, she could have slept in the airport. Alexandru wouldn't hear of it. He'd made the reservation, telling her it was a quiet place where she'd enjoy a relaxing and comfortable evening. He'd told her it embodied the true flavor of Romania, to make her stay memorable, and she'd simply gone along.

It was difficult to worry about details like where to stay. One place was as good as any. She had to hand it to Alexandru, though. He certainly knew his city. So far, it was definitely living up to his recommendation. Hopefully the relaxing and comfortable part held up too.

At the moment, a bed—any bed—would be welcome, even if she seriously doubted sleep was an option. Away from the hustle and bustle of the heart of the city, this quaint hotel might turn out to be a nice place to rest before continuing her difficult journey. Alexandru had sensed her real needs from across the Atlantic, even if she'd been oblivious to them. Quite the guy, and she hadn't even met him yet.

Maybe she would sleep and maybe she wouldn't. It was time to put one foot in front of the other. The sooner she moved forward, the sooner she could go home. She paid the driver and got out of the cab, holding the single suitcase she'd traveled halfway around the world with.

The woman who greeted Lura as she stepped up to the check-in counter was about forty, with dark hair cut short and curled around her friendly face. The woman gave her a smile that broadened as Lura dusted off her Romanian and gave it a go. Once again she said a silent prayer of thanks for her parents' emphasis on early language education. The words and phrases came back to her with surprising ease.

A foreign diplomat, Father had always insisted she have at least a conversational grasp of the language in whatever country her family happened to be stationed in. Her mother, a first-generation Mexican American, was fluent in her immigrant parents' native Spanish. Lura grew up speaking it as easily as she did English. Still did.

The choice of Sofia as her nanny was part of their grand plan to expose their only child to other languages as a small child. They weren't content with gifting Lura with her father's English and her mother's Spanish. Their aim for their only child was so much higher.

Their linguistic gift had served her well through the years, though frankly, she'd never really expected to use Sofia's Romanian. Though it came back to her quickly now, she didn't possess a skill with the language anywhere close to Vic's fluency. Still, it was enough to make her exchange with the desk clerk go very well, and she and the clerk seemingly became instant friends. The little things did make her grateful.

The room the clerk, Rita, showed her was small and clean, though it didn't have its own bathroom. Instead, it shared one with the guest room next door. Alexandru had neglected to mention that part of the hotel's charm when he sang its praises. She wasn't accustomed to sharing those details of her life and didn't much care for the thought now.

Not to worry, Rita told her before she had a chance to protest. The other room wasn't rented so the bathroom was essentially all hers. She hoped the relief she was feeling at that news didn't register like a neon sign on her face. Company was about the last thing she wanted at the moment, particularly when it concerned things like a shower.

She thanked Rita, then closed and locked the door before leaning back against its solid wood surface. For a long time she simply stood there while she concentrated on breathing in and out. No matter how hard she tried to keep it together, she was anything but together. She always advised her patients to take things one step at a time, and that's exactly what she should do now. If not…well, she didn't really want to think about that.

Finally, she pushed away from the door, picked up her suitcase, and tossed it onto the bed. While she still had enough energy to at least change her clothes, getting comfortable held a lot of appeal. Sleep was a great plan, even if she didn't honestly think it would happen. Since Alexandru's first call, she hadn't been able to sleep, and it showed bigtime. She had no illusions about her appearance; she looked like crap.

Since the bathroom was all hers, she might as well make the most of her solitary status. A warm bath in the old claw-footed tub would go a long way toward easing the tension in her body. Whether it would have the power to slow the racing of her mind, she didn't know. Sliding into the deep tub filled with warm water, she closed her eyes and let the tension flow away.

When she crawled out half an hour later, she did feel a little better. She toweled off and slipped into a T-shirt and sweats.

Back in her room, she brushed the long blond hair she should have cut years ago and stared at her reflection in the mirror. At least her shoulders weren't knotted up any more, but even the relaxation of the warm bath hadn't done a thing for her appearance.

Lord knows she hadn't been sleeping lately, but to say she looked terrible was a sad understatement. Though she was never a slave to tanning, at the moment the color of her skin appeared more like she was a slave to darkness. Given where she was, it was almost funny. If her face got any whiter, the folks around here might begin to believe she was a victim of Dracula. Or, rather, Vlad the Impaler, as they preferred to call him in this part of the world. Yes, she was most definitely in full-on Goth.

The dusky circles under her eyes were a good touch too. Looked an awful lot like somebody had punched her in both eyes. What a sight, and not in a good way. Tossing the brush to the dresser, she walked out to the small balcony for a little fresh air. The mirror was not her friend, and she certainly didn't need the reminder of the horrible state of her life.

Though the rail around the balcony was coated with a fine dusting of rust, she grabbed it with both hands and leaned out. The chilly winter air was crisp and clear, the sky just beginning to take on the scarlet hues of sunset. All around, the sounds of the city created a symphony of vibrant life. People were going about their daily routines of life and love while she stood watching, wrapped up in her own personal crisis. It was a dichotomy only she could appreciate.

Stepping away from the rail, Lura looked down at her palms, smudged deep orange from the rust. The flecks of color contrasted sharply with her pasty white skin. She should go in and wash it away, yet she didn't. All of a sudden, her legs refused to move. Instead, she tried to banish the orange stains: brushing, rubbing…harder, harder, harder. The rust refused to be cleared away from the soft skin.

Damn the stupid rail. A scream rose in her throat before dying away without passing her lips. As quick as the fury came, it passed.

What replaced it was worse. Her hands dropped to her sides and her shoulders slumped. Nothing was right about this trip. Or her.

She was not going to cry. Period. If she gave in to the tide of emotion lurking too close, it was certain to swallow her whole. All the way from the airport to the hotel, she'd managed to hold herself together in the cab. She could do it a little longer. Right?

Wrong. This time, being strong wasn't going to cut it. Everything welled up inside, a storm that had been building since long before the terrible phone call. The dam cracked, and when it did, the flood came.

Alone on the tiny balcony, she cried, tears streaming down her face as if mirroring the rain clouds gathering to the east. Nightfall pushed out what remained of the light, while in the distance, thunder roared, muffling the sounds of her sorrow…her guilt.

Lura dropped to her knees, stained hands pounding the balcony floor. The sobs she'd held back since learning of Vic's terrible death racked her tired body. The pain was so intense, she wondered vaguely if it would tear her in half. Tonight she just didn't care. If she could die right here, right now, it would only be right. She was the one who deserved to be dead. Her—not brilliant, caring Vic.

She'd come here knowing all along this would be a difficult trip. Only now did she realize how difficult. Vic had come to this country full of high hopes and the best of intentions. Not only were his skills as a doctor needed in a way that couldn't be matched in the United States, but the chance to spend six months in the country of his mother's birth was an opportunity too good to pass up.

He'd asked her to come, and she'd told him her caseload was too heavy to leave. He'd wanted to share his excitement with her, to have her be a part of a great and noble adventure. Instead, she'd sent him alone and with nothing but her shallow blessing. She'd sent him alone because she was too much a coward to tell him the truth.

And now here she was anyway. They would make the journey together after all. Except, rather than holding his hand, she'd be carrying him back in an urn.

Overhead, rain burst from the heavy blue-black clouds. Raindrops hit her face and shoulders, splattering the balcony like machine-gun fire. It was as if it was trying to force her inside, to push her away and make her go back where she came from. The rain pounded, telling her it didn't want her here, that she didn't belong in this place.

Despite the barrage, she didn't go in. She wanted to let the rain punish her, beat her flesh raw, anything that would make the pain in her heart go away. The physical pain was so much better than the emotional burden that nearly broke her shoulders.

God, it was worse than pain. Pure old-fashioned and very heavy guilt ate at her spirit. She'd sent her husband to this place with a soulless kiss and a false smile. Sent him away with relief because she'd known it would give her six months to try to figure out how to leave him. After five years of marriage, she longed for release, to be free of a man who was gentle, kind, and talented. He was everything most women wanted in a man, yet she wanted to be free of him. And why? Because she could no longer pretend. He deserved a woman who could love him for what he was: a man.

She wanted a woman.

He was a knight and she longed for a maiden.

He was a saint.

And she was a bitch.

The truth made her sick inside. Her heart, mind, and soul ached with the knowledge that she'd sent him here with everything except good intentions. What kind of woman did something like that? God, he'd deserved so much better.

The phone call that came into her office three days ago had changed her world in a way she never anticipated. Freedom was now hers. It came not with a signature at the bottom of a divorce decree but one at the bottom of a death certificate.

Tomorrow she would meet a kind stranger, drive some eighty kilometers to Tirgoviste to retrieve her husband's remains, and then take them back to Washington. For all he knew, she was a grieving widow. Her lie was safe.

Picking herself up, Lura headed for the bathroom. After she toweled herself dry again, she lay down on the bed. If she got even a minute's worth of sleep, she'd be lucky. With the balcony door open a crack, the cold night air wafted across her skin, and as Lura watched the shadows dance on the ceiling, she wished more than anything to turn back the clock.

CHAPTER TWO

Lura was wrong. She'd actually managed to sleep, and quite well, all things considered. Maybe it was the fresh Romanian air, or maybe it was just because she was exhausted. Whatever it was, the rest helped. By the time she was dressed, had her hair braided and her suitcase repacked, it was nearly nine. Alexandru was due to pick her up at half past the hour, and she didn't want to offend him by being late, particularly considering how gracious he was being to a complete stranger.

The sun was shining through the balcony doors, and she walked outside to take one last look before heading downstairs. The winter sunshine warmed her face, the air crisp and clean after last night's rain. Though it was winter here, so far, she hadn't seen any of the snow she'd fully expected.

If time wasn't a factor, she could easily sit here in the sunshine all day, the comfort of it making her feel more like she was home than across the world. The mountains in the distance rose high and intriguing, seeming to beckon her away from the comfort of the balcony. The peaks were snow-capped, reminding her of the view from her own front-room windows.

No time to dawdle. She had to take her bag and get to the lobby. A long trip lay ahead, and picking up Vic's ashes was the icing on a not-so-pretty cake.

Sighing, she turned around and left the sun behind her, pulling her rolling suitcase into the hallway. The door latched with a soft click that echoed in her ears. The sounds were trying to tell her something important, if only she would listen. She didn't want to, just as she didn't want to hear the whispers that swirled around her, choosing instead to believe it was just her over-tired, over-active imagination.

Besides, Alexandru was undoubtedly downstairs waiting for her. Important and real business was down the road. It was time to be attentive. That thought gave her a better grasp on the emotions that still wanted to bubble up and engulf her. She didn't want to go through that again. She was really good at helping others heal, but this physician wasn't all that good at healing herself.

Downstairs, a man stood gazing outside, his hands in his pockets. In black slacks and a black jacket, he seemed unaware of her as she came down the stairs. As she reached the bottom, he turned.

The picture she'd conjured up in her mind after talking to Alexandru certainly didn't do the man justice. In fact, he'd be downright insulted if he'd been able to read her mind. She'd pictured him as a middle-aged, stocky man of medium height with mousy brown hair and soft eyes. Dead wrong on all counts.

Smiling and watching her every movement, Alexandru Vizulea was about six feet tall with hair as black as coal and intense blue eyes the color of the ocean off the shores of Hawaii. He was slender, though not skinny, with a handshake that hinted at real power, the touch of his fingers as they wrapped around hers sending sparks up her arm. She almost jumped back at the unexpected sensation.

"Dr. Tappe," he said softly, still holding her hand. "So very good to meet you."

His English was flawless, his accent sending the words off his tongue with a roll. His eyes never left hers, and even if she'd wanted to, she was pretty sure she wouldn't have been able to pull her gaze away. *Intense* was the word that rolled through her mind.

"The pleasure is all mine," she answered in her best Romanian. Not bad, all things considered.

His already warm smile grew even warmer. "Splendid," he murmured as he released her hand and reached over to take the handle of her small rolling suitcase. "You must tell me how you learned to speak our language so well."

She was almost sad when he released her hand, the warm connection broken in an instant. Something about his touch was comforting, and irrational as that was, she liked it. "I'd be delighted. I don't know how to thank you," she said. Cutting her gaze to the suitcase, she told him, "You don't have to take my case. I can do that."

He just smiled and kept his hold on the handle. "Don't even give it a thought. Helping you is the least I can do for your kind husband. He did so much during his time here. He helped many people, many children."

Of course he did. Vic was—had been—drawn to children in need. It was his way, and though he never said so to her, she'd known in her heart the fact they never had a child together was a sadness he carried always. Without a child of his own, he turned to those he could help. "I can't tell you how much I appreciate what you're doing for me and for Vic."

"He is a fallen warrior and you are his widow. It is only right."

Not only did his choice of words take her off guard, but so did the realization that it was the first time she'd actually heard herself referred to as a widow. Her stomach knotted at the sound of the word, and not just because she'd lost Vic. Her stomach did a flip, and it took every bit of self-control she possessed not to throw up. If Alexandru had a clue what a rotten person she was, he'd probably make her walk to Tirgoviste and back.

"Well," she said as she looked away from Alexandru's intense gaze. "I guess we might as well get on the road. I'll just pay my bill, and then we can be on our way."

"It is taken care of."

She stopped, turning to look at him, her eyes narrowed. "Pardon me?" How, and more important, why would her bill be paid? Money wasn't something she had to worry about. Her soul, yes. Her checkbook, no.

"It is taken care of." His face was serious, his voice calm as if he paid the bills of strange women every day.

Lura wanted to argue with him, to explain she was more than capable of paying her own hotel bills, but something in his eyes and his voice stopped the words from passing her lips. Instead, she asked simply, "Why?"

He inclined his head slightly. "It is my honor to do such a thing." This was a man who took care of things according to his own personal code. Any argument on her part would be futile. He had his reasons, she was certain of that, but she would undoubtedly never know what they were.

She closed her eyes for a moment, took a breath, and said, "Thank you."

He nodded and waved one arm in the direction of the door. She walked outside and waited. She wasn't sure which one of the small cars parked along both sides of the road was his. It turned out to be a compact, black sedan of a make she wasn't familiar with. Inside it smelled of tobacco and leather, the telltale residue of a recent cigarette impossible to miss. She must have wrinkled her nose because, as Alexandru slid behind the wheel, he shot a glance her way and began to apologize.

"I'm very sorry. A bad habit I've picked up in recent times, I'm afraid. I say every day I will stop and every day I do not."

"Please." She laid a hand on his arm. "I'm the guest here and this is your car. You don't have to apologize for offending me. I don't want to impose on you any more than I already have. Besides we have about fifty miles together—I mean eighty kilometers—to keep each other company. I really don't want to make you uncomfortable in your own car."

He was peering out the driver's side window, appearing to assess the traffic with a practiced ease. "You, Lura Tappe, could never make me uncomfortable."

He didn't know her very well then. "You obviously haven't talked to many of my friends and relatives."

"I believe you do not give yourself enough credit."

"I made Vic uncomfortable," she whispered, but not quietly enough to escape his hearing. Alexandru cut a sideways glance at her, his intelligent eyes appraising.

Lura turned to stare out the side window more to escape his scrutiny than to appreciate the passing landscape. As they cruised out of the city on a stretch of long black asphalt that seemed to disappear into the steep mountains beyond, Lura watched in silence. Trees and bushes, some bare, some still retaining their foliage, were lovely, and any other time they would have been completely entranced her with their natural beauty. Today the view only made her sad. It was so beautiful, and she was such an ugly person. Self-pity was the name of her game at the moment. She was smart enough to realize it didn't help a damn thing, and yet she couldn't seem to shake it. Didn't really want to.

Alexandru reached a hand across the seats and took hold of hers. "I cannot believe that. He spoke of you like a princess."

Tears trickled down her cheeks despite her strongest self-talk to keep them in check. "I believe it, and unfortunately, that was part of our problem. Vic never really got me. He only saw what he wanted to see, and that wasn't even close to the real me. He saw a princess where a bitch lived."

Alexandru actually chuckled. "Not a bitch, I think."

"Then, what would you call a woman who sends her husband off to a country a zillion miles away just because it would give her chance to figure out how to dump him? If that's not a class-A bitch, I don't what is."

There, she'd finally said it out loud. The black, ugly truth. Now Alexandru would have no choice but to see her for the asshole she really was. He'd hear her words and know they were true—and he'd hate her just like any decent person should.

His laughter was a surprise that had her turning in the seat to stare at him. "I've waited such a long time for you," he said when his chuckles subsided. "Vic's words didn't do you justice. You are everything he described and more."

Lura narrowed her eyes and studied this very strange man. Waited for her? What in the world did that mean? "What?"

"Believe it, Lura. It's all true. I've been looking for you for a very long time, and trust me when I tell you you're not a bitch, even if you think you are. I've met more than a few in my life, and you are not one of them."

She wanted to believe him, to think that deep down beneath the lies and the deception, something good still survived. Doubts continued to weigh far heavier on her heart than hope, and she wasn't sure that would ever change. Nor did she really want to dwell on it at the moment. She just wanted to pick up Vic's ashes and go home. There she could bury herself in work so she wouldn't have time to dwell on unhappy, foul thoughts about herself.

Alexandru seemed to sense her mood. "There will be time enough for explanations, Lura, and I promise it will all make sense. For now, why don't you relax and try to rest?"

"Alexandru, seriously, you're not making a bit of sense. You don't even know me, let alone have been waiting for me." Even as she said the words, she thought about that first touch. What should have been a simple handshake…and wasn't. Why was that?

The intrigue was too much for her tired mind and heavy heart. She was on overload and couldn't deal with the effort it would take to try to figure any of this out. Despite the little bit of sleep she'd managed to pull off last night, she was tired. To just close her eyes and drift away into nothingness was a lure she couldn't resist.

Folding her sweater to use as a pillow, Lura leaned back and closed her eyes. Alexandru patted her hand again and she found the gesture comforting. She didn't even flinch this time, and within minutes the motion of the car lulled her into a deep, strange sleep.

❖

"Motherfucker!"

Riah's eyebrows shot up at the sound of Adriana's curse. Not so much because it was unusual to hear Adriana curse. No, it had more to do with the vehemence. It didn't require the services of a rocket scientist to figure out things weren't going well downstairs. At the sound of breaking glass, Riah quickened her step.

Adriana was sitting at the counter in her well-equipped lab with her head in her hands and shattered glass speckled with dried blood fanned out at her feet. Even from this distance, Riah could see her shoulders shaking and hear the sound of her sobs. Now that was unusual. Perpetual optimism was Adriana's middle name, and to see her hurting struck at Riah's heart.

She wasted no time standing in the doorway and closed the gap between them before putting her arms around Adriana. She pressed a kiss to her head and whispered, "What is it, love?"

"I can't fucking find it," Adriana said between sobs. "I've been trying for so long, and every time I think I've got it again, it all goes to shit. Why can't I get it? I'm so stupid."

She didn't need to ask what *it* was. The Cure. As in the discovery of what would finally release Riah from the darkness that had been her world for over five centuries. Adriana had discovered it, only to have it blown sky-high in an explosion orchestrated by Riah's vindictive first love. Ever since that awful night Adriana had been working to find it again.

So far, she'd failed.

Riah took Adriana's face between her hands and stared into her gorgeous though watery eyes. "You are not and never have been stupid. You'll find it again, love. You will. We all have faith in you, so you can't even blame it on me being blinded by love. You're brilliant and talented."

Adriana let out a long sigh. "How can I have done it once and now fail so miserably over and over? I'm letting you down, letting Ivy and Tory down. It shouldn't be this hard to make it happen again."

"No, you're not letting me or anyone else down. Not once since the first moment we met have you ever disappointed me. Quite the opposite in fact."

Adriana's eyes took on the sparkle that always made Riah's heart skip a beat. "You're sweet but so full of shit."

Riah kissed her and smiled, so happy to hear the familiar joking banter come back into Adriana's words. "I'm hurt." She put a hand to her heart and frowned.

"Yeah, yeah, yeah. Well, get over it, sister. If you're gonna be my bitch, you gotta toughen up."

Riah laughed and kissed Adriana again. "Have I told you lately how much I love you?"

"Have I told you how much I love the way you can always make me feel better? You're a one-of-a-kind vamp, Riah, and I love every immortal inch of you."

Riah stroked her cheek and studied her beautiful familiar face. Would Adriana ever know how she'd saved her? How her love and the hope she gave Riah made her want to live? Before Adriana, her life had been little more than mere existence, year after year of nothing but putting one foot in front of the other. It was this beautiful woman filled to the brim with a spirit that refused to be dampened who made her believe her own life had meaning.

"We're in this together, A. Don't ever forget that."

Adriana laid her head on Riah's shoulder and slid an arm around her waist. "Not in a million years."

CHAPTER THREE

His hair was as black as the night, the curls falling across broad shoulders and down his back from underneath a velvet cap ringed with perfect round pearls. Though she wasn't close enough to see the color of his eyes, his gaze was intense and probing, never leaving the face of the man who kneeled before him dressed in long robes of embroidered satin, a beautiful white turban wound around his head. Light flickered from the torches high on the walls, and in the massive fireplace, a fire roared.

She could only catch a word here and there, something about respect and homage. As the dark man spoke, the kneeling man began to shake as he dropped his head so low, his face appeared to touch the stone floor. She shrank back farther into the shadows of the tapestry hanging from the castle wall as fright sent a shiver sliding down her back. In the air a combination of body odor, cooked meat, and fear sent up a smell so strong that she gagged. She pressed a hand hard against her lips, tasting the blood as her teeth cut into tender flesh.

The beating of her heart was so hard and fast it seemed impossible that no one would hear it. Yet no one looked her way or seemed aware of her presence as she trembled in the shadows, wanting to run far away and yet unable to pull her gaze from the face of the powerful man. Sweat trickled down between her breasts, a damp trail that made the thick velvet stick to her body.

When he nodded slightly, seven soldiers came forward to encircle the man in the turban. Four leaned down to grab him, one at each hand and each foot. Together they stood, pulling on the man's limbs until he was spread-eagle and suspended a good three feet above the stone floor. The other three soldiers marched forward, a long pointed spike held parallel in their hands, an identical frown on each face. They positioned the point of the spike directly between the man's outstretched legs while they continued to hold firmly to the shaft. Only when the black-haired man nodded did they move. As one, the three rushed forward until the point of the spike disappeared into tender flesh. Inhuman screams filled the cavernous hall. She didn't know if they were the impaled man's...

Or hers.

Lura wasn't aware of falling asleep, but her scream brought her snapping upright. She gasped for breath—sick, dizzy, and very lost. After a moment, she realized the car was no longer moving and, as she blinked to clear the lingering bloody vision, discovered she was also alone.

The sun was still up, though shadows wrapped around the car were opaque and menacing. She sat up a little straighter and looked around. Where was Alexandru, and where on earth were they? She might be disoriented, but she was also pretty damn sure they weren't in Tirgoviste. By her calculation, they should have reached it by now. Morning was gone and the afternoon fading fast. Before too long the sun would begin to dip behind the mountains, trading the rays of sunshine for cloud-covered gloom. No, they should be there by now.

Glancing down at her hands, she was distressed to see them shaking. Great, that's all she needed. Wimpy old Lura all shook up by a nightmare.

Still, she could call herself all sorts of names and it wouldn't change the fact the fact that the dream, or whatever it was, had unsettled her at a very primal level. The stench of the room continued to burn in her nostrils, while the screams of the turbaned man echoed in her ears as if the scene had really happened instead of being simple REM-stage brain activity. She closed her eyes and pressed her hands to her ears, hoping they would shut out the inhuman screams. They didn't. After a moment she let her hands drop away and opened her eyes. Outside the car the shadows seemed to have deepened in the few seconds her eyes had been closed. This was turning into one long trip.

Shaking hands and all, she had to find out what the heck Alexandru was up to and where he'd brought her. Pushing the car door open, she dropped her feet to the ground and gulped in fresh air. The terra firma beneath her soles helped. Slowly, awareness started to push away the cobwebs of the nightmare. Really, it was a dream—just a dream like all the others. She'd had them as long as she could remember, probably always would. Didn't mean anything and was nothing to be afraid of. A simple case of an always active brain, awake or asleep.

Looking around, she wondered again where they were. Certainly Alexandru had to be close by. He wouldn't leave her alone in this strange place. Then again, how would she know? She didn't know the man except for a couple of telephone conversations and a few minutes in the car before she nodded off to sleep. So far all Lura had were two impressions of the man: he was quite good-looking and he was odd. Not much to go on, especially considering she was God knows where…alone.

❖

When Riah came into the library, Ivy was on the phone speaking rapid-fire Spanish and waving her arms as if whoever was on the other end of the line could see her. If not for the tension radiating from both Ivy's words and her body, the sight would have made Riah smile.

She looked over at Colin and raised an eyebrow. "Trouble?"

He shrugged. "All I've been able to catch so far is something about a cousin, a trip, and somebody being dead."

She chided him. "All this time with the woman and that's the best you can do with your Spanish? I'd have thought you'd be fluent by now."

He shrugged again. "My fluency has an expiration point, and it all hinges on pace. I don't do too bad until she gets to talking to family, and then she's like a speeding freight train. I'm lucky I got what I did. She talks so fast I don't know how anyone understands her."

Ivy seemed to have caught that last bit, even as she appeared to be in heavy conversation with the person on the phone. She cocked her head, smiled at Colin, and winked. Then she returned her full concentration to the caller and the words began to fly once more.

"See what I mean," he said as he ran a hand across Ivy's glossy black hair. "She talks like a machine gun. Pretty good-looking machine gun though."

Riah laughed, then turned away and walked to the windows. A bit of sunlight lingered outside, although here in the library the light was comfortably buffered for those who shied away from the day. Seeing the light always made her feel a little like she was still human. The lie soothed her.

When Ivy put the phone down at last, Riah turned from the window. Ivy's usually calm expression was tight. Again Riah proffered the question, "Trouble?"

Ivy shook her head slightly, a not-quite frown on her lips. "I don't think so, but the jury's still out."

Tension rolled off Ivy's body, and though her words were calm, she wasn't. Riah had known her long enough to see through the façade. "Something we can help with?"

This time she nodded. "Could be. My cousin, Lura, flew to Romania a couple of days ago to pick up her husband's ashes. He was killed in some kind of freak accident over there while doing some doctor-type volunteer work. Cool guy who had no clue his wife liked women."

Riah raised an eyebrow. "A marriage for appearances?"

Ivy shook her head. "No, I don't think so. I doubt Lura realizes she's a lesbian. Me, I've known for a long time, but what could I do until she made peace with it herself? I wasn't all that surprised when Vic went to Romania without her. What did surprise me was his death. A real shame. I really liked the guy. Everybody did. He was just one of those people you're drawn to. Lura headed over to bring his ashes back home."

So far Riah hadn't heard anything that explained Ivy's discontent. "The problem?"

"Good question, and frankly, I'm not quite sure there is a problem. That was my aunt Penelope on the phone, my mother's sister. Anyway, she hasn't heard from Lura since her plane landed, and she's pretty worried. It's not like my cousin to drop off the face of the earth."

"Should your aunt be worried?"

Ivy waggled her head from side to side. "I don't think so...I don't know."

"But what?" Riah could see a flicker of something akin to alarm in Ivy's troubled expression.

"I have a not-so-good feeling something isn't right. Lura's a doctor like her husband, and plenty capable of taking care of herself."

"I still hear a *but* in there."

"But it makes me a little nervous, her not calling and all. I know things were messed up between her and Vic. Still, it's not like her to make her parents worry. She's pretty tight with my aunt and uncle. Lura was always uber-responsible. The shock of Vic's death surely has her rattled, yet I have to believe she'd talk to her mom."

Riah didn't often see Ivy nervous about anything, especially since becoming a vampire. She was confident, powerful, and usually right. Riah could always count on Ivy in any situation, regardless of how tense or dangerous. Seeing her friend's obvious unease made a bad feeling start to creep up her spine as well, and she'd never even met Ivy's cousin.

❖

Under any other circumstances Lura would be pissed off. Strangely, right now she wasn't. Curious, yes. Uneasy, yes. Angry, No. Alexandru was different, but even so there was something about him she inherently trusted. She couldn't explain it; it was just gut instinct.

One of her favorite professors in medical school always insisted a really good psychiatrist used not only her brains and education, but her gut instinct as well. Hers was telling her now that Alexandru hadn't left her. He was close by and he was waiting for her.

As the sun edged its way across the clear blue sky, pushing shadows out longer and longer, Alexandru came over the top of a hill a few hundred yards from the car. In glow of the sun, he was a proud figure walking with the grace of a nobleman. It was like something she'd seen in a movie.

Who was he really? Where did he come from? How did he come to be her knight in this time of pain and loss? So many questions and not one single answer.

"Hello, lovely one," he said as he stopped in front of her. "Feeling better?"

Lovely one? What exactly did he mean by that? He didn't even know her, so what was with the term of endearment? Or maybe he didn't mean anything at all by it and she was overthinking everything because…well, because she was a train wreck and overly sensitive. Truth be told, she was bone weary and out of sorts. A perfect combination for taking anything and everything out of context.

Time to get over it—to get over herself. He probably meant nothing more by his kind words than a gentle greeting for a grieving woman. He was trying to make her feel better, and she was being a bitch about it. Tired or not, she couldn't excuse her behavior. Her mama had taught her better.

She pushed herself up and out of the car, giving him a weak smile. "Yes, thank you."

His smile was gentle, friendly. If he sensed her earlier grumpiness, he gave no indication. "Good."

She raised an eyebrow and glanced around. "Ah, Alexandru, where exactly are we?" She might not know her way around this country, but she was pretty sure they weren't on the road to Tirgoviste anymore.

He took her arm and walked toward the hill he'd just descended from. "I hope you do not mind, but we've taken a little detour. We are at the town of Snagov."

A little detour? She honestly didn't have the time or the desire to go anywhere except exactly where she needed to. It wasn't like she was on a sightseeing tour. Far from it, and he had to know that. "Snagov?"

His smile was slight as he gazed out, his eyes trained on something she couldn't see. "Yes, Snagov. Isn't it beautiful? Come, we'll take a little boat ride."

The last thing she wanted to do today was hop in a boat for a pleasure cruise. Her frustration level started to climb once more. She was about to tell him they had to get back on the road when she caught sight of the boat he was heading for. It wasn't exactly the type of boat made for lake cruising. It was a rowboat.

"Ah, Alexandru, a rowboat?"

Undeterred by the reluctance ringing loud and clear in her voice, he smiled and his face lit up, making him even more handsome. Too bad she wasn't into men. "We have to walk the grounds of Snagov Island. It is a beauty you won't soon forget."

"Do we really have time?" She was trying to be diplomatic and polite, though it took effort.

"Do not worry." He squeezed her hand as he helped her into the boat. "All will be as it should be."

Well, that didn't exactly answer her question. A protest was poised on her lips and then died. Why not just take a little detour? It wasn't like Vic was going anywhere. Besides, if she knew Vic, he'd been here too, and taking a bit of time to see the island could make her feel as though she was walking with him. A little less guilt, maybe. Or not.

As Alexandru rowed, the boat swayed from side to side, and a cool breeze blew through her hair. The shores of the island grew closer with each slap of the oar through the frigid water. She wrapped her arms around her body and stared ahead. There in the distance, the Snagov Monastery rose tall and beautiful. The pale walls almost glowed in the light of the fading day as the many steps that led to the arched doorways rested deep in shadows. Even from this far away, the building was impressive.

Despite her weariness, curiosity about the church tickled her mind. Perhaps a quick prayer might help ease her aching heart. Not that she was overly religious. Still, it couldn't hurt. If they hurried, it wouldn't cost them too much time, and they'd be back on the road fairly quickly.

Alexandru brought the boat up alongside a long wooden dock. It bumped the side and he jumped out, tying it securely before holding out a hand to her.

At the end of the dock, she stepped out onto the grassy shore, looked around, and asked, "What's so special about this place?" It was scenic, she'd give it that. Special? She didn't see it.

His gaze never strayed from the chapel. "Many things make this island special. Perhaps the most important detail, at least to the people of Snagov, is that we're standing in front of the reputed burial place of Vlad Dracula, son of the dragon."

All right, she got that one of the major tourist draws to this country was not just the legend of Dracula created by Bram Stoker, but also the mysterious prince who was the real man behind the fictional creation. Under different circumstances, the historical significance would interest her. But these weren't normal circumstances by anyone's definition, and she wasn't an American tourist looking for vampire chills and thrills. No, she needed two things, and two things only: to get Vic and to get home.

"The vampire," she stated, less than enthusiastically. Somehow it had seemed more interesting before Alexandru had thrown in a vampire legend. The lovely historic monastery was unique and the island itself quite beautiful. Wrapping it all up in legends and folklore tarnished it for her.

Honestly, Alexandru didn't strike her as the type to be interested in old myths and glorified legends, preternatural or otherwise. Her first impression of him as a serious, stalwart man seemed dead-on, only now she wondered if she'd been mistaken. Either she was off her game, or he'd seriously misjudged her by thinking this was something she'd appreciate.

"Not a vampire," he said, turning to study at her with dark, solemn eyes. "Exactly."

His gaze captivated her. In it she still saw the serious man who'd offered unwavering hospitality and empathy for her loss. But buried beneath the obvious was something she'd missed earlier and couldn't quite define now. Strangely enough, it didn't frighten her. Instead, it piqued her curiosity.

Getting sidetracked wasn't a good idea, even if she wanted to know what he was up to. She kept her awareness on the here and now, and would figure out the rest of it later. "I didn't mean it literally, but remember I'm from the good old USA, where Dracula is very nearly a cult hero. I'm just not one of the flock who finds that interesting. I prefer to live and breathe in a world more real."

Lura didn't worship fictional heroes like Count Dracula. Her grasp of what was real and what wasn't prevented her from getting sucked into the crap people made up, Stoker included, even if his novel was a classic. Vampires didn't exist, period. Dracula, the real one, was just a man, flesh and blood like everyone else. She'd counseled her share of lost souls who embraced the Goth and vampire cultures, and she didn't buy in.

"A shame," he muttered, turning away so that all she could see was his strong profile. "The world has so many layers and dimensions. And for the record, in my humble opinion, he was hardly a hero."

Exactly her point. "I'm surprised you'd say that." Vic had told her often how the real man, while brutal and vindictive, was at the same time a savior to his people. He protected them from invaders even when they were far outnumbered. His tactics had been brutal, without question, but he'd lived in brutal times and probably did what he believed he must. Who was she to judge when she'd never had to live in Dracula's world?

His face turned sad. "You wouldn't be if you knew the whole story. So much death."

True enough, but how would anyone ever know the real story? History wasn't always written to the facts. The victors had a way of consistently glorifying their own actions while omitting anything that hinted at failure or their own bleak secrets. The old saying that the winners wrote history was born of a deep truth that denied subsequent generations the history they deserved.

She thought back to the stories Sofia had shared with her. Granted, Lura had been a child in those days and the stories tempered for her young mind. Still, she'd grasped Sofia's pride in her country's legacy and the man who'd saved them from the invading Turks. Her admiration of his time had filtered through clearly in her words.

"They revere the man in these parts…that much I do know."

He nodded. "Yes, they do, and for good reason. The legends of Dracula, good and bad, have brought much to this place. I'm speaking of the reality of what folk legends can do, and that, my dear Lura, is something completely different from the stark reality of a monster."

Her name as it crossed his lips brought goose bumps to her flesh. Instinctively, she crossed her arms across her chest, rubbing her hands up and down her forearms until the warmth returned. "So why, Alexandru, why are we really here?"

In the last few minutes, she'd come to believe there was a backstory to this little venture off the beaten path. Alexandru had suggested the detour casually, and yet she had the sense it was anything but simple.

"I apologize," he said in a tempered voice. "I had no right to bring you to this place, but I wanted to see it once more. To stand here in this time and in this place and to drink it in until it filled my whole being. My own journey of discovery started here, and thus it will end here as well."

His words were so filled with ghosts and regrets she almost put her arms around him. Resisting the uncharacteristic urge, she stuck her hands in the pockets of her jeans and said, "I still don't understand. I thought we were just going to drive through to Tirgoviste, pick up Vic, and return to Bucharest in order for me to take him home."

His smile banished the sadness. "No, I don't suppose you do understand, and it would take a terribly long time to explain. Just suffice it to say that I was here a very long time ago, and I needed to bring my voyage full circle."

Full circle, yeah, she understood the concept. "I get that," she said as she put a hand on his arm, his skin warm. "If I couldn't feel you right now, I'd still believe I was dreaming like I was in the car." The thought of the dream made her shudder. "Speaking of which, I'm surprised you didn't hear me scream. That was one strange nightmare."

"Scream?" His face suddenly filled with concern. "I did not hear you."

"Just a dream. No big deal. I have them all the time, always have. Especially when I'm exhausted. Since the call about Vic, I don't think I've slept for more than a couple of hours at a time. It was inevitable that one of them would knock my feet out from under me."

"Come." He extended his hand. "Let us walk. It will relax you."

Lura looked at his hand and his face, then put her hand in his. The gentle pressure of his fingers entwined with hers was comforting. "Where are we going?"

"Darkness is falling and it's not safe to try to navigate the lake with no visibility, so we'll stay at the home of a friend."

What? Stay on this island all night? "You mean we're stuck here?" Her stomach sank.

"Yes." He made a quick stop back at the boat to grab her suitcase, which apparently he'd put into the boat while she'd slept.

"My suitcase?"

He shrugged. "I've been caught off guard here before and I prefer to be prepared just in case. Tonight is such a case."

She blew out a long breath and let him guide her with a firm hand in the direction of a narrow road some distance away from the lakeshore. "I give up."

His voice was calm and soothing. "Not to worry. We will have a wonderful place to rest. Mircea is on a trip but leaves his home open for my use, should I be on the island."

"Stay here?" The near-panic in her voice sounded loud and clear, even though she tried not to sound like a frightened child. Why had he brought her to this place anyway? Before she'd nodded off to sleep things had made sense in a warped, this-is-fucked-up way. But from the moment she opened her eyes in the car, nothing made sense. Now this. Could things in her life get anymore messed up?

The corners of his mouth turned up a little as he tucked her hand in the crook of his elbow. "Yes, you will have a wonderful rest, and we will be on our way before you know it. Trust me, Lura. Things will work out as they should."

"Vic…" she whispered as he tugged on her hand.

"All in good time." He spoke in a soft voice. "It will be fine, I promise you, Lura."

For some odd reason, she believed him, and at this point, what could she say? They should be getting close to Tirgoviste about now, and instead they were on an island where Dracula was said to be buried. As far as she could tell, they were on the island alone. Surely more people were about somewhere, but as the sun began to set, she had no idea where. Not a sound, not a light, nothing.

How Alexandru knew where to find the place was a mystery. She didn't see a driveway when he tugged on her arm, turning her to the left. Yet there it was, winding between trees and bushes. They followed it until a small, tidy cottage popped up out of the night. Lura stopped and stared while Alexandru disappeared into the house. A minute later, lights spilled from the ornate paned windows.

"Come," he said from the doorway where the yellow glow of lamps beckoned from behind him.

Lura let go of any lingering reluctance and gratefully accepted his invitation to step inside. Like the hotel Alexandru had guided her to, his friend's house was cozy and inviting. Though it was small, the minute she stepped inside, warmth wrapped around her like an old, comfortable friend.

"Sit." He motioned toward a stuffed chair with a beautiful woolen throw tossed across the back. In deep blues, greens, and golds, it was a work of art. "I will make you a cup of tea, and then we'll have some time to talk. I have much to tell you before our journey continues."

CHAPTER FOUR

Wallachia, Romania
1456

Most in the castle slept, and for that small blessing she was grateful. The wait had been long, but at last the night was upon her. How she longed to see her brother's face and to know that he was well. For such a long time they had been apart from each other. Many days she despaired for his return.

His journey was destined to be and she, nor any other, had the right to question the wisdom of it. Despite the rightness of what he was doing, the danger of it weighed heavy on her heart. What if he failed? What if he did not find her? What if? What if? What if? The doubts were enough to make her head ache until she cried out in pain.

The Prince's party lingered far into the night with plentiful wine, food, and many groping hands. Unlike many of the other women, she was spared the indignity of the vulgar attention. No word was spoken, and yet all knew they were not to touch her. Any other choice was not really a choice at all. *He* alone claimed that right. Even now, her skin crawled as she thought about his hands touching her flesh and...

No, she wouldn't think about it or what could be. Her thoughts would be on getting to her brother and bringing him home once more. Of keeping her secret once he returned. She feared what he might do if he learned the truth.

Dressing in a black gown and tying her hair into a woven scarf, Nicoletta left her chambers and hurried down the corridor. At the end of the stone passageway, the sounds of laughter—drunken laughter—echoed off the walls. Her hands trembled as she listened. Pressing her back tight against the wall, she moved silently. To draw attention to herself would be a death sentence. The Prince would see her sneaking out of the castle alone as a sign of betrayal. No one betrayed him and lived to tell of it.

Glancing into the room as she slipped by, Nicoletta saw three men stretched out in chairs before the fire. A bottle of wine was tipped over onto the stone floor, the drink flowing freely like a deep crimson river. One of the men held a second bottle that he waved in the air as he spoke loudly, telling a ribald story that had the other two laughing loudly. From the neck of the bottle bright-red wine flew like rain, though none of them seemed to notice.

She knew all three of them, and the sight of their flushed faces made her skin crawl. Josef Yalina and Matea Branta were nobles with large nearby estates. Both were pigs who kissed the Prince's boots and in return were allowed to do as they pleased.

The third man was the Prince. Even from this distance, the difference between him and the two nobles was clear. Dress him in rags and he would still be a royal. Power radiated from him like the rays of the midday sun. If one did not peer too closely, the sight of him could be intoxicating. For her, the closeness had revealed something that would always make her want to retch. She longed for the day when she had been able to look upon him and see only a handsome face and regal bearing.

Her brother possessed power too, though his was of a different nature. All knew of it and respected it. No one spoke of it. Ever. To do so was to risk the wrath of the Prince. Few dared to cross either the Prince or her brother, and rightfully so. The Prince was vicious without the wine. Drunk with it…the thought made her shudder.

She yearned to understand why her brother had to leave her and go away to another world for so long. He never explained other than to say he was on a pilgrimage to find the woman, and she learned not to push him for answers. It did no good. When he chose not to speak, even the Prince could not pry words from his lips. Not even with his threats or his stakes. She admired that about him. She hated that about him.

On another night like this one, true black with only a few stars dotting the sky, her brother had walked between the stones and disappeared. She had waited for hours, thinking he would simply travel a distance and return. When the light of day fell upon her and the sun warmed her body, she knew it would not be so. He had passed through the stones and was gone somewhere beyond her reach.

Where? She did not know.

All she had to cling to was his promise that he would return on this night when the moon was full and directly above. When a shooting star cut through the black sky. Then he would come back to her once more and the prophecy would be fulfilled. He would bring with him the woman who was to save them all.

Time was growing short and the stones were still far away. Her journey was a long one, and she did not dare linger any longer. She peered into the room once more and, certain no one looked her way, slipped by and out into the night.

The path was well known to her, for she had followed it a hundred times since he had gone away. Always she hoped to meet him along the rough and rutted road. Always she returned alone.

Not tonight. He would come. The truth of it tingled within her bones. She could almost see his face and feel the strength of his body as she hugged him to her. When she returned to the castle this night, he would be with her and everything would change.

❖

A comfortable silence had fallen between them as Lura watched the fire Alexandru coaxed into a blaze in the big fireplace. She felt a little like she was drowning in the flames that licked at the logs piled high in the grate. The feeling wasn't all that unpleasant.

She finally drew her gaze away from the hypnotic flames and studied Alexandru. He seemed different here, more at ease. Not that he'd been tense or uptight, that she'd noticed, since meeting him this morning. Still, in this simple cottage far from the city he seemed naturally at peace. He wasn't a city boy, that was for certain.

"Where do you come from," she asked, breaking the silence at last. Their small talk throughout the day had mostly revolved around her, and it occurred to her now that he'd told her little of himself. She was curious to know what made this man tick. Why he had taken her cause upon his shoulders when he didn't have to?

He smiled and said, "My family comes from a part of Romania that was once known as Wallachia, the land that brought Dracula into this world. Once upon a time this place was divided into a number of kingdoms, of which Wallachia was one."

She thought on the reference to Dracula. "The way you say his name is so different. Everyone else in these parts describes him as a prince of a guy, even as bloody as he was. By the tone of your voice, I get the feeling you disagree with that characterization." It was true. She noticed an edge to the way he said the man's name absent in anything else said. Made her wonder all the more about him.

His nod was slight. "You are very astute. Yes, I know the legends. I've heard them all and understand how the people today see him as a savior. Truthfully, the man was a demon, bloodthirsty and power-crazed. His body was of princely blood. His heart was not." Again, the biting words had an almost personal feel to them.

She tucked the throw around her feet as she leaned closer to the fire. "I thought he saved the land from the Turkish invasion." Sofia's stories had possessed a magical spin to the Prince who saved her homeland from invaders.

Again, he nodded, his brown eyes intense. "It is true. His methods, though brutal, were very effective in turning back the Turks, at least temporarily. In some ways he saved many of his countrymen's lives. If that were all of the story, then I'd embrace him as a hero. Unfortunately, it is far from the complete chronicle of the man, and that is why I have a problem with how they worship him in this century. Time has erased so much of the reality, taking away the tarnish and replacing it with gilt."

"You believe the legends about his killing for fun?"

This time he shook his head, which surprised her, given what he'd just said. The history books were full of various accounts of brutality that seemed to edge just past what was needed to maintain order and avoid anarchy. Those accounts seemed in line with Alexandru's interpretation of Dracula.

His eyes met hers with a hardness she hadn't seen before. His words were just as harsh. "I don't believe, Lura. I know."

Wow, there was something very concrete in his statement. No sitting on the fence here. She said lightly, "You say that like you actually knew him."

He raised a single eyebrow. "Let us just say I have a little more background on the man than most people."

She sat up straighter in her chair and nodded. "So that's it, you're an historian." He did have that air about him. Not arrogant or snobby, just quietly knowledgeable. It made sense and accounted for the way his words came across as personal.

He inclined his head. "Yes and no. I think of myself more as a traveler, which gives me the opportunity to pick up history through my personal adventures."

Traveler? Across miles, oceans, and continents, perhaps, but this conversation was crossing centuries. So far Alexandru was proving adept at not giving a straight answer to the vast majority of her questions. "You're quite a mystery man, Alexandru Vizulea, full of crooked answers and more than a few surprises."

His dark eyes danced. "I'm not sure, but I believe that is a compliment, no?"

Lura laughed, surprised at the sound coming from her lips. She'd had nothing to laugh at even before Vic's death. "I suppose it is in a kind of backhanded way. I only know that since meeting you this morning, I'm starting to feel a little bit better, and that says a lot."

His face brightened, though his eyes were still dark and somber. "I'm glad. I hope you will still feel the same tomorrow."

Why wouldn't she? Then again, she didn't want to think about tomorrow. At first she'd been irritated to discover they were trapped on this island for the night. As the evening wore on, she'd settled in and appreciated the peaceful cottage and the warm fire. Her taut nerves began to relax, something that hadn't happened since the call about Vic. Tomorrow would be soon enough to bring him home. With that thought in mind, she excused herself and went to bed.

She sank down on the soft bed and rubbed her face with her hands. Outside the bedroom door, Alexandru moved about quietly. After a few moments, even those sounds were gone. Silence draped around her. Sighing, she lay back and prayed for sleep. It came, taking her away to blessed oblivion.

Sometime later, she didn't exactly know how much later, she kicked the covers off and tried to untangle her legs from the crisp white sheets. A few moments passed in the total darkness before she remembered where she was. It had to be late into the night, because it was jet black in the tiny bedroom.

She'd been sick when she boarded the plane in Seattle, disgust, despair, and self-loathing filling her every fiber. The time in between had done nothing to dull those feelings. Duty, however, had propelled her forward, accompanied by the guilt of having driven Vic to his death.

Now she was confused. She expected to be in a small Tirgoviste hotel, the ashes of her husband packed in her suitcase, ready to head back to Bucharest for a flight home. Instead here she was lying in small, soft bed in the middle of a Romanian island with a strange man, wanting little more than to stay put for days. Somehow it all felt right, and that was the oddest thing of all.

The wind kicked up as she straightened and pulled her legs to her chest, wrapping her arms around them. The shutters rattled and the wind whistled by. Once again she sensed the world outside was trying to talk to her and tell her something that was just out of earshot. Shaking her head, she almost laughed. Supernatural imagination wasn't typically her style, yet here she was thinking about spirits in the wind talking to her.

The dim light of a full moon directly overhead poked its way through the small window shutters, casting golden streaks across the floor. She got up and walked as softly as she could to the window. Easing the shutters open, she stared into the night.

Off in the distance she saw him standing there, a shadow really, the figure of a tall man who appeared to be watching the house with a steady gaze. No overactive imagination at work here. She knew who she was seeing—Alexandru. What on earth was he doing out there at this time of night?

Did he see her? Then again, how could he? It was bleak inside the house, and she didn't have so much as a candle to light the room. If it wasn't for the moonlight, she wouldn't have spotted him.

For a few minutes, she stood and watched him, wondering if he would come back to the cottage. Curiosity got the better of her and, looking around for something to put over her lightweight nightclothes, she spied a lovely robe on a hook behind the door. It was gorgeous really, long and lush velvet, a color she couldn't quite discern in the shadowy room. She slipped it on, tied the belt tight around her waist, and headed for the door.

The grass was cold and damp, and Lura wished she'd put something a little more substantial on her feet besides the sandals she'd brought along, thinking they'd pack well. That part of her plan was perfect; they did work well in a suitcase. Not so well on long damp grass with the beginnings of frost. As cold and crunchy as the grass was, she'd have been much more comfortable in her hiking boots. But it wasn't like she planned to be out here long, so what did it matter if the slides and her feet got wet? At least the heavy robe was nice and warm.

Hurrying along, she kept him in sight as she moved farther away from the cottage. What was Alexandru so interested in that he'd come out in the middle of the night? So far, she hadn't seen or heard a thing that merited leaving the warmth of the cozy bedroom. She'd almost reached him when he turned and started walking away.

"Alexandru," she said loudly. "Wait." Kind of rude when he could see her trying to catch up with him.

He didn't even turn, just kept walking in the direction of a large rock outcropping. Was he just going to let her run behind him in a robe and slippers? Really…what kind of host left his guest to wander around in her nightclothes? And Alexandru himself, what exactly was he wearing? From here it looked like it was some sort of thigh-length jacket over tights. Tights? Obviously she was way more tired than she realized, because no way was she seeing what she thought she was.

"Alexandru?" She yelled a little louder this time. He had to hear her. He wasn't that far away.

Finally, he turned and glanced back. His eyes seemed to meet hers—a little hard to tell for sure in the inky darkness—and for a moment she thought he would stop. He didn't, not even when he reached the outcropping of large rocks. His pace never slowed.

And then he was gone.

CHAPTER FIVE

R iah watched Adriana come out of the bathroom rubbing a towel over her wet hair and wearing nothing at all. The sight made Riah's breath catch in her throat. Adriana was so beautiful. Skinny wasn't the word she'd use to describe Adriana because she was curvy and full breasted. All woman. The combination was breathtaking.

It wasn't just her physical beauty that made Riah's body ache at the mere sight of her. No, it was the whole woman—mind, body, and spirit. In all her time on this earth, she'd never encountered someone quite like Adriana, and she was grateful every day when she awakened to find her still here.

"What?" Adriana asked when she caught Riah's stare.

Riah smiled and shook her head. "Nothing. I was just thinking how much I love you."

"Back atcha, girlfriend." Adriana tossed the towel toward the bathroom before launching herself on the bed next to Riah. She smelled fresh and clean. "Been waiting for you to open those pretty eyes of yours. Took your sweet time too, lazy bones."

A tingle slid down her spine. "Have you now?"

Adriana lightly touched Riah's bare breast. "Oh, yeah." Then her head dipped to take a nipple into her mouth.

Riah arched back and moaned. One simple touch was all it took to send her to a very happy place. Her hands went to Adriana's short black hair, the dampness and sweet scent of vanilla still clinging to it. The hot feel of her lips on her breast contrasted to the coolness of her hair against Riah's palms. She moaned again.

Adriana raised her head and smiled wickedly. She began to slide off the bed. "So you probably want to get downstairs, see what's going on."

She barely kept the begging out of her voice. "No."

The wicked smile grew. "Oh…no? You tired? Need a little more rest?"

The tease. She liked it. "No."

Sliding back onto the bed, Adriana dangled a handful of scarves she'd grabbed from the nightstand. "Um, well then, what shall we do?"

Before Riah could answer, Adriana began to use the scarves. The beautiful four-poster bed was in their room for more reasons than being a fantastic piece of furniture.

Satisfied with her work, Adriana stepped back and studied Riah as she lay with her hands and feet tied to the bedposts with the silk scarves. She licked her lips and said, "Looking good, vampire, real good."

The game was breathtaking. Oh, she could tear away the scarves with barely a flick of one hand, but she wouldn't. This game was more than sex; it was trust and love and sex all rolled together. Adriana had taught her that, and it made her heart soar.

So did the touch of Adriana's lips and tongue as they worked across every inch of Riah's body. Her nerves were on fire, the desire building until she thought she'd explode. When Adriana moved between her legs, she didn't think she could hold on much longer. The moment her tongue touched her center, it was over. Any pretense of control was gone. She came with a cry that would probably wake anyone who happened to still be asleep anywhere in the house.

Later, when the scarves were returned to the drawer and Adriana was loose-limbed and breathing heavy too, Riah wanted to kick back and enjoy the moment. Except she couldn't.

Despite the mind-blowing sex, she was catching Ivy's unsettling mood. Maybe because it was so out of character for her. Ivy just didn't let things rattle her. It was one of the things that made her so good at her job as the coroner in Grant County, a position she'd held until she was turned. It was also what made her so incredible as a hunter after her life changed.

Now, Riah was feeling as uneasy as Ivy. It was possible she was simply picking up Ivy's jittery vibes, or maybe it was something else.

She'd had a lot of years to learn how to tune out others when she chose. After all this time, she was a master at it. That truth made her all the more nervous. What exactly was she picking up on if it wasn't Ivy's trepidation about her cousin?

Not something she wanted to put a name to. The Spiritus Group had endured three particularly bloody battles since forming, and it would be nice to have a rest for a change. A little vacation of sorts. Didn't appear that was going to happen. She had a bad feeling her wishes and reality were at odds. Evil just didn't want to take a break.

Adriana, on the other hand, wasn't about to let sleeping dogs lie either. Recovering from their interlude, like Riah, she was alert and on edge, her spider senses picking up on the unease as well. Without talking too much, they rolled out of bed, showered, and dressed. Fifteen minutes later, they were downstairs joining Ivy, Colin, Tory, and Naomi, who were already up and brainstorming.

Frowning and rubbing her hands together, Adriana said, "Okay, chickies. Something has our vamps in a twit, and I think we need to figure out what it is."

"Hey," Tory said from across the room. "Maybe you should be a bit more specific about the vamps you're referring to. I am definitely not in a twit."

She nodded, the frown still pulling down the corners of her mouth. "Duly noted. As I was saying, two of our vamps are wound up tight, and I believe we all need to figure out why and what we can do. Hunters of the preternatural persuasion in a twit…not a good idea, boys and girls."

"I'm not in a twit either," Ivy said, a small frown shadowing her usually beautiful face. "I'm just worried. No, that's not even right. What I am is really worried. This isn't like Lura. She's the responsible type. Always made me look like a scofflaw. If I didn't love her so much, I'd probably hate her, if you know what I mean."

"Yeah, I think we all get that." Adriana nodded at Ivy and then turned her attention to Riah. "What's your excuse, gorgeous? If you don't mind me saying, you're a little on edge."

Adriana's deep eyes met hers. Riah wished she knew what it was she was feeling or, more specifically, what was causing her to feel this way. It was at least partly a response to Ivy's concern. They were so close, it was easy to feed off each other's emotions. Unfortunately, something else was rippling in the air, and more than picking up on

Ivy's unease, it was that indefinable thing that had the tiny hairs on the back of her neck standing up. She held Adriana's gaze for a long moment and then slowly shook her head. "I don't know. It just feels like something's not right."

"Well then," Adriana declared. "What are we gonna do about it? Sit here and pick our noses, or figure out what the fuck is going on? In case you haven't figured it out already, I'm on the side of getting off our asses and hitting the road."

Colin was leaning against the doorframe, his long legs crossed at the ankles and his arms across his broad chest. "I think we need to find Lura."

All of them turned to look at him. Tall and lean, he was typically a man of few words. When he did offer up suggestions, he was dead-on the great majority of the time. After Riah had gotten over her initial repulsion of him—not because he was a man but rather because he was a vampire hunter who'd arrived to take her head—she rather liked him. Even more than that, she respected him.

"You mean head to Romania?" On the other hand, respect aside, if Colin was suggesting the old country, Riah wasn't sure it was a good idea. And that was aside from the fact it was one incredibly long plane ride. Many other unvoiced reasons played into that scenario.

"Yes, that's exactly what I mean. We charter a plane and we go find her."

Adriana walked over and slapped Colin on the shoulder. "See now, that's what I'm talking about. Like the man said, we get kickin' and get going."

Finding out where Lura had disappeared to was a good idea. Doing it in the flesh, not so much, and Riah wasn't giving in without a fight. She did not want to go to Romania. Ever. Again. "I don't think we have to fly to Romania to track down your cousin." In this day and age they had any number of alternatives to being there in the flesh.

"I do." Ivy stood next to Colin, putting a hand on his arm. "You don't have to go." She looked straight at Riah as if she could read her mind and knew why it wasn't possible for her to make this trip. "But I do. She's family. If something has happened to her over there, I've got to help make it right."

Crap. They didn't understand what this meant to her. It wasn't just Romania. She didn't want to set foot in Europe, period. This was her home now and, more importantly, her sanctuary. She'd come here for a reason all those centuries ago, and a few hundred years hadn't changed anything. The rest of them might not understand the significance of what they asked, but she was pretty sure Tory did.

One glance at Tory's face and her suspicion was confirmed. Two of the vampires in the room wanted nothing more than to stay with their feet on the ground in the good old USA. The others would have to understand.

"Don't be a party pooper," Adriana said as she slung an arm around Riah's shoulders. "I know you hate everything on the other side of the pond, but trust me, gorgeous, we'll protect you. Nothing's going to hurt you when we're all together."

The unfortunate side effect of loving a free-spirited, brave, and beautiful sorceress was, she was hard to say no to. Adriana's enthusiasm and adventurous soul always won, even when Riah promised herself to stick to her guns. Like now.

Riah closed her eyes, took a deep breath, and caved. "Okay, let's go find Lura." She'd simply have to ignore the growing dread in her stomach. Maybe it was nothing and she was just overreacting, based on her personal history.

Or maybe not.

Lura stopped and squinted. Surely it was just a trick of the night. It was black and cloudless here. The few stars that dotted the sky gave off very little light. The moon, shrouded by clouds, didn't help at all either. Anybody would question what they saw in the murky night. Just like thinking a guy was wearing tights, Alexandru's disappearing act was probably nothing more than a trick of the nighttime shadows, low visibility, and unfamiliar surroundings.

Sounded very sane and rational except for the fact that not only was Alexandru gone, but so was any hint of noise. As in *any* sound at all. When she'd followed him from the cottage, his footsteps on the frost-covered ground had been audible in the otherwise quiet night.

When he'd turned to look at her as he'd stood between the two giant boulders, she'd sworn she heard the swish of his coat. Then he'd stepped through the stones and everything went deathly silent; the only sound she could hear now was her own rapid breathing. Perhaps the light could mess up visual perception, but auditory? Not likely. She shivered and wrapped her arms around herself. This was turning into one of the strangest nights of her life.

A burst of cold air enveloped her, gone as fast as it came. Fear tickled at the back of her neck. She grimaced and looked around. Nothing out here gave her any reason to be scared. There was a big pile of rocks; Alexandru had stepped through them, obscuring him from her direct line of sight, and that was that. All she had to do was trace his path through the rocks and he'd be right on the other side. No monsters, no demons.

The best thing she could do to put her mind at ease was follow through on that thought. It would all shake out in a minute. The only problem...she couldn't get her feet to move. The effort to pick them up and walk forward was almost too overwhelming to handle. She wasn't sure if it was the complete silence or the isolating darkness that gave her the heebie-jeebies. Something was definitely giving off some freaky vibes.

Even as a child, she'd possessed a vivid imagination and could scare herself silly. Education and adulthood hadn't diminished her ability to imagine both the best and the worst. Right now it seemed to be in overdrive, and frankly, she was too old to be letting it incapacitate her. She was a trained professional, although anyone who saw her at the moment would seriously wonder about the licensing board that had awarded her credentials.

Then again, in her own defense, she was out in the pitch-black night, wandering through an unfamiliar field, in a foreign country, in her nightclothes, and, worst of all, alone. Imagination working overtime? Maybe. Questionable decision to follow Alexandru out here? Definitely.

A breeze picked up in intensity once again, ruffling the velvet robe and bringing with it the faint scent of fire, probably coming from the cottage fireplaces. She pulled the robe tighter around her body and thought seriously about turning around and running back to the cottage. Would definitely be the smart thing to do. Lord knows she'd done enough stupid things lately. Didn't need to add another one to the count. Time to use her brain instead of her emotions.

Lura turned her head in the direction of the cottage and stared off into the distance. It was warm, the bed comfortable, and surely if she returned, Alexandru would be back soon and they would have a good laugh about her nighttime imaginings. It made perfect sense to hotfoot it back to warmth and safety.

She shifted her gaze back to the boulders and the hushed blackness beyond. It was so incredibly odd. After a moment's hesitation, with a mournful sigh, she picked up the long skirt of the robe and followed the path Alexandru had taken only minutes before.

When she reached the boulders, she paused. The air was colder here, the scent of fire stronger, even though not so much as a flicker of a flame pierced the dimness. The wind must be carrying the smoke across the island. She cocked her head toward the rocks. Was she hearing something from inside the stones? Storm winds? A voice? A moment before it had seemed deathly silent. Now, she strained to listen.

She slowly inched closer, certain she heard voices coming from a long distance away. Peering in, all she saw was a black, yawning nothingness. Shouldn't she see something?

As she placed one foot between the boulders, a whirlwind rushed up so severe she had to touch the cold stone to keep her balance. The moment her fingers connected with the cold surface, light exploded in her head and a cacophony of sound made her cover her ears. Over the roar, she couldn't hear her own screams.

Riah settled back into the soft leather of the seat and stared out the small window as the lights of Spokane grew dimmer. Soon, the plane had climbed to cruising altitude and the vastness of the sky wrapped them in a comfortable cocoon.

Since Kara Lynch and Cam Black Wolf had joined the Spiritus Group, air travel was pretty easy most of the time. Cam was a pilot who just happened to have her own plane. Of course, her favorite little plane had nearly been destroyed by a vindictive werewolf who managed to punch a hole in gas tank that almost took out both women during a flight to Montana. Only Cam's cool head and experience with the plane had saved them both, and she'd put it down with little more than a bump. That plane had been repaired, but these days they'd jumped up a bit with a bigger version that had plenty of room for most of the group. They never knew when they'd need to hop on board and wage a battle.

Tonight, Cam wasn't at the controls. The international flight required more than Cam's current certifications and a whole lot bigger plane. Lear jet rented, everyone on board, and Cam hanging out in the cockpit, they were now headed for Bucharest. It had taken them less than three hours to pull it all together and be on their way. Riah, along with Ivy and Tory, could safely rest during the daylight hours, and night would once again be falling by the time their plane touched down.

At least she hoped she'd be able to rest. Didn't want to lay a bet on it actually happening. This whole trip made her nervous. She hadn't been on European soil in over two hundred years, and she certainly wasn't looking forward to it now. If she never stepped foot on that continent again, she wouldn't shed a single tear.

Then again, evil didn't seem to have a sense of geography. In fact, it was pretty much an equal-opportunity employer, not discriminating based on sex, race, religion, or location. The job of the Spiritus Group was to stop evil—all evil—regardless of where it was found. In short, it was time for Riah to "man up."

She'd do it because it was important for many reasons. Didn't mean she had to like it, though she wasn't going to pout about it either. Vampires with over five centuries under their belts did not pout. It was undignified.

With at least another twelve hours to go before they arrived in Bucharest, Riah closed her eyes and hoped she could ignore the torrent of emotion racing through her body long enough to capture a bit of rest. She tried to quiet her mind. They had a better chance of getting in and out quickly if they were operating at a hundred percent.

Fingers touched hers, and she didn't have to open her eyes to know they belonged to Adriana. The warmth of her hand against Riah's was enough. She breathed into the comfort and let her mind drift.

CHAPTER SIX

Nicoletta's heart raced the moment she spotted the shadow moving from between the stones. She recognized the shape and the movement even after all the time that had passed. Alexandru.

She ran to him, and he opened his arms to welcome her. The feel of his solid body strong and real against her own brought tears streaming down her face. He was all she had in the world, and it seemed he had been gone forever. Her tears soaked into the cloth of his fine shirt.

He placed a kiss against her hair and whispered, "Quiet now, little one. I am home."

"I thought you might never return." She sobbed. "I was afraid you had left me forever." Her body quaked with the force of her pent-up emotion. For many seasons she had kept strong. She could do it no longer.

He held her out at arm's length, and under the light of the moon, he looked much younger than she remembered. Had it been so long she could not even know his face? He smiled and her heart sang. "I would never leave you, Nicoletta. Never. We are family."

She understood and was grateful that she was no longer alone in the world. "Did you find her, brother? Did you find her?" He had to, because if not, it was all in vain.

He nodded and a smile lit up his face. "I did, sister."

Relief rushed through her. At last. Alexandru was a great man, a true magician, but she often did not understand him. He was patient with her and explained how important it was to find the woman. Despite his teachings, she hated that he had to leave her and disappear into the beyond that would take him places she would—could—never go. All she had to comfort her during his absence was the faith that one day he would return.

During the long days and nights of his absence, she could not banish the dire thoughts that when he disappeared between the stones, promising to return on this night, he would not. That he would be gone for eternity. The very thought made her stomach lurch. Each night she prayed for his return and hoped God would grant her favor.

He must have sensed the direction of her thoughts, because he laid his palm against her cheek. "I swear never to leave you to face this world alone. You have my solemn promise, beautiful sister."

She smiled and put her hand over his. "I am never alone as long as you are in my heart."

A clap of thunder made her jump and scream. Alexandru simply looked up at the sky and then turned back to the stones. He left Nicoletta to stare after him as he retraced his path. If he walked through a second time, she would be lost. He could not leave her again; she could not survive without him now that she had once more gazed upon his beloved face. She started to follow, to stop him, and then halted when a figure stepped from between the rocks.

Rodolphe dropped the woman's lifeless body to the ground. Once, she had been pretty. Not any longer. All that made her special had been drained away, leaving little behind but a shell. He turned his back on her and walked toward the river beyond.

Catherine hesitated. Leaving a body so openly exposed was not a good idea. Certainly no one could harm them, and yet it felt somehow wrong. She wanted to do something for this poor girl, whose sole misfortune it was to catch Rodolphe's eye.

It was too late to help her, but Catherine refused to leave her for the wolves. She bent down and picked her up. She was so light, just a sprite of a young woman. Or at least she had been. Her long brown hair nearly touched the ground as Catherine walked to the river's edge. Her gown was in shreds, her skin so white it looked like fresh fallen snow. In life she had been pretty, but in death only a ghost of what she had been.

"What are you doing?"

"We cannot leave her here for scavengers." Catherine did not turn to look at him. She knew the expression that would be on his face. Distaste. Disappointment. She disappointed him at every turn.

"Do not be absurd, she is nothing. No one will even miss her. Leave her and come with me."

"No," she shot back. *"I will not leave her like rubbish. She was someone's daughter, someone's sister. You destroyed her, but I will not let you disrespect her."*

His laughter was hearty, cruel. *"A daughter? A sister? Like you?"*

The pain that shot through her heart was mixed with anger. He always knew how to hurt her where it would draw invisible blood. He never left a mark on her body, only on her soul. *"Yes,"* she said softly as she slowly lowered the young woman's body into the river. *"Like me."*

"And you believe anyone misses you?"

She closed her eyes and took several deep breaths. When she opened her eyes, the woman was gone, the current carrying her down and away. *"Rest in peace,"* she murmured before turning to face Rodolphe.

"We are not monsters," she told him.

He raised an eyebrow and a smile turned up the corners of his mouth. *"No, my sweet."* He ran a finger down her cheek. *"We are royalty, especially here in the motherland."* He waved his arms wide.

The motherland. He had been so eager to bring her here, to share with her the land where it all began. To drink the blood of those who served the great master.

Since the moment they had arrived, Rodolphe seemed to glow in a way she had not seen before. Catherine did not share his embrace of this place where the terrain was still extreme and the people suspicious. The glances they sent their way were cold and knowing. They were not welcome in this country, and while Rodolphe laughed it off, the chilly reception made her feel cold.

He took her hand, tucking it in the crook of his arm. *"Come, my pet. A boat awaits, and it is time for us to visit him."*

She managed to suppress a shudder and instead walked alongside Rodolphe. He helped her into the carriage that would take them to the waiting boat. They would cross the waters by the light of the moon to reach Snagov Island, the final resting place of Prince Vlad Dracula.

Riah came awake slowly. The dream—the memory—didn't want to leave her. The trip to Wallachia had been so long ago, and yet she could recall every detail as if it had been just days ago. She'd been Catherine Tudor then, the last daughter of King Henry VII, who, as far as the world had known, died at birth. Only a very few knew she'd been given to a favorite of the King as the prize for a winning bet.

She'd been raised as the only daughter of the wealthy childless couple, only learning her real identity when her brother, King Henry VIII, arranged to have her fall victim to a vampire. Her brother, knowing of her true identity, didn't want another sibling who could potentially challenge his claim to the throne. She had to be eliminated, the way of succession kept clear and uncluttered.

Rodolphe was supposed to have killed her. Instead, he made her his partner. No, not his partner…his pet. He'd taught her to hunt and to kill. He'd turned her into a vampire who needed to feed on blood to survive. He believed he'd found a perfect complement to his own depraved personality, only he'd been wrong. He took her life, but he never came close to capturing her soul.

Riah had come to hate what she was and the thing that had made her. It was here in the land now known as Romania that she put an end to his reign of violence and terror. She left Catherine Tudor behind as she boarded a ship for the new world, never expecting to set foot here again. On that long-ago night, dread had made her sick to her stomach. The same feeling assaulted her now while she gazed out the window as the lights of Bucharest grew bigger and brighter.

As suddenly as it started, it stopped. The roar of noise certain to pierce her eardrums fell away until Lura was once again surrounded by total silence. Had she hit her head somewhere along the line, explaining the sounds, lights, and smells?

When she'd followed Alexandru from the cottage to the stones, the night air had been thick as coal, but this was even more so. Not to mention a distinct drop in temperature. On the island, the brush of winter was beginning to fall, yet on the other side of the rocks, it was downright frigid. Winter was in full command.

She pulled the robe tighter around her and tried to get her bearings. Wasn't happening. She was so disoriented by both the deep night and the silence she didn't have a clue where she was anymore. It shouldn't be this weird; it was only a few feet between where she stood now and where she'd come through the stones, yet it was as if she'd stepped into another world entirely.

Glancing behind, she could make out the large rocks, except something wasn't quite right. She squinted and tried to see clearly. Then she spotted it. The space between the rocks where only moments before she'd walked was different. How exactly, she wasn't sure. But definitely different.

Shaking her head, she turned back around. A flickering light was just ahead. What kind of light was it? Certainly not a flashlight. She moved toward it, grateful for any kind of illumination. The closer she got, the more it came into view. A torch…a torch? Who in the world used one of those outside of a good Gothic movie? Not in this day and age.

Then she saw it. Alexandru was heading toward her, a petite woman dressed in clothes so black she nearly disappeared into the night a few feet behind him. She held the torch aloft, its light dancing off the little bit of her face not obscured by a full hood. In that tiny glow, Lura glimpsed a lovely face and deep, deep brown eyes, lips full and red. She was alluring and beautiful, a dreamlike image in what had to be a dream. She kept walking.

"Alexandru?"

He met her before she'd taken more than a few steps, a smile lighting up his face. He took Lura's arm, patting her hand reassuringly. "At last. I've been waiting for you. I believed you were not far behind me, but it took you longer than I thought to follow through the stones. Come. I have someone you must meet."

Yes, it felt like he was touching her, but really, she had to be dreaming, didn't she? It was weird here, off in a way she couldn't put a finger on. All of a sudden another realization hit her. Alexandru wasn't speaking English or the Romanian she'd been conversing in since landing in Bucharest. It was more a strange version of Sofia's native tongue. Distinctly different from the dialect she'd learned at Sofia's knee, yet she was still able to follow his words.

When he urged her forward, she resisted for only a second. Strange as everything was at the moment, she was intrigued by the lovely woman holding the torch. "Lura, this is my sister, Nicoletta."

Turning to stare at him in the flickering light, she repeated, "Your sister?" Beyond the fact that his family was popping up out nowhere, where exactly had she come from?

His smile was warm. "Yes, we have been apart for a very long time now, but tonight we are home."

Seriously, this was all going beyond bizarre. Lura liked to think she had an open mind, but this was outside the bubble. Granted, in the thick of night, it was hard to make out much of anything. Still, there were no cars, no other houses, no nothing that she could see. It was as if this Nicoletta had appeared out of the clear blue sky. Well, more like the pitch-black night sky.

It all seemed strange and somehow wrong. She had nothing to base that on except instinct, and it was screaming. "I don't understand, Alexandru. Where did she come from? I thought we were essentially alone on the island."

"Brother." Nicoletta interrupted before he had a chance to respond. "We must not linger here. It is too dangerous, and we must travel far too great a distance before sunrise. Let us get her to safety, and then we can share with her the reason for this journey."

Nicoletta reached out and touched Lura's other arm. She flinched and took a step backward. The electricity that shot through her arm was hot…exciting.

"Do not worry, I will not harm you. We must hurry. It would not be safe to be found in this place." Nicoletta's words were low and intense, an edge of fear in them that chilled Lura to the bone. She wasn't pretending, though what exactly they had to be afraid of she wasn't sure.

Alexandru's next words didn't help either. "She's right, Lura. Please, follow us. I know you have many questions, and I promise to answer them when we are safe."

Whatever they were afraid of, she wasn't. They were what? A hundred yards, maybe a hundred and fifty yards from the cottage. How much trouble could they get in so close to shelter? It seemed to her they were both exaggerating the situation more than a little.

Despite the comfort of his touch, she shook off Alexandru's arm. "I'm not following anyone anywhere. This is crazy, and you know it. We can go back to your friend's cottage where it's nice and warm. Then you can explain how your sister appeared out of thin air. It's stupid to stand out here in the cold."

He shook his head. "I'm afraid it is not that simple. Please," he pleaded with her. "Trust me. We must go." The urgency in his voice was deep, and the twinge of panic she'd felt when she'd stepped between the rocks returned. Something about all of this was a long way from being right.

Good sense told her to turn around and head back through the rocks. Curiosity said something entirely different. Gut instinct leaned in the direction of trust. Alexandru was on her side, and well, she did want to know more about the pretty mystery sister who sent her nerves tingling with a simple touch.

Curiosity won. "Fine." She picked up the skirt of her thick robe and began to follow. "I hope Nicoletta has a pair of jeans and a sweatshirt I can slip on. This thing is a pain in the ass, and I'm cold." She shook the velvet skirt, sending sparkling bits of frost flying.

Nicoletta glanced over her shoulder at Lura, giving her a puzzled look. So she liked jeans better than some girly velvet robe. What of it? This wasn't exactly the Middle Ages, even if Nicoletta was dressed for it. She liked good old twenty-first century comfort clothes: a nice pair of well-worn Levi's, a comfortable pair of hiking boots, and a warm hoodie. She almost groaned thinking about them.

"Come, Lura. We will talk when we get back to the castle." Alexandru didn't turn to look at her, just kept moving forward at a clipped pace.

Castle? Where exactly would that be? She hadn't seen anything more imposing on the island than the monastery. He didn't give her a chance to ask, taking off at a stride that brooked no resistance. It didn't leave her much in the way of choices and so she followed him, almost running, wondering the whole time what she'd gotten herself into. He'd seemed so normal earlier.

CHAPTER SEVEN

Two centuries, give or take, had a way of changing things. Granted, it was full-on nighttime outside and things always looked different when the light was gone, but this wasn't the same place she'd been in so long ago. Back then, Wallachia was falling under the influence of Russia, and the times had been turbulent and dangerous. Everyone was scared, their style of life changing in ways over which they had no control. For her and Rodolphe, it all combined to create an environment for perfect hunting. He'd been ecstatic. Her...not so much.

It also proved to be perfect for doing the one thing that would assure her freedom from Rodolphe. Not even a trace of hesitation had stopped her back then, and even after all this time, she wasn't sorry for what she'd done. She'd made the right choice and, if she had it to do all over again, wouldn't change a thing.

Riah closed her eyes and tried not to think about him or that horrible last night. Wasn't working. It was as if the simple act of touching the ground here brought everything back in an avalanche of memories and regrets. Not a single regret for killing him, only many for what had come before.

Rodolphe brought her roses. The bouquet was huge, the flowers deep red and fragrant, tied with a soft golden cord. Catherine held them to her nose and inhaled deeply. He knew how much she missed her gardens and occasionally brought her the gift of flowers.

Why, then, did she feel so empty? Even her beloved roses failed to lift her spirit. She sat on the brocade couch and held them close, the thorns biting into her skin, making tiny spots of blood dot her chest.

*He stood behind her and caressed her shoulders. "Ma chérie,"
he whispered in her ear as he dropped kisses along her neck. "You like
the roses?"*

"Yes, Rodolphe, they're very beautiful."

*"Like you." He used a finger to turn her face to his and kissed
her softly.*

*His hands loosened the laces of her dress and slid the gown off
her shoulders after he took the roses and set them aside. He licked
the blood from her skin, then lowered his mouth to a bared breast.
Catherine closed her eyes and allowed sensations to wash over her. He
nipped lightly and she shuddered.*

"Come," he said when he raised his head.

*She took his offered his hand, stood, and stepped out of her gown.
He went down the hallway and she followed him to their bedchamber.
Next door, she heard the soft cry of the child, the other gift he'd brought
her this night.*

*The child was beautiful, no more than a year old, with pale-
blue eyes and flawless skin. Earlier, Rodolphe had proudly presented
Catherine the infant, a delicacy rarely taken by any vampire. Children
were forbidden, a vampire law unspoken yet universally understood.
Rodolphe heeded neither man's law nor vampire law.*

*He was standing in the middle of the room, naked and aroused.
Catherine didn't think she'd ever seen a more handsome man and never
would've believed she'd want a man like she did Rodolphe. It was more
than the fact he was her maker; he was charismatic and alluring, a
lover like no other. Though not a day went by she didn't long for Meriel,
she found some satisfaction in the touch of her lover.*

*Inside the door, she paused and reached behind to take hold of the
weapon propped against the wall. Firelight reflected off the gleaming
blade. Caught up in the passion of the moment, Rodolphe didn't notice.
It was so heavy in her hands.*

*She closed the space between them. Tears blurred her vision as she
brought her arms up, holding the sword with both hands. A confused
look, one she'd never seen before, crossed his face. As realization
dawned, darkness veiled his expression. One hand came up, the silver
ring with the flashing ruby, reaching out.*

*She didn't hesitate. With all her power as both a vampire and
a woman, she stepped into the swing. When his severed head hit the*

ground, it rolled across the stone floor, coming to rest on the lush bearskin rug laid out in front of the fireplace. Catherine turned away. The sword slipped from her fingers. In the next room, the child cried.

Riah's gaze swept over the once-familiar landscape, and she wondered about the ancestors of the child. Did they still live? Did they ever sense how precarious their existence was? Probably not. She'd saved that child, but like so much of what she did, it had been done undercover. No one ever need know of her hand in anything…even though her desire for anonymity really hadn't gone so well in recent years.

Her face on the front page of a newspaper wiped away years of hiding in plain sight. The old legend that a vampire's image couldn't be captured was a fallacy perpetuated by vampires themselves. A simple reflection in a mirror had saved the life of more than one vampire when confronted by an angry mob. Unfortunately, she hadn't always been quick enough to avoid a camera flash.

Here it was different. Hundreds of years of absence wiped anyone off the radar, and she liked it that way. No pictures in the newspaper in this land. No old photographs with her face peering out. As far as most people knew, she'd never stepped foot in Romania before. She only wished the horrible feeling wafting over her would go away. Two hundred years wasn't long enough to wash her clean.

In the moonlight she was a vision. Dressed in a flowing gown, long hair the color of sunlight spilling over her shoulders, she made Nicoletta's breath catch in her throat. She was a vision straight from her dreams. Never had she set eyes on a woman more beautiful.

Alexandru reached out a hand to the woman, who took it without hesitation, as if they were friends of many years. Together they stood near Nicoletta, and the golden light spilling on the woman's face highlighted her shiny hair, beautiful dark eyes, and full lips. It was all Nicoletta could do to breathe. Her heart raced as the woman's gaze met hers, and an image of their lips touching flashed before her eyes.

Her voice as she spoke was firm and confident. Nicoletta liked that about her. She was not like any she knew, and what of the *jeans* she spoke of? Alexandru would have to explain to her what that meant. The dressing gown she wore now, while of a strange style and oddly belted, was beautiful, the velvet thick and rich. Why she would want to wear any other garment when she possessed something so lovely, Nicoletta did not know.

First, they must hurry back to her chambers. They would have to return to the castle by daybreak and be certain to have the woman dressed in an appropriate gown before the others awoke. The robe she wore was fine for bedchamber attire, but to meet the Prince? Never. She shuddered to think what he might do if he encountered her in that garment.

The thought of the Prince made her stomach roll, and for a moment she thought she might need to find a bush. She dared not let her body betray her. There was no time for her needs. This was about Alexandru and the woman he had brought through the stones. If the prophecy was true, she was the one, and Nicoletta intended to keep her safe so they would know the truth of it. She prayed he was right about the light-haired beauty. If she was not and he must leave here once more…she wished not to think of it. This beauty must be the one, for she could endure this life alone no longer.

She all but pushed the reluctant woman into the boat tied to a tree at the water's edge. For some reason, she stopped on the shore and didn't seem to want to go any farther. They did not have time for a soft soul who was afraid of the lake. Time was passing much too quickly and they had to get across. Before Nicoletta could speak, Lura picked up her skirts and stepped into the boat. She breathed out a sigh of relief.

Alexandru took the oars and began to row, slicing through the water with quick, powerful strokes. He had them across the lake as silently as the fish swam beneath the surface. Like her, he felt the urgency of returning to the castle before the light of day shone upon their faces.

Once on dry land again, Nicoletta wasted no time. She hurried through the night, her feet sure and quiet against the hard earth. She did not turn to see if they followed, for she knew they would. The horses were right where she had left them and she mounted quickly, motioning for Lura to get on behind her.

"Oh no, no, no," Lura muttered. "How about a car with nice seats and a heater? Riding a horse isn't exactly my thing. Especially not in this outfit." She picked up the skirt of her robe. Alexandru did not say a word as he knelt beside the horse, linked his hands together, and stared at Lura expectantly. He was ignoring her reticence. Nicoletta understood Lura's confusion and could do nothing about it. She just wanted them both to hurry. The woman did not seem to understand the danger they were in out in the woods.

Lura sighed as she put a foot into the hold Alexandru offered. He hoisted her to the horse's back as if she weighed nothing, and her arms circled Nicoletta's waist, holding so tight they nearly pushed the breath from her chest. She did not mind, for they could be on their way, and the feel of her body pressed so close was lovely.

Alexandru had lost none of his prowess in his time away, and he seemed to float through the air and onto the back of the second horse. He was off and racing into the distance without so much as a glance back at them. He knew the way as well as she. The sight of him soaring on horseback through the moonlit night made her heart light. How she had missed him.

She guided the horse across the ground with sure, solid direction. In the time since Alexandru had disappeared between the stones, she had covered this same path many more times than she could count. Darkness had no effect on her, for she would know the way even if she were blind, and in the thickest recesses of this deep night, it was almost so. Her horse, burdened with its two riders, caught up to Alexandru quickly, and they rode side by side down the rough road.

Every little bit, a quiet, muttered oath came from behind her. Several times it was Alexandru, and those exclamations made her smile. While his carriage on the horse still seemed natural, her elder brother apparently had gotten soft in his time away. Where once he too would have been able to spot a low-hanging branch and duck, now he suffered the sting and cuts of the treacherous wilderness as it sliced across his face. She hoped he was not wounded too deeply, for they would have much to explain as it were.

The woman struggled more than Alexandru. She followed Nicoletta's lead and did not fall victim to any of the branches. Still, sitting astride the horse did not appear to be a thing of comfort for her. Not like it was for Nicoletta. She loved the animals and the freedom she felt when she was high upon their backs. It made her forget her place, her role, and she could ride as free as any man.

It was clear that wherever Lura came from, racing across the uneven ground in the deep of night was not something she was accustomed to doing. Nicoletta would gladly help her just for the chance to touch her, but time was not a luxury. She concentrated more on whisking them through the land to the castle borders.

On the outskirts of the city, she halted and led them to the stable, where her friend would tend to their horses. No words were exchanged as she handed the reins to the sleepy man whom she trusted with her life. Soon, they were on foot and moving in the direction of the castle.

At the base of the wall, she paused and listened. The dogs, thank almighty God, were on the other side. It was not that they disliked her; in fact, they liked her too much. Her own fault for often visiting them with bits of meat in her pockets. Should they see her this night, in their haste to come to her, they would draw attention their way, and that she could not risk.

"Sonofa—"

Nicoletta clamped a hand over the woman's mouth at the same time she kept her from falling face-first into the ground made soft by a mild snowstorm that had passed through some hours earlier. The snow did not stay upon the ground; instead it had melted, making the muddy mess beneath their feet. She pulled Lura tight against her body, the feel of her warm in the cool night. The sensation was as intoxicating as the wine the Prince drank.

"Be still," she whispered into her ear. "We must not allow anyone to know we hide here."

The woman nodded and Nicoletta moved her hand way from her lips. She still had one arm around her midsection as she held her tight against her body. It was safe to let her go, but she did not wish to break the contact. In a moment she would release her. In a moment.

The murmur of voices that had made her stop and draw into the shadows grew louder as three men approached. She could not see well enough to make out their faces, though soon enough she recognized at least one voice. It was Bohdan, and just the sound of him made her blood run cold. He was the soldier, the ever-eager-to-please soldier the Prince had sent for her on the last full moon. He had come happily with a smile on his face that she would never forget. How could she? She saw it in her nightmares night after night. It took the strength of heaven not to roar when he gave her that same smile each time she had seen him since.

She did not realize she had stiffened until the woman covered her hand with her own. The gentle pressure of her fingers brought Nicoletta back. She dropped her arm from around Lura's waist after she returned the reassuring squeeze.

Talking loudly and boasting of some conquest that she cared not to know the details of, Bohdan and the other two men moved by the open gate. She leaned around the gatepost and waited until they were out of sight. Then she motioned for them to follow.

Her feet seemed to barely touch the ground as she crossed the courtyard and flew up the steps, slowing when she reached the long passageway. Only then did she spare a moment to look behind, just to be certain they had not been followed. Thus far, they were safe. No one in the castle appeared to be awake, thanks be to God, and they easily made their way to her chambers.

When she slid the beam across the door, she allowed herself a long breath. They had made it and Alexandru was once more with her. All was to be right once more.

"And who, pray tell, is this pretty wench?" A deep voice came from behind her.

Nicoletta almost screamed and then caught herself. Squaring her shoulders, she turned and met Bohdan's cold gaze, almost level with hers as he sat in a chair nestled beside the fire. Her heart raced, her hands trembled. She would let him see none of it. If there was ever a moment for bravery, this was it. The Prince might very well be the Devil, but this man was one who would sit at his right hand.

"You know my brother, Alexandru." She inclined her head to where he had moved and now stood by the frosted window.

"Indeed, though he has been away a very long time and that does not answer my question. Who is the woman?"

She did not know how to explain Lura, and her mind raced, trying to come up with something this brute would accept. She could not tell him she came from another time and place. Nor could she reveal the true reason her brother had stepped through time with their visitor. He would not believe her, and worst of all, he would like nothing better than a reason to take her life. Bohdan enjoyed spilling blood almost as much as the Prince did. Alexandru stepped in gracefully, saving her from a lie she was not ready to make.

"So good to see you, Bohdan. I trust your family is well? Your lovely wife, Isa? Any children born during my absence?"

Bohdan's face clouded at the mention of his wife. A vein throbbed at his massive temple. "Do not speak of Isa. She is not your concern. The woman?" His voice was hard and loud. His patience, never long, was at its end.

Alexandru inclined his head and spoke softly. "This is my dear cousin, Lura, from London. We arrived just tonight. Lura for an extended visit and I—" he shrugged, "I believe I am back home to stay, though we shall see."

Cousin? Her brother's thoughts were much quicker and more imaginative than hers. It did not come to her to introduce Lura as family, but it was the perfect way to explain her presence, not just at the castle but in her chambers as well.

Bohdan's scowl grew deeper. "You say you return home with your cousin, and yet you sneak through the castle like thieves. What are you hiding? Why do you not come during the daylight like a proper gentleman?"

What were they not hiding? She prayed the big man would just leave. She knew him too well. He never did anything without a horrible reason, and there was not a question of his reporting their nocturnal activities to the Prince. Bohdan was like a child trying to curry favor from a parent. He would run directly to the Prince and tell him of their late-night appearance. The thought made her stomach cramp again. She wondered briefly if she would ever not feel sick each and every time she thought of the Prince.

"Not thieves, Bohdan," she said. "We simply tried to be thoughtful of the Prince and his many guests. Alexandru and Lura did not want to disturb anyone with their late arrival. By the time the Prince was awake, they would be bathed and dressed in clean clothing appropriate to be introduced to his majesty."

Relief rushed through her body as she saw the conflicting emotions flicker across his face. He knew she was not wrong. It was right to present her family to the Prince only when they were neat and properly attired. Bohdan could not argue that with her, and he would have no way of proving it was all a lie, even if he suspected as much.

As he pushed his big body up from the chair and moved to the door, flicking the locking beam away as if it weighed no more than a butterfly, she allowed a silent sigh to pass her lips. He wanted to argue, to press them harder, and yet he had nothing more with which to further his quarrel. With one last scowl bestowed on all three of them, he wrenched the door open and left. For once she had won the battle with the big ugly man. Deep in her heart she knew it was never likely to happen again.

CHAPTER EIGHT

Okay, would somebody enlighten me? What was all that about?" Lura had stood there like some kind of voyeur, watching the massive, craggy-faced man try to intimidate Nicoletta and Alexandru. Didn't have to be a psychiatrist to know he wasn't a nice guy. To their credit, they held their ground, and in the end, he'd had to give in and grudgingly leave.

Actually she wanted to know more than simply what the big oaf of a man was all in a tizzy about. Everything since they'd stepped through the stone outcropping had been...well, off. The castle they were in now was in remarkable shape. Someone had done a fantastic job of restoration, and it was clearly evident that all was in keeping with the time of its construction. Had to be a serious tourist draw and one she suspected was quite successful.

Still, it felt different from any reenactment facility she'd ever visited before. Smelled different too, a mixture of smoke, greasy food, and what? A Porta-Potty past ready to be emptied? She cringed and tried to banish that thought.

And there was the big oaf, who was one pissed-off guy. Keeping in character? Possibly. Didn't feel like it. His anger felt real and dangerous. Not the kind that actors usually employed in a place like this, where making the paying tourist feel comfortable was paramount.

Then there was their undercover arrival. So what if they came skulking in at midnight. BFD. Why would anyone else around here care? This trip to pick up ashes was getting weirder by the moment.

On the other hand, her initial gut instinct about Alexandru was still holding strong. She liked the man, plain and simple. And, for no reason that she could rationally explain, she trusted him. By extension, she trusted his sister. Of course, she'd be a fool not to acknowledge that when it came to the sister, it wasn't all gut instinct. Some of it—maybe a lot of it—was because she was hot. Didn't mean she didn't still need an explanation for *The Twilight Zone* episode they appeared to be living in tonight.

Nicoletta shook her head and didn't quite meet her eyes. "We do not have time to explain. Daylight will be upon us very soon and we must get you properly attired. Alexandru, hot water, please."

Lura watched Alexandru jump and run. "Really? Water? That's what you're worried about right now?" She was so tired and everything was so out of whack. "Can't we just call it a night, grab a few hours of sleep, and then go get Vic's ashes?"

"Please," Nicoletta said, a note of pleading in her voice. "We must have you ready. Time is passing, and he will be asking for us at any moment." She'd moved to a tall chest with double doors she'd pulled open to reveal a trove of gowns. She was pawing through them, obviously looking for something, though Lura couldn't tell exactly what that might be. From where she sat it was a box stuffed with a lot of fabrics in different shades of dark.

"Him who?" The ugly guy?

Nicoletta didn't look away from the interior of the chest. "The Prince."

Yeah, well, that answer cleared things up not at all. Lura ran her hands through her hair and, for just a second or two, closed her eyes. Patience, she told herself. Getting upset wouldn't solve a thing. This was all going to make sense at some point.

She opened her eyes and put her hands on her hips. As nicely as she could muster she asked, "Who exactly is this prince and why do I care?"

After spreading a gown that she'd pulled from the chest across the bed, Nicoletta brought a lovely bowl to the small table by the fire and set it down, her hands a flurry of movement. "Prince Dracula. Vlad Dracula. This is his castle. His home. He will want to see Alexandru and be introduced to you as soon as he arises."

She wanted to laugh but was too tired to work up the effort. "Prince Dracula. Of course it is. You guys never let the Dracula crap go, do you?"

Alexandru came back through the door carrying a steaming bucket and poured some of the hot water into the bowl before setting it on the floor. Neither of them seemed to hear her or pay any attention to her, for that matter.

He spoke directly to his sister. "You have everything you need to ready yourselves. I must be on my way. My clothing is in my chambers?" When Nicoletta nodded, he turned and started toward the door.

Seriously, did they not see her? "Back up the pony there, Alexandru. You're on your way where? You're not leaving me here with the Mistress of Vagueness. I want to know what's going on and I want to know now."

He paused and looked back at her, his soulful eyes full of pleading. "Trust me, Lura, please. I promise you are in good hands with my sister. Right now, it is critical for me to hurry and change before the Prince comes looking for us. It would not do well for us to meet him as we are."

"What's this Prince's big problem? Dracula, my ass," she muttered. Besides, what exactly was wrong with how they looked? Well, beyond the fact that he was in some weird tights and she was wearing a bathrobe, albeit a really nice bathrobe.

Nicoletta's face faded to an alarming shade of white. "Please, do not speak so. The Prince will not tolerate it." The way her words trembled made Lura feel crappy for being such an uncooperative bitch.

Suddenly, Lura was so exhausted she could barely keep her head up. This trip had started out on a bad note, and now it had morphed from bad to weirdly messed up. If she could just get Vic's ashes and go home, maybe this crazy nightmare could end. Playing make-believe in a Romanian castle was nowhere on her agenda, and the way Alexandru and his sister were acting was getting on her last good nerve.

Nicoletta touched the neckline of Lura's velvet robe and began to slide it off her shoulders. The trembling in her voice was gone, replaced by a gentle firmness. "I know this makes little sense to you, and I promise we will explain everything when we can. For now, please,

please, please do as I ask. You must freshen yourself, wipe away the dirt of our journey here, and put on a proper gown before it is too late."

"She is right, Lura. We will all clean up, and then I will return as soon as I can. This will make more sense when we have time to explain." Alexandru was out the door before Lura could say another word. Really, he had to stop doing that.

All the fight went out of her. There was no point. She was getting nowhere, and if she wanted to find out what was really going on here, she might as well just do what both Alexandru and Nicoletta asked her to do: trust them.

As Nicoletta pushed the robe away from Lura's body and pulled the nightshirt over her head, exposing her breasts to the cool air, she didn't resist. Sinking to the edge of the bed, she sat. Nicoletta's hands were soft and soothing as she ran a warm rag across Lura's skin. She should protest, but she was too damned weary. It had nothing to do with the way the other woman's hand felt against her skin. Nothing at all.

Soon, too soon, the warm cloth and gentle hands were gone. Instead, Nicoletta helped her to her feet, and the robe fell in a velvet puddle to the floor. Nicoletta held up a heavy gown in a beautiful shade of crimson, and Lura touched it. It felt like fine wool that must weigh a ton. Nicoletta appeared to very seriously want her to put it on. Rather than even try to argue, she simply picked it up. Sometimes it was a whole lot easier to play along.

Surprisingly, the dress fit well, and it wasn't nearly as heavy on as it had seemed when Nicoletta pulled it from the wardrobe. The wool was so finely woven it was soft and comfortable, almost as if the dress had been made just for her. She wished there was a mirror in the room so she could see what she looked like. Not that she'd have had time to stop and stare even if a mirror had been handy. Nicoletta had her back down on the bed and was fussing with her hair the second she was trussed up all snug and pretty.

"What now?" She winced as Nicoletta's comb tugged through a knot in her hair.

"Your cap." She kept combing, oblivious of Lura's winces.

Really? It was clean even if it was a little messy from the horse ride. She preferred it down and loose. Hats weren't her thing. "I don't wear caps."

Nicoletta ran her fingers quickly, gently down Lura's cheek. "Please, again I ask you to trust me. I know that we are asking much of you, and I have given you my word that you will understand all that is happening very soon."

Lura sighed, having already given up. Until they had their audience with *the Prince*, she wasn't going to get squat out of either of them. That much was being made very clear to her. She shut her eyes and held still while Nicoletta fussed with her hair and the silly little cap.

Finally, Nicoletta seemed happy with the hair thing she had going on. Once she was done with all the combing, pulling, and gathering of her hair, the cap didn't feel all that bad.

Nicoletta pulled Lura to her feet just as the door to their room was flung open. She frantically tugged at Lura's hand, tension radiating through her touch. Took her a second before she realized why. A man— tall, strong, and imposing—stood in the doorway, and Nicoletta was bowing her head as she urgently tried to get Lura to do the same.

Riah didn't like finding out they'd missed Lura. Fate appeared to be making sure she didn't leave this place any too soon, and for her, right now was already too much time back here. Still, something about this whole adventure wasn't right. She felt it in her bones, an icy sense of fear that Ivy's cousin was in danger.

So far, all they had been able to find was that she'd left with a handsome black-haired man in an older sedan. The desk clerk at the hotel had heard Lura call him Alexandru. Beyond that, the only other clue they had to go on was a text Lura had sent to her mother telling her that they were headed to Tirgoviste to pick up Vic but had to spend the night on Snagov Island because they couldn't get back to the mainland. That little tidbit of information gave Riah alligator-sized shivers.

Snagov Island had always bothered her, and if she could avoid the place, she did. The wind that blew cold and ominous, holding a vibe beneath that wasn't right, was only one reminder. She couldn't argue against the island's beauty, and she had little doubt that the march of time had erased any of it. It had always possessed what they liked to refer to these days as old-world charm.

On the other hand, she was equally certain time had not erased the menace.

If they had a better choice, she didn't see it. They'd have to follow the only clues they had, and that meant a road trip to both Snagov Island and Tirgoviste. Hopefully they'd find Lura sooner rather than later. If only she'd answer her cell and send a text letting them…or anyone… know she was okay, then this madness could end.

"Whatcha thinking about, beautiful?"

Adriana put a hand on the nape of her neck, her fingers caressing the tender skin. Riah rolled her head, loving her gentle touch. A thousand years could pass and she'd never, ever tire of the feel of her, flesh against flesh. More than that, she'd never grow weary of this feeling of contentment, of being whole for the first time ever in her very long life.

People, humans, took so for much for granted. They threw away beautiful relationships because they were too much work or too hard. There was no time to put into a healthy, happy relationship. What she could tell them. But it wouldn't do any good. How long had it taken her to figure it out? Only five centuries, give or take. If she was that dense, then it was only fair to cut humans a little slack. They rarely got one century to figure it out, let alone five.

She gazed into Adriana's eyes and smiled. "Just thinking about the last time I was here and how much I never wanted to come back."

Adriana kissed her. "Yeah, but you came back for a friend, and that speaks volumes about you, lover."

"They might not be very good volumes."

Adriana was shaking her head. "That's where you're wrong. You're always putting yourself down, and I don't get it. Maybe you were a bad girl once upon a time, but there isn't a single person alive who would know it or remember it. What you've done for so long more than makes up for anything terrible you might have done with Rodolphe. Give yourself a break for once."

A break? The only break she'd given herself was the day she surrendered to her love for Adriana. Truthfully, it was enough. For everything else, she'd be trying to make amends for as long as she walked the earth. It was a life sentence, and she was just fine with that. After all, she'd earned it.

"Come on." She took Adriana's hand. "Let's go have a meeting of the minds with the others. We have a bit of journey to make and some plans to solidify."

Much later, Riah pulled the rental car into the tidy parking area near the launch for the small boats that took the curious to Snagov Island. They weren't alone. They parked their car next to another, cold and quiet. A black sedan. Just like the one Lura had left the hotel in. Trickles of unease that had been flowing through her since setting foot in Romania now intensified about a thousand percent.

She didn't have to point out the obvious to anyone. The silent stares directed at the car told her everything. No one said a word, just moved toward the lakeshore.

Dusk was settling when they made it to Snagov Island. A rented boat, sunscreen, big coats, and wide-brimmed hats protected Ivy and Riah from the sun, not that it was horrible, considering the day was gray and overcast. Still, it was better safe than sorry. Ivy wasn't anywhere near ready to tolerate sunlight, and Riah found it uncomfortable even if it didn't kill her. Being an old one had some distinct advantages.

At least they had only two vampires to worry about at the moment. Tory had stayed behind with Naomi, Cam, and Kara just in case Lura returned to Bucharest. They'd all decided it wasn't a bad idea to divide and conquer.

The little motorboat propelled them quickly across the open water, and when the boat bumped against the dock on the other side, Colin jumped out to moor it before extending his hand to help each of them to their feet. She walked down the gently swaying dock, stepping off where the wood planks met grass now brown with winter's arrival.

The moment her feet touched the island's soil, lightning shot through her toes to head. In an instant everything she'd been sensing up until now solidified into a terrifying reality. Something was very wrong here, and Lura was right at the center.

God, how she wanted to go home. Now.

"She's here." Ivy turned and studied the landscape. "She's here somewhere, I know it." Her words echoed what was in Riah's heart and mind.

Colin was standing beside Ivy, scanning the rise and fall of the island's terrain. "I don't know, babe. It seems pretty deserted."

Riah closed her eyes and concentrated. As if pulled by an invisible string, she opened her eyes, turned, and began walking, stopping only when she came to an outcropping of rocks. The buzzing had started minutes ago just before she began her trek across the long, open area, and the closer she got to the stones, the louder the buzzing became until it morphed into a deafening roar inside her head.

Though she didn't look back to see, she could feel the others as they followed in silence. They'd worked together long enough now not to need explanations for every move, every instinct. When she stopped, so did the other three. As she stared at the blackness beneath the massive rocks, one word kept rolling through her mind: damn. Slowly she turned to face the warriors who had her back every day and every night. "We have a problem."

He was a striking man whose presence seemed to fill the entire doorway. His features were sharp, hawk-like, with narrowed, menacing eyes. He looked remarkably like the pictures of Vlad Dracula she'd seen in different places since arriving in Romania; he had to be a much-removed relation. Amazing to think so many hundreds of years later, one of his descendants could be such a dead ringer for the guy. Again, the amazing authenticity of the castle and its period actors impressed her.

"Alexandru," the man bellowed.

Alexandru stepped around from behind the two men who flanked him like twin towers and bowed deeply. "My Prince."

Lura wondered where he'd come from. One minute the hallway was empty, and the next Alexandru was back dressed in a beautiful black topcoat thing that really set off his handsome face. He still had on those odd leggings, but since the other guys did too, she wrote it off to staying in character with the period of the reenactment.

"Tell me why you came in darkness, sneaking about like a criminal trying to rob me. You disappoint me, Alexandru Vizulea."

Alexandru bowed even deeper and spoke in a soft, reverent voice. "My Prince, I meant you no disrespect. Our travels brought us here quite late, and I did not want to disturb your slumber. I intended to present myself at dawn's first light."

"And yet here I am, chasing you down, and this." He pointed at her. "You bring a stranger into my castle? What right do you believe you have to insult me so?"

"Again, my Prince, no disrespect. The lady and I intended to present ourselves straight away. May I present to you Lady Lura Tappe. She is our dear cousin from London."

London? Seriously, where did that come from? Left field, for sure, and he had to quit telling people that. She certainly couldn't pull off an English accent, even under the best of circumstances. She was as American as it got. Saying she was a cousin was one thing. That she was a cousin from London, well, that just didn't make any sense, and why did it matter anyway? Wasn't like any of this was real. Nicoletta was squeezing her hand so tight Lura had the urge to yank it away. She didn't. Despite the desire to step forward and speak for herself, to end the British-cousin charade, at the same time she had the feeling it was important for her to play along.

Something here wasn't quite what it seemed. This might look like a well-scripted reenactment scenario, but it didn't feel like one. In fact, it felt pretty damned real, and that sent a chill racing up her spine. So, if for the moment she needed to be the cousin from London, so be it.

"Lady Tappe?"

Nicoletta tugged on her hand again, and she got the hint. Lura bowed and kept her eyes low as she said in her best Romanian, "A pleasure to meet you, sir." Hopefully he didn't notice the distinct absence of a true English accent.

When he stepped forward and gripped her chin hard with strong fingers, she instantly thought, *that's gonna leave a mark.* He yanked her head up until her eyes met his. He smelled of soap and musk, of a man strong and proud. Some might call him sexy, but she'd be more inclined to go with creepy. The kind of man she dubbed a step-back guy. Those were the type that made her want to take a step back without any reason other than instinct.

"My Prince," he said slowly, his dark eyes intent on hers.

"My Prince," she repeated, unable to pull her gaze away from his even though she wanted to run in the opposite direction.

He dropped his hand and turned his back on her as if the strange exchange had never happened. "You will come to the great hall after the morning meal."

Lura resisted the urge to rub her face and, rather than say the wrong thing, said nothing at all.

Nicoletta, her gaze still on the floor, saved her from any further interaction with the man. "Of course, my Prince," she said in a voice Lura could only describe as subservient.

The Prince, and the two with him, turned and strode away quickly, the slap of their boots against the flagstone floors loud in the quiet morning air. Lura straightened up and stared at Nicoletta and Alexandru. Both stared back, their faces pale and somber. A brief silence followed before Lura blurted out, "What the fuck was that?"

CHAPTER NINE

Nicoletta's knees weakened as soon as the Prince was out of sight. It took a supreme effort not to crumble. She lowered herself to the chair and waited for the trembling to subside. The words the woman spoke were in a language she didn't understand, but her tone of voice was no mystery. Trouble lurked just beneath her beautiful face. It was in her eyes, the set of her shoulders, the spread of her feet beneath the gown's full skirt. Before she did or said something foolish, they had to make her see and understand. If not, all of their lives were in danger.

"Lura, please let us explain." The pleading in her voice was not flattering. She hated ever sounding like a desperate woman. But it did not matter. She would use whatever she possessed to make Lura understand.

Alexandru came over and put a hand on her head. She pressed into the warmth of it, tears forming in her eyes. It had been so long since she had felt his touch, and until this moment, she had not realized how she had longed for it. While he had been away, she had no one she could confide in or turn to, even if she wanted to. Not a soul to hold her when her spirit was crushed.

"I will tell her," he said softly. Then he cocked his head and studied her face. His intense gaze lingered on hers. "What is it, sister? Something is not right."

How could she tell him? How could she tell anyone? Her shame was so great, even though she had been the one dishonored. It made no difference to her heart. She was ruined, and no one would have her now. Could ever love her. Her fate was set and nothing could change that, not even Alexandru and the power God had graced him with.

But this was not the time to discuss her or her failures. This was about the woman. Lura. The stars had told of her coming and of her saving them all. What was happening now was so much larger than one small woman who meant nothing, when the one who meant everything was here at last.

"All is fine, brother. Let us share the prophecy with Lura. Help her to understand."

"Understand what?" Lura asked. She used both hands to rub her face. Nicoletta could clearly see the tiredness in her body. No, that was not right. Lura was not simply tired. Exhaustion was settling over her features like storm clouds rolling in for a bitter winter storm. Nicoletta felt for her and wished she could hold her in her arms and let slumber wash away the lines in her face.

"Sit," Nicoletta said softly. "Let me brush your hair as Alexandru tells you what you must know."

Lura shook her head. "I don't need my hair brushed. I need to know what kind of shit's going on around here."

"Please," Nicoletta said. "Sit. You will feel better." It had always comforted her when their mother brushed her hair. She hoped it would do the same for Lura.

With a big sigh, Lura sank to the chair and did not protest further as Nicoletta removed the cap she had covered Lura's hair with before the Prince came in. She ran the brush gently through her hair, careful not to pull. The silky texture of Lura's golden tresses was heavenly against her fingers. If only they could sit here and pretend it was simply another day. How lovely that would be.

As she brushed, Alexandru stood staring out the window, and for the longest time he said nothing. His words when they came painted a picture that until now had seemed a fantasy. Yes, she had heard the prophecy before and thought that she understood. She had been living with it since the night Alexandru had disappeared through the rocks. Still, it had seemed like a dream; only tonight the dream became very, very real.

And she was terrified.

❖

The expression on Ivy's face said it all: no Lura. Among the four of them, they'd quickly perused the island and hadn't found a soul. Ivy wasn't a happy camper. Join the club, Riah thought. The last place she wanted to be right now was here. Just being on this island made her stomach roll. Something disturbing and heavy weighed down on her shoulders, and she wanted to shake it off.

This wasn't about her though; it was about Lura. If she just kept reminding herself of that little fact, things would go down so much easier. They'd track Lura, get her back to the States, and then she could go back to her normal life, such as it was.

Ivy put her cell phone back in her pocket and looked at Riah. A deep frown put lines in her face. "That was Cam. They flew over to Tirgoviste and checked around. Lura never made it there and she's not here, so where did she go? And what the hell is that noise coming out of those rocks?"

Riah had heard stories even way back when about the singing stones. She'd thought it was all a bunch of crap when she and Rodolphe had been here. Written it off as silly superstitions of the poor and uneducated.

When the legends persisted through the years, she'd given it a little more notice. Maybe it wasn't just something uneducated people came up with to explain a phenomenon they didn't understand. A couple of times she'd actually dug into a bit of research, and that's when she'd discovered wormhole theory. More specifically, traversable wormhole theory. In other words, a way to move from dimension to dimension.

She gave them a quick down-and-dirty of her research findings. She told them how a wormhole can connect two points in space time. Of how, in theory, a person could move through a traversable wormhole from one time to another.

"You're not fucking serious?" This from Colin, who typically took anything strange or unusual in stride. Apparently she'd just located the point where he could no longer suspend disbelief. "You think we can time travel through there?" He pointed to the blackness between the stones.

Truthfully she didn't have a clue. All she really knew was that the theories never went away, and while she hadn't taken them too seriously before, now she wondered if perhaps she'd dismissed them too quickly. "I think it's possible, and I think that's what happened to Lura and the mysterious man."

Ivy was shaking her head, though her eyes were on the suspected wormhole. "Why would she even consider going through there? It doesn't make sense."

She got the struggle going on in Ivy's head, not to mention Colin's and Adriana's. This was a whole new logic to follow. She'd had a lot more time to digest the possibility, and all of a sudden she was asking them to blindly trust her.

Her gut instinct tracked back to her visit here with Rodolphe. The universe had a warped sense of humor, and it was taking her full circle. "*He's* buried here, and I'm pretty sure he's the key. The power has always radiated around him, even long after his death. If there was ever a place for a wormhole, this is it."

"He…" Ivy's face reflected confusion, but only for a moment. "Oh, shit. You mean *he* as in the king of bloodsuckers?"

Riah nodded. "Yes, Vlad Dracula."

"Fucking A," Ivy muttered. "That's all we need."

"I don't like it either," Adriana said as she leaned close to the rocks and peered between them. "We're on shaky enough ground as it is, with you vamps here, but throw in the king of them all, and I don't get a warm, fuzzy feeling. See what I'm saying?"

"Indeed I do, and trust me," Riah told them. "There was nothing warm or fuzzy about Vlad the Impaler. Not a real charming man."

"You knew him?" Ivy looked stunned.

Riah shook her head. "No, he was gone before I ever made it here, but he hadn't been gone long enough to erase his legacy. I saw what he did, felt him in every breath of air I took here. He was both a savior and a curse, and I don't think any of that died with him."

Ivy seemed to think about what she'd said and then asked, "So why do you think he still figures into the mix?"

For that one, she didn't have a very good explanation. "Call it a hunch."

Colin put an arm around Ivy's shoulders. "Good enough for me."

She felt like she still had to justify what she wanted them all to do. "This is territory I've walked through before. If this place is telling me something, then we should all listen."

Ivy relaxed and nodded. "You know, I think you're right. As much as I'm in favor of following Lura's itinerary, I'm inclined to give your hunch a try. Something's wonky here, and we need to find out what it is. Maybe it's Dracula or maybe something else, but let's track it down whatever it is."

Adriana likewise threw in. "I'm in, and I say let's roll. The sooner we do this thing, the sooner we can go home. I don't know about you guys, but I don't really like it here. This has got to be one of the strangest places we've gotten sucked into yet."

Riah inwardly sighed in relief. They had to step through, the draw too great to ignore. She didn't know what was on the other side of those rocks. But she was about to find out, and she just hoped at least some of them lived to tell about it.

CHAPTER TEN

So, you two are trying to tell me I've just traveled back to the court of Vlad Dracula, as in the real Dracula? Did I get that correctly?"

Alexandru and Nicoletta nodded in unison. Lura looked from one to the other, searching for signs of the madness that surely had to lurk beneath their otherwise normal-looking exteriors. She didn't see anything, and she was a licensed professional. Alexandru was still handsome and bright-eyed. Nicoletta, still beautiful. Not a hint of insanity in either one of them. Of course, she'd been in practice long enough to know mental illness didn't always show on the outside.

"Really, guys? Dracula? I'll buy a re-creation scenario, and a pretty damned good one at that, but trying to make me believe this is real…Well, even as messed up as I am right now, I'm not stupid enough to buy into that as an explanation for the mega weirdness going on around here."

Nicoletta was gazing at her with a decidedly confused expression. Before she could say anything more, Alexandru fired off something rapid she couldn't quite catch. Took her a second to realize he was actually translating her words for Nicoletta. Her Romanian was good, but somehow her tirade needed some clarification for a native speaker.

The confusion cleared in Nicoletta's face, only to be replaced by a frown. "This is real," she said to Lura. "I am real." She took Lura's hand and held it to her chest. "Do you not feel me? Am I not warm and alive? Do you not feel the beat of my heart?"

Lura wanted to yank her hand away. The sensation of Nicoletta's hand against hers was disturbing in a good way, but she didn't want or need that kind of distraction right now. Besides, using the very obvious attraction to get her to buy in wasn't fair at all.

"Yes, you're flesh and blood. I feel you all too well, but in this time and place, not hundreds of years ago. We're right here in Romania in the twenty-first century. Alexandru and I drove from Bucharest to Snagov…in a car. "

"What is this car?" Nicoletta asked. The confused expression was back and damned if it didn't look genuine. If Lura didn't know better, she'd almost believe Nicoletta didn't know about cars.

Alexandru was shaking his head. "Later, sister, I will explain what Lura speaks of." To her he said, "Give us the day, Lura, please. Play along with us and we will talk again this night. You may tell us then if you still believe we tell you an untruth."

Oh, well, why not? It wasn't like she was making ground anyway. They blocked her at every turn. She shrugged. "Sure. Convince away. Vic's ashes aren't going anywhere. But tomorrow, Alexandru, I'm heading to Tirgoviste to pick him up with or without you. Then I'm heading home. Understand?"

He nodded, relief flooding his features. "If that is still your wish tomorrow, it will be my honor to escort you home. You have my word."

She wrinkled her face as she studied him. What was it with his manner of speech all of a sudden? He didn't sound like the man she'd met in the hotel lobby. This guy was far more serious and his words so terribly formal. They were, it appeared, getting farther and farther down the rabbit hole.

Honestly, the best thing she could do was pack it up and head back to Snagov right now. Drop the charade and get on with learning to live with her altered reality. This whole detour was beginning to get tedious. Except something seemed to tug at her to stay. She guessed the suspicion of crazy she'd pointed in Alexandru and Nicoletta's direction probably needed to be pointed her way as well.

It was then Lura realized Nicoletta was still holding her hand. She didn't let go.

❖

The moon was high as Colin guided the small boat quickly across the lake, the quiet hum of the little outboard motor the only sound.

They'd returned to the car, grabbed what they thought they might need for the journey ahead, and now were on their way back to the island.

The church in the distance grew larger and larger as they neared the dock. Riah's throat tightened and her head buzzed. When she was a child she'd had terrible headaches, and her mother had tried to soothe them away with warm cloths dipped in lavender water. Five hundred years without a headache and now one came creeping back in like an old hated friend.

A cool breeze brought gooseflesh up on her arms and carried the scent so familiar to fresh water. As they neared the shore, the sound of water gently lapping the shore was the only sound besides the buzz of the little boat motor. Any other place and it would be a romantic, moonlit boat ride. Nothing romantic about this. Not even close.

Adriana reached over and ran her hand down Riah's hair. "What's wrong, baby?"

Even the touch of Adriana's hand hurt. "Headache."

On the small boat seat, Adriana shifted and studied her face in the buttery moonlight. "Say what?"

"I know. Haven't had one since before the change."

Adriana's face grew serious. "That's not a good sign."

"Nothing about this is good."

The boat bumped against the long wooden dock and Colin jumped out, grabbing the line and securing it with the mooring rope. One by one, he helped them out. The dock rocked side to side as they steadied themselves. She took a deep breath and headed one more time toward shore.

As before, the moment her feet touched the solid ground, vibrations roared up her legs. This was very bad. The pain in her head grew stronger.

Even in the thick of night, the spires of the monastery rose in the blue-black sky. As she stared, a fierce wind rose, whipping her hair in a wild dance. It was cold and uninviting, almost as though it was trying to push them back to the boat. How she wished she could do just that.

"Crap," Adriana muttered as she pulled her jacket close. "Wasn't expecting this place to turn into a freezer."

Riah looked around and shuddered. Winter here could be harsh, and long ago she'd experienced its frigid embrace. This was different. "It's more than the winter weather rolling in."

"I sure hope so." Ivy chimed in. "I'm banking on those flipping rocks holding their own kind of hocus-pocus and pointing us squarely in Lura's direction."

"Let's hope you're right." And she did, except Riah wasn't sure if it was so they could find Lura quickly or get herself back home immediately. She suspected it had more to do with the latter.

She didn't stop to analyze. Not hesitating, she began to hustle in the opposite direction from the monastery and toward the stones. All of them kept their heads down against the wind, steps as quick and light as possible. If all went as she hoped, they'd find Lura on the other side of those rocks and return within a few hours at most. She wanted to be back on the mainland well before daybreak.

Off to the left, Riah noticed a cottage, and while that wasn't unique for the island, this one had a single light flickering in a window. That did get her attention. This time of year few, if any, stayed out here. It was too cold and too remote. Great for a hermit. Not so great for anyone who wanted to participate in the human condition.

Not giving it too much thought, she veered off, pausing only briefly to ask the others to follow. They did. Once again, she was moving on nothing more than pure instinct. An unseen force drew her this way and she knew she had to follow.

At the house, her knock went unanswered. The front door swung open, its lock not engaged, and they stepped inside with the confidence of those who believed they had a right to be there rather than the strangers they really were. A quick survey found it empty. Whoever had been here and turned on the lights was gone.

"She was here. How did we miss this earlier?" Ivy's voice came from a small bedroom in the rear. She emerged with a rolling bag, the long handle clutched in her hand. An identification tag hung from a strap. "It's Lura's."

Riah nodded. The buzzing in her body was even greater now. They were very, very close. She shut her eyes and concentrated. If she could focus, maybe a solution would come to her.

Without a word to the others, she left the house and walked back outside. The buttery moon flowed down on the grass beginning to turn frosty, almost as though lighting a path just for her. She tilted her head and studied the play of light, thinking how much it reminded of her the proverbial yellow brick road. It'd worked for Dorothy, so why not her?

She began to walk, the light taking her away from the cottage and up a small rise to where it disappeared between the outcropping of rocks. Vaguely, she heard the others as they hurried to catch up with her. She didn't know if they were talking to her or to each other…didn't care. She was focusing strictly on the rocks.

Back at the opening in the stones that earlier had been a black void, she paused. The roar enveloped her like a cowboy's lasso, pulling her in and drawing her ever closer to the yawning abyss. The sound was deafening, and she no longer knew if she stood alone or with the others. As she stared, a pinpoint of light pierced the deep nothingness.

Vaguely, as though coming from far away, she heard Adriana's questioning voice. Her words were lost on Riah as an irresistible tug to follow the light through the rocks pulled at her. She took a step. The pinpoint grew larger, the roar louder. She took another and her breath caught. Could it really be? Without looking back, she stepped through.

The sickness rose, and Nicoletta could do nothing to stop it. She crumpled to her knees on the hard stone floor and retched into the bucket. The last thing she ever wanted was for Alexandru and Lura to witness her shame. Not that it made a difference. Nothing mattered when it came to her. She was a ruined woman. Any hope for a happy life was gone.

Her eyes closed, she waited for the rolling of her stomach to pass. It would, it always did. Just a few moments, that is all she would need, and then she would be ready to face the Prince…and Lura.

Lura stroked her head, and the shock of her touch made Nicoletta start. Her head tipped back and she looked up into eyes so deep and haunting it was like gazing up into a beautiful bright sky. She wanted to say something, but words failed to come to her. What could she say to explain any of it? Or take away the burn of shame in her face?

Lura's fingers brushed against her cheeks. "Are you all right?"

Nicoletta sighed and nodded. "I will be." The tenderness and concern she saw in Lura's face made her heart ache. How she wished her life were her own. How she wished it could be different from what it was.

"You're certain?" Lura's eyes still studied her face with intense, caring scrutiny.

"Yes, I am well." As much as she enjoyed the feel of Lura's touch, she pushed up and off the floor. Standing, she smoothed her skirt and looked over at Alexandru. She dreaded what she would see there—the horror, the dismay. When their eyes met, shock made her look twice. She saw not the expected disgust, only deep concern.

"Sister?" He knew. It was in the single questioning word. The expression of compassion on his face made her want to weep.

She shook her head. "It is nothing, Alexandru. I will be well and we must go. He will be waiting." She could not make the words he wanted to hear pass her lips and prayed he would not force to do so. Her shame was great enough without saying it before God…and Lura.

She took Lura's arm and pulled her toward the door. "I beg of you, just do as we do and try to please the Prince. We do not want to anger him. I pray you listen well."

Lura rolled her eyes, but Nicoletta was grateful that was the only sign of resistance. With her golden hair once more in the pretty cap, she was a proper lady for her appearance in front of the Prince. "I don't get it, no matter what you two say, but for now, I'll play along. I expect an explanation soon."

She squeezed Lura's arm gently. "I thank you."

Still holding onto Lura, she guided them down the corridor. Most doors still remained closed, although the scents of foods cooking wafted through the air. Her stomach rumbled again, and she hoped she would make it through the audience without the need of another bucket. Any other time, the smells would make her long for the morning table. Now they sent a coil of unease into the pit of her stomach.

In the great gallery, Prince Vlad sat sprawled in his finely carved chair with the thick velvet cushion, food piled on a table next to him, a tall goblet in one hand. The trembling of her body was more than reaction to the smells that roiled her stomach. Her eyes lingered on the ornate goblet, and she wondered if he drank wine this day or something else. She sent a prayer up to God it was mere wine.

He looked up from an animated conversation with a man who had recently come to the castle. His eyes narrowed as his gaze swept up and down. She shivered, feeling as though he looked at not her clothed body but at her flesh, cool and naked. No matter how long she lived he would always make her feel so. She hated it.

His hand came up, and his long fingers waved them forward. Her instinct was to turn, pick up her skirts, and race away, but instead she held tight to Lura's arm and moved toward him as he commanded with the simple gesture. At a suitable distance, she stopped and bowed her head, urging Lura silently to do the same. She did.

"My Lord."

When she brought her head up, his black eyes bored into her as if he were seeing into her soul. The look made her cold. He was not content to simply take her body; he wanted to possess her soul as well. He could not have it.

Just as quickly, though, his gaze slid away and locked on Lura. She saw the flicker of interest that crossed his face, and her heart sank. As she had feared, Lura's lovely face and golden hair were alluring to a man who felt the need to possess all. She had insisted on putting the cap back over Lura's beautiful tresses not only because it was proper but also to hide the golden locks from the Prince's eyes. It did not seem to have been enough. *Please, God, let him not desire her.*

"You." He pointed to Lura. "Come to me."

Nicoletta squeezed Lura's arm gently as she nudged her forward. She feared letting go of her but had no other choice. If the Prince called for Lura, she would have to go. To do otherwise was to anger him, and that was far more dangerous for everyone.

Lura stepped up and, much to Nicoletta's relief, dropped her head in a gesture of respect. She relaxed a little. If she showed proper respect he might lose interest quickly.

"Your name."

In a quiet voice she answered. "Lura Tappe."

"Lura Tappe. A strange name for a woman with a strange accent. Your cousin tells me you come from England, and yet I've not heard an accent like yours before. So tell me, Lura Tappe, where do you come from?"

Nicoletta cringed at Lura's soft answer. "Washington state."

The frown that creased the Prince's face worried Nicoletta. With a step forward, she was at Lura's side. "She is from the far west, my Prince. A little village."

His head snapped around and he glared at her, his black eyes full of fury. "I did not ask you to speak. Be silent."

She nodded and turned her gaze to the stone floor, her hands held tightly together to keep the shaking from the Prince's notice. Her prayers so far were going unanswered. God could not forsake her now.

"I do not know this place you speak of. You are family to our fair Lady Nicoletta and her brother, Lord Alexandru? Have you no husband?"

"I have no husband." The sadness in her voice wasn't lost on Nicoletta, though it seemed the Prince noticed it not.

A slow smile spread across his face and a chill raced down her spine. She wanted to protect Lura and did not know what to do. She dared not interrupt again, and yet she feared what might happen next. He could not hurt her. If he did? She could hardly breathe.

Heavy footsteps interrupted any further interrogation. Three burly men burst into the gallery, two of them dragging a fourth man by his arms. His face was bloody and swollen, his tattered clothing caked with mud. He was so thin, the bones in his shoulders poked through his tunic.

"My Prince," the first man said as he dropped to one knee and bowed his head. The long sword at his side clanged on the stone floor.

"What have you brought me, Mircea?"

He stood and pointed a beefy finger in the directions of the bruised and bloody man. "A thief. We caught him poaching from the castle grounds."

"My family," the injured man whispered hoarsely. "I have to feed my family."

Prince Dracula looked unmoved. "And you think stealing from me is the answer?"

"I am sorry, my Prince. I did not intend to steal from you. I only wanted to feed my children." His voice was weak and full of despair.

"Then you should have come to ask of my help, not steal from me."

"Never again, my Prince." Tears began to drip down his filthy cheeks, leaving long streaks. "I swear to you I will never again take from your land."

Prince Dracula stood and stared down at the man while wiping away the crumbs of his bountiful morning meal with the back of his hand. "And so it shall be. You will never again steal from me or anyone else." He waved his hand, and Nicoletta wanted to run screaming from the hall. She had seen that command too many times before.

Reaching for Lura's hand, she squeezed it. No matter how hard she tried, she could not stop the shaking, especially after the man was dragged screaming outside, where a stake was being prepared.

CHAPTER ELEVEN

S on of a bitch." Riah stopped in her tracks. Okay, it was true she
could hang out in the sunshine and not turn into a pile of dust.
One of the perks of being an old one. Still, this was a lot more than just
stepping outside. This was full-on sunshine without a hat, sunscreen, or
protective clothing, and it should at least sting.

It didn't.

On one side of the stones it was a cool, black night, and with a few
steps through, she was transported into daylight bright and light. Here
she stood just like a regular old human being. Something was incredibly
weird. In a way it was good. The problem was, she had a very healthy
distrust of things that seemed too good to be true. Somewhere, there
was a catch.

She was scanning the landscape, her eyes narrowed, when sounds
behind her made her spin. Tumbling through the stones came Ivy,
Colin, and Adriana.

Ivy started to back up, a look of terror on her face. Colin quickly
embraced her, trying to shield her from the sun with his much-larger
body. The sunshine could end her existence so quickly it was frightening.
The new ones simply could not tolerate the killing rays of the sun.

Riah watched in fascination as the light struck Ivy's skin and did
nothing. By all rights, her beautiful Hispanic friend should be writhing
on the ground in agony, her flesh turning to blackened ash. She wasn't
even twitching.

"What the…?" Ivy said as her face turned up to the bright sky.
"How can this be? Where exactly are we?"

Riah shrugged. "Been wondering that myself for the last few minutes. I don't think we're in Kansas anymore."

"And?" Colin said as he unwrapped his arms from around Ivy, his own face full of wonder. "Where exactly are we, then?"

She turned full circle and stared, the germ of an idea starting to take root. It didn't seem possible, and yet everything she was seeing told her it was so. Memories hundreds of years old seemed to be coming to life before her eyes, vivid and quite real. Of an island with gently rolling hills, acres of green grass, and a beautiful, well-used monastery.

This was no flashback. "Ladies and gentleman, welcome to Wallachia."

"Wall lacha what?" Ivy said, still sporting an expression of disbelief that she hadn't gone up in a puff of smoke.

"Wallachia, the kingdom of the quite real Vlad Dracula."

"Get out of here," Colin said, his hands on his hips. "And what's with the night/day thing. And…why are we *all* standing around in the sunshine without anyone going up in a puff of smoke? This is a brand-new twist for me, and ladies, I've seen a lot."

"A little more than a paradigm shift, I'd say," Adriana put in, her face mirroring amazement. "We just did a little time-warp thing, didn't we?"

"Good call," Riah said as she put an arm around Adriana's shoulders. "What made you latch onto the idea of time travel?" She'd already worked it out in her own mind but was surprised that anyone else had too.

"That." Adriana pointed to the monastery in the distance. It was tall and beautifully intact, as if it had been recently built.

"Holy crap," Ivy muttered. "Are you kidding me?"

Riah listened carefully, breathed deeply. No, definitely not kidding. It might have been nearly five centuries since she last stepped foot here, but she had a pretty good idea where…or rather when she was. The centuries were rolling back as if she were hitting the back button on an old movie.

Her immediate thought was *holy* crap. The stories about the wormholes were true. She didn't know how or why and, frankly, didn't care. All she did care about was that they were here and hopefully so was Lura. Nothing physically or intellectually confirmed it. Only her heart felt her presence, and that was enough to push her forward. Now all they had to do was haul ass, find her, and get back. Easy peasy, as Adriana would say.

"I don't know what kind of power those rocks hold, but we're definitely not in the twenty-first century any longer. This is the world, more or less, that I came from, so you'll need to follow my lead. Let me do all the talking. Anybody have a problem with that?"

Adriana laughed. "Yeah, well, that's not exactly a problem. First of all, gorgeous, have you noticed yet that none of us speak the lingo? And that was before we took a giant leap backward."

Truthfully, it was going to be a stretch for her as well. She was good at languages, always was, but it'd been a very long time since she'd been here, and the dialect was a distant memory. She'd muddled through well enough after landing in Bucharest and she'd silently patted herself on the back for the accomplishment. This was something completely different. From up-close-and-personal experience, everything changes, including languages. Nothing stays static. Hopefully the nuances of this place in time would come back to her sooner rather than later.

Ivy's face suddenly stilled even as she seemed to be enjoying the feel of the sun on her skin for the first time in a year. "Hold up the cavalry. Let's not ignore the obvious. I should be a pile of ash right about now, so why am I still standing here? This is just so not right in the preternatural reality that I've been living in."

After a long silence, Riah finally admitted the truth. She wanted to be able to provide a good explanation, but she just didn't have one. "I don't know."

Ivy tilted her head and studied Riah with intelligent, questioning eyes. She blew out a long breath and said, "You know this is fucked up, right?"

"Yes." Again silence hung as a feeling inside Riah took hold. "Yes, and there's something else I do know that you may not."

"Like…"

Riah had nothing except gut instinct to base her answer on and yet didn't hesitate for a second. "She's here." The words as they left her lips felt as true as if Lura were standing right in front of her.

"She who…Lura?" Ivy looked around in confusion. "Where?"

Like Ivy, Riah turned to look full circle, not that she expected to find the woman they sought anywhere nearby. "She's here. I don't know exactly where, only that it's the truth. All we have to do is find her."

Three expectant faces stared back at her, and she wished she had something more to give them. She didn't. It was all a feeling. Sure, it was a strong feeling, but nothing concrete that would make them believe with the certainty she felt. If there was ever a moment for blind trust, this was it.

Apparently, they thought so too. Ivy squared her shoulders, took Colin's hand, and looked out toward the lakeshore in the distance. "Well, then what are we waiting for? Let's get rolling and find my cousin."

Great idea. Little problem. Riah saw it immediately, though it appeared to have escaped the notice of the others. "Have you looked at what we're wearing? Not exactly local fashion, if you know what I mean."

"Crap," Adriana said, and then stared at her own hands as she turned them over and over. "I have a hunch I'm not exactly going to blend in here in medieval Eastern Europe, and I presume that's where we are."

"Neither is he." Riah nodded in Colin's direction.

"What's wrong with me?"

Ivy tilted her head and raised an eyebrow. "Does the term *giant* mean anything to you, love?"

He opened his mouth to protest and then snapped it shut, muttering a single "oh" before he did.

"Yeah," Ivy said, a wry smile on her lips. "If we're when and where I think we are, you, my dear man are head and shoulders above everyone else and will stick out like a sore thumb. Don't get me wrong. I love you, sore thumb and all, but somehow we have to find a way to make you blend in a little better."

Riah ran her hand over Adriana's face and stared into her gorgeous eyes. "You too, beautiful. While people of color aren't entirely foreign here, neither are they commonplace. A single black woman would draw far too much attention, I'm afraid."

"Do you know where we need to go?" Colin asked.

Riah nodded. Though not a hundred percent certain, she had a pretty good idea. "Tirgoviste."

"That's like forty miles away," Ivy exclaimed. "And we're on foot. And on an island. We are so screwed."

Colin drew her close. "We're going to have to find proper clothes and horses. Probably a boat, unless you ladies feel like a swim."

Riah shuddered at the mere thought of slipping into that water and shook her head. "No swim. There's usually a boat somewhere along the shore, or at least that's what I remember. For now, we need to take cover and move as invisibly as possible. It would be hard to explain all of this." She waved at their very modern attire.

Adriana grabbed her hand and tugged her toward some nearby trees. "Well, what are we waiting for? Let's kick it in gear. If Lura's with your buddy Vlad, I'm thinking the sooner we get to her, the better. He might have been a savior against the Turks, but everything I've ever read about the guy gives me the heebie-jeebies. Let's find us a boat, some clothes, and some horses...in that order."

Riah knew exactly what she meant. Warm and fuzzy, Dracula wasn't. Bloodthirsty and dangerous? Absolutely. "Time to roll out."

And that's exactly what they did.

Lura managed to make it back to Nicoletta's chambers before she tossed her cookies...a technical term taught in medical school. Earlier, she'd thought both Alexandru and Nicoletta were nutbags...another technical term. Not anymore. Her world had taken a decided shift into the land of insanity when that man, that poor man, had been impaled on a roughly hewn stake. His blood had poured down as the stake was hoisted and secured, his body writhing as the life drained out of him. She'd never seen anything like it and hoped to God she never did again. It was nothing even the most skilled special-effects artist could recreate. The sounds, the smells, the sight were a horror that would not ever be erased from her memory.

Nicoletta's tears mixed with hers as she kneeled beside Lura holding a damp cloth to her head. Her touch was soothing and helped her to calm down, even as the shaking in her body refused to subside. At last, she rocked back on her heels and stared into Nicoletta's gorgeous brown eyes.

"What was that?" Her words were as shaky as her hands.

Nicoletta held a palm to her cheek, and Lura pressed into the reassuring touch. "He tolerates nothing but truth and honesty."

"But he staked that man...alive! He was starving, and all he wanted to do was feed his family."

She nodded, her eyes reflecting deep sadness. "It is the way of the Prince."

The way of the Prince? What a goddamn cop-out. Surreal didn't even begin to describe what she'd just witnessed. All morning she'd been going along with Nicoletta and Alexandru, believing the whole time that their story of shifting to the past was nothing more than that: a story. How wrong she'd been.

The blood pouring down the ugly wooden stake was real. She saw it every time she closed her eyes, smelled the rancid odor of terror and death. She might be able to convince herself this was all a façade, but she'd never be able to reconcile any of it with the man whose life had slipped down the rough surface of the stake.

Nor would she ever forget the expression of the man who'd ordered his death. Any doubt about the truth of Alexandru and Nicoletta's story of where she was now had vanished in the space of time it took to rob that poor wretch of his life. She understood with crystal clarity that she was in a time and place far removed from her world.

Worst of all, she understood at last that the man who filled her vision with blood and terror was, in fact, the very real, and very vicious, son of the dragon, Vlad Dracula.

How could this be happening? As if it wasn't bad enough that Vic was dead or that she'd been waylaid on the way to pick up his ashes. Oh, no, she had to step through some wormhole, space/time wrinkle, or whatever the fuck it was, and end up in a Middle Ages nightmare.

Why couldn't she have found herself back in ancient Rome in a nice palace with maybe an orgy or two? Just the kind of thing to make her forget what a bitch she was.

True to form, no Rome. No palace. Definitely no orgy. Her journey into the world of the paranormal didn't take her anywhere fun. She'd managed to drop into the lap of Vlad the Impaler. She'd be lucky if she got out of this mess without finding herself on the pointed end of one of those hideous stakes.

"All right." She captured Nicoletta's gaze. "I get it. We're not in Disneyland."

Nicoletta's face clouded. "Disneyland?"

"An amusement park," she started to explain, and then stopped. "A place in my world where people go to have fun. I'll tell you about it another time."

"As you wish."

"What I'm trying to say is, I finally understand what you and Alexandru have been trying to tell me. I get where I am."

Relief seemed to soften Nicoletta's features, and for the first time, Lura realized how truly lovely the woman was. Lovely but haunted. Something in her eyes spoke of pain and heartache. A man, perhaps? For some reason that thought made her want to put her arms around Nicoletta and protect her. She didn't want to dwell too much on why. She had enough on her plate without taking on slaying dragons for a beautiful woman.

"We must be careful." Nicoletta took Lura's hand.

Even with the soothing touch of Nicoletta's flesh against hers, the horror of the man impaled on the tall spike returned and her stomach did a flip. She might not fully understand what kind of hades she was neck deep in right now, but Nicoletta's earlier cautions made perfect sense at last. Whatever it took not to catch the attention of the Prince was precisely what she planned to do. She might be a lot of things; stupid wasn't one of them.

CHAPTER TWELVE

As Riah anticipated, a boat was on the shore pulled up away from the water, and they were able to launch it so that they could row across to the mainland. They made it across in no time at all. From centuries past she recalled how small boats would dot the shoreline both on the island and the mainland. Her recollection hadn't been wrong and now they stepped to dry land. Things from there seemed to go their way. A real treat considering the obstacles they typically ran into.

Their first piece of luck was finding clothes. Stealing wasn't high on Riah's list, but sometimes it was the only option. The second bit of luck: no one in residence. The manor house they stumbled on was what they needed most: vacant and well stocked. Whoever lived here was apparently gone at the moment, taking along any servants they might employ. Fate was smiling on them. She'd take it and not question why. Sometimes explanations just weren't necessary or needed.

Riah directed their choices like a good movie wardrobe chief. After all, she was the only one of the group who'd actually been here, even if it was a few decades later, judging by the styles she found inside the manor house. Still, things hadn't changed that much by the time she and Rodolphe landed on Wallachian soil. She remembered very well what was and wasn't proper. Stylish wasn't as much a concern as propriety.

For that reason, she and Ivy chose the nicest dresses they found, while Adriana and Colin were guided to the oldest and most tattered clothing. They would have to give the impression of servitude. Dressed too richly, they would be questioned. A black woman and a giant man were simply not everyday sights in this place. Ivy's Hispanic heritage was easier to camouflage, and she'd easily be able to pass herself off as a woman of substance.

Ivy's short hair was a bit of a challenge though. Refined women did not cut their hair in such a way. The longer, the better. They solved the problem with an embroidered cap that covered most of her head. It worked well to hide the shortness, and as long as she kept it on, no one would be the wiser.

By the time Riah was finished with her, Ivy was a proper lady of standing. Her black dress with gold collar and sleeves was an excellent fit and gave her a somber but elegant look. She was all nobility in the gown, and by the look on Colin's face, it was a successful choice. No one would question her authority dressed so appropriately.

Riah discovered ribbons in one of the drawers that were the same rich burgundy color of the soft wool dress with the slashed sleeves she now wore. Weaving the ribbons into her long hair, she soon looked like a very well-to-do European noblewoman herself. It was amazing how fast it all came back to her.

After some discussion, they decided that Adriana would do better going undercover as a boy. She'd draw less attention as a boy servant, and so they scoured the estate until they found shirt, shoes, and pants. Her rather generous chest was a bit of a problem they solved by binding her with a length of cotton. By the time they were done, the curvy beauty Riah shared her bed with was gone, replaced by a scruffy boy wearing shapeless clothes a mere step up from rags. The metamorphosis was stunning.

Unwilling to give up all her twenty-first century goodies, Adriana managed to fashion a bag out of cord and a piece of soft leather. She hung the contraption around her waist, and it actually worked with the whole waif motif. Riah smiled when she saw her in the grubby duds, little bag resting on her hip. Damned if she wasn't sexy in that getup. Might have to remember that after they got back home. Role-playing could be fun when life and death was off the table.

If they got back home.

She shook her head to banish the negative thought. They got here through the rocks and they'd return through the rocks. Whatever magic was in those stones, it would hold long enough for them to make the reverse journey. It had to. She was going to keep focusing on that thought. No reason to believe it wouldn't work.

Getting Colin into character proved to be a greater challenge. He was simply too big to blend in easily or find clothes close to his size. They finally found a shirt that sort of fit and gave him a little more of a servant appearance. They couldn't do much about his pants. Nothing they uncovered came even close to fitting him, and forget about the shoes. Nobody in the fifteenth century had a size-thirteen foot. If they got into a pinch, he'd just have to stash his shoes and go barefoot. It wasn't great, but it'd just have to do.

"This is the best we can hope for," Riah said when they stood out in the courtyard, the clothes they'd come through the rocks in folded in their arms.

"I say we stash these somewhere," Ivy said, nodding toward the clothes. "We can put them back on when we get ready to take a run at those rocks again."

"If we can get back here in one piece," Adriana muttered.

Riah gave her a hug. "We'll be fine. I know we will." She hoped she sounded more convinced than she felt. Maybe if she said it enough times she'd actually believe it.

Adriana kissed her cheek. "If you say so."

"I've kept you safe so far, haven't I?"

Adriana rolled her eyes, hands on her hips. "Oh, please, Vampira. I've covered your ass more than once."

Riah loved the way this woman made her feel. Whenever her confidence was shaken, Adriana could say or do exactly what she needed to help her center once more. "I love you too," she said, and kissed her. "Now, let's tuck these away somewhere we'll be able to find them again and then get on our way before whoever lives here comes back. We really don't want to get caught with our hands in the cookie jar. These folks do not take stealing lightly, and they'd be real quick to cut off said hands."

"Borrowing." Adriana corrected her.

"Our borrowing is their stealing, and trust me. I'm real fond of my hands and would like to keep them right where they are."

"Would be nice if they had a few horses we could *borrow*, since we're in the borrowing mood," Colin said. "I'm not looking forward to walking all the way to Tirgoviste."

"Hey," Riah said with a smile. "At least you have comfortable shoes to walk in. Have you looked at the nightmares Ivy and I have to wear?"

Ivy lifted her skirt and shook a foot in his direction. "These might look all sweet and pretty, but trust me, big boy, they feel like crap. I'd give anything for one of my nice pairs of Brooks Adrenaline runners right about now." A look of wistfulness flashed across her face.

"Shhh," Riah hissed. She narrowed her eyes and listened intently. Oh no, just as she'd feared. "Someone's coming. We have to get out of here, and right now." She picked up her skirt with one hand, tucked her contemporary clothes under her arm with the other, and began to run toward the thick trees. No one missed the urgency in her voice, and not another word was spoken. They all just followed her lead, running as silently and as quickly as possible.

Once she was certain they were all out of the direct line of sight of the incoming riders, she paused and listened again. The shouts of several men penetrated the deep woods. Two? Maybe three? Damn, she'd so hoped they'd make a clean exit from the manor house, though she'd known someone would have to come along before nightfall because of all the livestock to be tended to.

"We don't have much time," she said as she began running once more. "If they haven't discovered our theft yet, they certainly will soon, and those horses you were looking for, Colin? Well, they have them, and they'll be hunting us down like foxes."

Her prediction came true, though. As it turned out, it was only two men, each one riding his own horse. They easily caught up to her and the others on foot, their ground travel no match for the finely bred animals.

Riah was loath to do it but didn't see that she had any choice. Even with the great beasts beneath them, the two men had no way of knowing the advantage was not theirs. They weren't hunting down common thieves or ladies in delicate shoes barely passable for walking, let alone running.

She caught Colin's eye and he nodded. Both of them stopped running and readied themselves for the oncoming riders. They each took one. Colin's arm shot up at the same time he made a vertical leap any NBA coach would kill for. He caught a thin man with long black hair around the neck, dragging him from the horse's back. Riah drew on her own strength to capture the foot of the second man, pulling him off in one swift motion. In a matter of moments the two were on the ground and unconscious. They never knew what hit them.

Such a quick and easy takedown should have provided a sense of relief. It didn't. The unfortunate part was, she hadn't come here to hurt or kill anyone and resented the fact they'd been put in a position to do just that. It worried her, not just that they were here but what their actions might do during the events to follow. Killing someone could have devastating effects on the future, and she didn't care to be responsible for that. The potential ramifications of every move they made were mind-blowing.

For now, they were lucky. No one had to die. The worst of it was a bloody nose, the result of a well-placed punch to the face. The guy would recover, after a horrendous headache. At the sight of the blood streaming down the man's face, Riah hissed and, just as quickly, quieted.

"Do you feel it," she asked Ivy, staring in wonder at the crimson blood glistening on the white skin of the man's slack face.

Ivy's eyes were wide and she nodded. "I don't get it. What's going on here? It's all wonky."

She didn't get it either. First it was the walking in sunlight. Now this? The wormhole had allowed them to time travel, and she'd swear that's all they'd done. Suddenly, it seemed so much more complex than that. It was as if they were in another dimension, not just another time. One in which she and Ivy were no longer creatures of the night but human again. How that could be, she didn't know.

Standing over a bleeding man, the metallic scent of blood thick in the air, by all rights both she and Ivy should be craving it like any alcoholic staring at a bottle of booze. She wasn't. Neither was Ivy, who, being a young vampire, had nowhere near the control Riah had been able to cultivate through centuries of practice. The calmness that flowed over her now shouldn't be and yet it was.

"I don't give a shit why you two are kickin' it in human mode," Adriana said as she peered back the way they'd come. "Call it a righteous gift and then move it. We need to get out of here before someone else shows up, not to mention it's getting cold enough to freeze my little tootsies, if you catch my drift."

Not quite as sensitive to the cold as humans, she didn't notice the dropping temperature until Adriana brought it up. She was right. It was growing cooler by the minute. Colin had thought quickly enough to grab the reins of both horses the men were riding before they'd had a chance to race back to the manor house. They were no longer on foot, which gave them an even greater advantage.

"Adriana's right," Colin said. "Let's haul it out of here."

In a way, she wanted to stay put so she could try to figure out why all the rules seemed suddenly skewed. She'd spent so many years as a vampire, trying to even think as a human again was a foreign concept, throwing her normal patterns of logic into disarray. Understanding the new rules before she went any further seemed important.

Adriana didn't give her time to dwell on it. She grabbed Riah's hand and dragged her to a gray mare. "Come on, beautiful, let's get going. Tirgoviste isn't getting any closer while we're all standing around wondering about shit we have no control over."

How she loved the way Adriana's mind worked and, as usual, she was right. Even thousands of miles and centuries away from home, Adriana zeroed in on what was most important. Ivy already sat behind Colin on the second horse, a beautiful black gelding. Riah mounted their horse, thinking how it seemed like just yesterday she'd ridden, when in fact it had been at least a hundred years. Some skills just never fade.

Wasting no more time, she glanced at the two unconscious men and then raced away, Adriana's arms tight around her waist. Everything else might be screwed up, but the feel of Adriana pressed against her kept her grounded. As long as they were together, human or undead, nothing else mattered.

"We cannot stay here, brother."

Nicoletta could feel the disquiet that rippled on the air, no matter where she went in the castle. It was this way whenever the Prince was in residence. Power rolled off him and flooded the castle as though a raging storm filled the halls, and it affected everyone.

Some in the castle thrived on the chaos that seemed to follow the Prince. Others, like Nicoletta, hated it. Wallachia was a hard land and yet a beautiful land. The threat of invasion by the Ottoman Turks always lurked in the background, and even Nicoletta could not deny that the Prince's bloody ways had held them at bay for most of her life.

Still, she longed for a day when she did not jump at the tiniest sound or could sleep soundly through a night without awakening with worry.

Such dreams were out of her reach. Her life was here, and things were as they were. But perhaps not forever. This woman, Lura, would change their world; it was written in the stars. Her life was more important than anything else. Nicoletta did not know what Lura's role was in the impending change, only that she was the key. Alexandru had told her so and she believed him.

That she also made Nicoletta's heart pound—was that also written in the stars?

Alexandru stood looking out over the courtyard, silently surveying the comings and goings of those already awake and at work. Today was to be a beautiful, clear day. The meadows were covered with a very light blanket of snow, crisp white and perfect, the sky blue and cloudless. The fresh scent of air washed clean by the quickly passing snowstorm was refreshing and welcome. It would all melt away soon under the rays of the sun, but for this moment, it was a picture of perfection.

He finally turned and looked into her face. "No, sister, whatever is to happen will happen here."

The urge to scream was strong. She hated this castle and every moment she was forced to stay here. Every corner she turned she saw another face, and each one, in her mind, looked upon her with accusing eyes. It was as if each and every one of them knew her shame. She wanted to run and hide, to leave and never return.

"We must leave. We cannot risk her safety. He will destroy her."

Alexandru's eyes narrowed and he stepped forward, capturing her face between his hands. She did not like the way he peered into her face as if he could see into her soul. "What is it, Nicoletta? What has happened during my absence?"

She kept her eyes steady on his, though it took every bit of strength she had not to flinch. Telling him the awful truth was impossible. Never would she be able to do that. The secret was hers to take to her grave.

"Dear Alexandru, while you were away, nothing changed." It was not a lie, and it was the strength of the truth that kept her voice from trembling. What happened to her was not new. She was far from the first, only one in a long string of obedient women that the Prince had demanded. Many had fallen before her, and many more would fall at his hands after her. An old story whispered from the lips of many throughout the land.

The only difference for Nicoletta…well, she did not want to think about that. Pain welled up inside, nearly choking the breath from her throat. Not a physical pain. No, it was something much, much worse.

Alexandru did not need to know. Not just because she was ashamed. Should she share the truth with him, he would take her shame as his own because he had not been here to protect her honor. As her only living family, he would defend her from any and all who meant her harm. He would stand against the Prince in her name, and if he did, her brother would die.

She would not—could not—allow that to happen. Nothing would have been different even if Alexandru had been here. He might think he could have protected her and he would have been wrong. It was the way of things in this place. They could not be changed by those as powerless as Nicoletta or her brother, despite the gifts God had bestowed upon Alexandru. They were not enough to defy Vlad Dracula and live.

"I do not believe you. Nicoletta, you are different. Something happened during my journey, and you will tell me."

She touched his face and gave him a sad smile. "And you have been gone a very long time, Alexandru. Everyone changes over time. It is so for me. Time has made me different." That much was not a lie. Perhaps just a little misdirection. The last thing any of them needed at the moment was to be concerned over any misfortune that had befallen her. Lura's safety and well-being were far more important than her condition.

"True, but your way of avoiding an answer to my question has not changed at all."

She laughed, and it made her heart a little lighter. This was so much like when they were children. It had never failed to amuse her to play word games with her older brother. That had surely not changed. Nor had his ability to see through her. He knew her better than anyone and always had. He had been the one to care for her when their parents died in a raid orchestrated by the Prince's brother, Radu the Handsome.

In some ways, she had felt sympathy for Radu. After all, the Ottoman Turks had stolen both he and Prince Vlad from their beds in the middle of the night. Dragged away, they spent years under the reign of the Ottomans. She, who had been raised by stern yet loving parents, could not imagine how it had been for the two young princes. In the beginning, only Vlad was returned. Radu had remained as their prisoner.

She wondered, however, if Radu truly had been under their dominance. For years she had believed it was so. The night her parents were butchered, her faith wavered, and for good reason. If he had still carried this land in his heart, how could he have had a hand in the death of her parents, loyalists to the court of Prince Dracula and his father before him? How could he have turned on his own brother as he did?

In a way it mattered not. The Prince and Radu the Handsome had both brought fear to the land. Different kinds of fear, but fear nonetheless. Alexandru knew this despite being gone for years. That much had not altered in his time away. Only the name of the ruler was different. Though Radu the Handsome had taken Wallachia away from his brother by force, God did not smile on him. His life was gone as quickly as a flash of lightning, and once more, his brother, tall and cruel, lorded over them all.

If she thought about how she had changed during that time, she could understand why Alexandru questioned her now. She had little choice but to embrace strength in order to survive. Every day she had to watch and worry. Every day her strength was put to the test. Now, it would be even more so. Not just because of Lura but because of the secret she had shared with no one.

She did not intend to now.

"Brother, it is just the state of things around us. So much trouble. So much worry. I think about it day and night. I know not what Lura brings to us, only that her importance has been written in the stars. It matters not what happens to you or to me, only that we keep her safe."

With a nod, he gave her a sad smile and stepped away. "You speak truth, dear sister. I know you hide something from me, and when the time comes, you will share. Until that time, let us go to our friend and keep her from danger."

A little flutter went through Nicoletta. They had known each other less than one day, and yet something about Lura made her heart light. She wanted to be with her, to touch her, to hear her voice. Others talked of love, and she had never understood anything beyond the love of one's family. Since last night, she was beginning to fear that she finally understood. She had always believed it would be a man who entered her world and changed it. The last thing she expected was that it would be another woman.

CHAPTER THIRTEEN

"A ll right, boys and girls. I don't know about anybody else, but my ass hurts." Adriana stood unsteadily on her feet, both hands rubbing her rear end. Despite their odd and dangerous circumstances, Riah almost laughed.

"Oh, you big modern babies," she said with a smile. "We've probably only covered half the distance we need to, and you're already whining. You have to toughen up if you expect to last very long around here."

Adriana's eyes narrowed. "Are you fucking kidding me? I have to ride that beast another couple of hours?"

Riah pulled her close and kissed her. The warm, sweet taste of her lips was comforting, familiar. "You, my sweet, have to ride perhaps only another hour."

Pulling away, Adriana studied her with eyes filled with something akin to distrust. "And why would that be, my beautiful vamp?" She was still rubbing her butt.

Riah couldn't help the smile as she studied Adriana in her boy-clothes, her face now spotted with dust kicked up from the rough road they'd been following. "Because you can't be seen riding astride this lovely horse with a noblewoman."

Adriana threw her hands into the air. "Oh, isn't that just fucking great? I've been kicked back a couple of centuries and the black woman is once again a servant."

Kissing her again, Riah hugged her tight at the same time. "You'll never be a servant to anyone. You just get to play one here in the old country."

"Fuck the old country," she muttered, but didn't pull away. "When I get you in bed," she whispered against Riah's lips, "we'll just see who's the master and who's the servant."

Riah shivered just thinking about it. "Deal."

They all took a seat on the ground, not caring that it was damp, and let the horses nibble on the grass crisp and yellow from the snow and cold. From a nearby pond they were able to drink, the icy cold water rejuvenating. The stop, in Riah's mind, was as much for the animals as for them. She'd grown up riding horses, not that it did her any good now. Though the skills came back to her quickly, the conditioning didn't. She'd just taken a century or so off but was feeling it as much as the rest of them.

Oh yes, her ass hurt too—not that she intended to admit that to Adriana.

With very little encouragement, she could drop on the ground and relax for hours. It was a little cold and wet, flakes of snow fluttering down every so often, but she still wouldn't mind a little nap. This being human again was tiring. Rest wasn't going to happen. No time. Too dangerous.

That thought got her up and off the hard ground. Sore ass and all, it was time to be back on the move. The quicker they got to Lura and returned to the rocks, the better. She hoped whatever doorway through time that had brought them all here would still be open enough to take them home again.

Being one of the old ones had let her live through many waves of history. Interesting in many ways, yes. At the same time, it didn't mean she wanted to go back and live through those times again. The only way to survive as long as she had was to assimilate into the current environment. She'd outgrown medieval Europe eons ago.

No, she wanted warm showers, fast cars, and modern technology. She wanted her computer and her state-of-the art morgue where she could do her important work. She wanted to go back to her lab where she and Adriana could work side by side until they once more discovered the cure to what held her captive to darkness. She didn't want to be here.

After they traveled for hours, the daylight began to recede, and as it did, a deep sadness washed over her. Though as an old one she could tolerate sunshine, she couldn't spend a day in it. She'd exposed herself to daylight only in small increments. This was the first time in over five hundred years she'd ridden a horse, face exposed, skin warmed, throughout an entire day. It was an odd feeling. Not unpleasant.

When daylight bloomed again tomorrow she had no guarantee she would once again be able to stand in the light of the sun. Whatever magic was carrying her and Ivy through the countryside unscathed on this day might fade along with the rays of today's sunshine.

"How are we going to find our way in this?" Adriana said, a worried expression creasing her brow. "It's getting as dark as molasses, and we sure don't have a clue as to the lay of the land."

Not an exaggeration. In this world where fire was the only source of illumination, when the sun set in the country, only the light of the moon and the stars could break up the all-encompassing blackness. Not so oddly, she found it comforting, bringing back memories she'd have thought had long faded into oblivion.

With those memories came thoughts of Meriel, and though once upon a time they might have made her smile, now they made her shiver. She'd thought Meriel murdered on a muddy stretch of road just like this one, five centuries earlier. Not too long ago, the four of them had nearly lost their lives as they discovered the fallacy of that closely held belief.

Like Riah, Meriel had become a creature of eternity that very same night. After centuries at Rodolphe's side, Riah had freed herself to ultimately use her sentence to undeath in order to try to help others. Meriel had gone another direction altogether. The evil that filled Meriel's heart still made Riah sad. Once she'd loved her deeply. In the end, she'd pitied her, and then she'd taken her head.

Turning her gaze to Adriana, the melancholy fled and her heart lightened. It was true that when one door closed another opened. She'd found the strength within herself to make peace with her past and with her feelings for Meriel, only to discover the kind of love she'd only dreamed of with Adriana. It was a miracle that happened for other people, but one she never believed could be a reality for her. She thanked her lucky stars every single night.

"Earth to Riah. Come on back, girlfriend."

"Sorry," she said as she brought her attention back on the here and now.

"Finding our way...in the dark? Any great thoughts? You're the only one of us who's been here, done that."

She hugged Adriana and kissed the side of her head. "Not to worry. We just have to keep heading north and we'll run right into Tirgoviste."

"And we will know which way north is how?"

"You spend too much time in the city, beautiful. All we have to do is follow the sky."

Adriana rolled her eyes. "Of course we do. Whatever was I thinking?"

"She's right." Colin was helping Ivy mount again. "Navigation by the night sky, people have been doing it for centuries."

Adriana stared up at the deepening sky and grumbled, "Yeah, well, where I come from, we use a Garmin. Quicker, easier, and a heck of a lot more accurate."

Riah kissed her again. "Ever hear the phrase 'when in Rome'?"

Adriana was using a tree stump to awkwardly crawl back up on their horse. "Stupid Rome," she muttered.

Lura would give Nicoletta credit for one thing; she knew how to lie low in a large castle teeming with people at every turn. They were everywhere and all bending over backward to not rock the boat with the good prince. What the fuck was up with that guy anyway? He had classic narcissist written all over him. She'd love an hour with him in her office, running a test or two. A serious personality disorder, or more like two or three, going on there.

She remembered her nanny telling grand stories of how Prince Dracula defended the country from the invading Turks and saved what was to become her homeland. Lura was just a child when Sofia lulled her to sleep with vivid tales, and her descriptions always made her think of a great man on a big white horse who smiled and made all the people happy. The kind of man who kissed babies and embraced old women. She had a completely different idea of what constituted the prince.

Not exactly what she was seeing when she faced the man in the flesh. Happy was about the last thing she noticed about him, and she hadn't seen a single white horse. Babies would certainly scream, old women would hide. Sofia's stories and reality were worlds apart.

In the castle, people constantly scurried with heads low and voices quiet. That was odd enough all by itself. Throw in how Nicoletta would grab her arm and drag her into shadowy corners any time she thought the Prince might be nearby and it got even stranger. Nicoletta's fear of the man was palpable, and she wished she could do something to help ease it.

Finally, they were back in Nicoletta's private chambers. The sun was beginning to dip below the mountaintops, and candles were lit to illuminate the rooms and hallways. The flickering light across Nicoletta's face softened the worry lines that creased her brow. Though Lura tried not to stare, she just couldn't help it. She longed to reach over and run a finger down Nicoletta's smooth, pale skin. Something in her eyes was sad, and Lura understood. Boy, did she understand. She could take a patent out on that one.

A stab of pain roared through her, followed by a wave of shame. This was the first time she'd thought of Vic in more hours than she could count. What a bitch. If Nicoletta had any idea what kind of woman she really was, she'd throw Lura to the wolves. She'd let the Prince run a stake through her too and be all the better for it.

"What are you thinking?" Only then did she realize Nicoletta was staring back at her.

"I was thinking there's no way I'm this savior you and Alexandru are so convinced I am."

"Of course you are." The sadness that only a moment before seemed to fill her expressive eyes was replaced by a brightness that shone. It turned her from simply pretty to stunning.

She didn't share Nicoletta's obvious confidence. "Impossible. I'm not a good person."

"Why? Because you believe you did wrong to your husband? Because your feelings toward him were not those of a woman for a man? Because in your heart you desire the touch of a woman?"

Shock made her momentarily mute. How could this woman possibly know? She'd told no one of her deception. While it was true she'd been planning to confess to Vic before she came out of the proverbial closet, she never got the chance. If the person who knew her best didn't know her secret, how could this woman? As drawn as she was to both Nicoletta and Alexandru, she was a little scared of them too.

The words came slowly. She wasn't sure she really wanted to hear the answer. "How do you know?"

Nicoletta came forward to stand in front of her. She took Lura's hands in hers, the warmth of her skin comforting. Somehow just touching her helped. For so long she'd felt lost and alone—an imposter who spent her life helping others with their inner demons when she couldn't begin to make peace with her own.

In this strange world that in so many ways was an impossibility, it all seemed right. Nicoletta chased away the overwhelming loneliness. She no longer felt like a lying imposter.

"I know," she said in a small voice. "I know because I too feel as you do. I feel what they say we should not. I long for what is not proper. I want what is not to be spoken of."

Tears pricked at the back of her eyes, and Lura's hands tightened on Nicoletta's. "Is it true?" She could hardly believe she was hearing the words. Hope surged.

Nicoletta nodded. "It is so. That is how I know what is in your heart and your head. You married this man you thought you loved, but here—" she tapped her chest, "in your heart you longed for something else, someone else."

"Yes," Lura murmured as a tear slid down her cheek. How was it possible that Nicoletta could see so clearly into her heart when no one else ever had?

Nicoletta ran a finger down her cheek. "You longed for a gentle touch and lips as soft as your own."

"Oh God, yes." She was trembling now.

Nicoletta slid her arms around Lura and laid her head on her chest. Lura leaned her chin on Nicoletta's head, and her own arms found their way around her small body. Her heart beat so hard she was certain it could be heard in the passageway outside their chamber.

"I know because I have felt as you do."

The impossibility of all this pounded at Lura's brain. How everything in her world was so right and so wrong all at the same time boggled her mind. They'd never taught anything like this in medical school.

Was all of this a strange dream brought on by the stress of Vic's death? At any moment now she was going to wake up in the quaint hotel all alone, her face puffy and red from crying. Downstairs would be a very normal, very twenty-first-century Alexandru waiting to take her to pick up Vic's ashes. No Dracula. No Nicoletta.

Or maybe not. If this was a dream, it was a damn good one, and she didn't want to wake up. The woman in her arms felt very real, the warmth that crept through her just as real. So did the pounding on the door.

They jumped apart just as the door to the chamber flew open. Two burly men stepped inside, followed by the Prince. He walked through, and it struck Lura once again how noble his bearing was. He threw off power like a dog shook off water. It went everywhere, filling the room and prickling at her skin.

Atop his long black hair that curled slightly, he wore a striking hat of fur, its brim decorated with pearls that caught the light of the candles. His jacket was likewise trimmed with the same fur and held together with buttons that looked to be made of gold. If not for his eyes, he would be the perfect vision of royal masculinity. Not that his eyes weren't male. No, but the deep-black emptiness of them sent a chill into her bones. The package was handsome, but somehow the soul was frightening. Foreboding sat like a stone in the pit of her stomach.

He turned those black eyes first on her and then, with an almost imperceptible shrug, toward Nicoletta. The eyes, so empty a moment ago, filled with a look that made the chill in her bones go glacial. He nodded at Nicoletta, then spun on his heel and left. He never spoke a word.

She experienced a brief moment of relief when the Prince left the room, only to be filled with a new terror when the two men stepped forward, grabbed Nicoletta by the arms, and dragged her out the door. Lura started to follow but stopped when the men slammed the heavy door in her face.

CHAPTER FOURTEEN

The night seemed to grow deeper the farther they traveled. At one point, Adriana's drooping weight let Riah know she'd fallen asleep. With her arms firmly around her lithe body, Riah held tight to her and let her sleep. It would do her good. They would all need to be on high alert once they reached the city.

Here in the uninhabited woodlands, they could travel easily, particularly under the cover of night. No one was near to question the four strangers who were stranger than most. Once daylight exposed them, it would take a lot of quick thinking to keep to their presence in the shadows. Their only advantage was her knowledge and experience with the times. It wasn't much, but it was more than Lura had at her disposal.

She worried about getting to Ivy's cousin before something terrible happened. This was a violent time in history, and a bloody man ruled this land. Granted, he often had little choice, and she could cut him some slack for that fact. It didn't diminish the danger.

At other times, however, she questioned the choices he consciously made. The level of his violence, at least to her, appeared to be in excess of the needs of the situation. But that was neither here nor there. What she did or didn't think about Vlad Dracula had little bearing on anything in their present circumstances. She just needed to worry about getting their band of warriors safely out of this city and back through the rocks. A plane was on the other side of those stones that she had every intention of being on as soon as possible.

Her mind was wandering in that direction as they moved through the trees, and at first she didn't hear the rustling off to her right. Slowly it penetrated her deep thoughts and she peered ahead, narrowing her eyes. Must be wildlife, frightened into motion by the sound of their horses. She hoped.

Shifting on the horse to focus more intently, her movement stirred Adriana, who slowly opened her eyes. "I can't believe I actually fell asleep on this thing," she muttered.

Riah wasn't surprised at all because she knew the beauty of a horseback ride. "This thing is a horse, and this magnificent animal is our friend."

Adriana patted the horse. "In my head I'm all over that. My ass, on the other hand, not so much. And for the record, this horse doesn't feel friendly at all. Smells kinda funky too."

"He smells like a horse, and that's wonderful. Now, sleep more if it helps. You'll need all your wits about you when we arrive in Tirgoviste."

Yawning, Adriana shook her head. "Naw, what I got was okay, but truthfully, sleeping upright on the back of a horse trotting through a pitch-black countryside in another dimension? Well, sweetheart, that might be normal for you, but not for this city girl."

Riah laughed softly. "I don't suppose it is." She stiffened and peered around. "Did you hear that?"

Adriana rolled her head as if trying to work out the kinks. "Didn't hear a thing beyond the *thump thump* of Silver's hoofs."

"Silver?"

"Ah, come on. You gotta remember the Lone Ranger and his trusty mount Silver."

"That one must have slipped by me."

Adriana's head dropped once more to Riah's shoulder. "Too bad. Kind of a fun show when you're a kid."

Sometimes Adriana forgot that Riah had never been a kid and seemed amazed by the thought when it occurred to her. Actually that wasn't technically true. She had been a child, like everyone else, except it had been at least half a millennia ago for her. By the time the Lone Ranger made his appearance on American television, she'd been around for centuries and was far from interested in TV shows.

Straining to catch the sounds again, she urged her mount forward, dismissing them as normal wilderness activity. Short of running into bears, wolves, or even a lynx, she wasn't too concerned. The smaller wildlife wouldn't give them much in the way of trouble. They still had a fair distance to go so it wasn't wise to get sidetracked over squirrels and rabbits.

Turning to make sure Colin and Ivy were still close behind, she heard the whish right before Colin let out a cry. What was it? Even though she'd grown up in this world where darkness dropped like a blackout curtain and the sounds of the night were filled more with nature than man, she'd been gone too long. What once was natural was now strange and foreign. Then the lightbulb hit a hundred watts and she understood. Despite the heavy skirts of her gown, she easily whipped her leg over the horse and was on the ground lightning fast. Adriana was right behind her, although her dismount was more like a tuck and roll than a graceful leap. Still, similar to Riah, she bounced up and ran once her feet touched earth.

The smell of blood hit her before she was within three feet of the spot where Colin had tumbled from his horse and hit the cold earth. Ivy knelt by his side, staring at an arrow that had pierced his shoulder, through and through.

Moments before she might have been less than alert and passing off the sounds within the trees as normal. Not now. Though the steps were light on the forest floor, she knew they weren't the sounds of animals. No squirrels and no rabbits. Their stalkers were of the human variety. She popped back up and spun. When the second arrow came whirring through the night air, she was ready and deftly avoided its sharpened tip. The breeze it created blew cool on her skin, the scent of man carried along with it.

"Take cover," she whispered to Adriana. "Get Colin into the trees and tend to his wound. Get that thing out of his body." God only knew what was on the arrow, and she wanted any kind of dirt or debris out of him. This wasn't the place to contract an infection.

Ivy and Adriana didn't ask questions. Together, they grabbed Colin by his armpits and began to drag his big body toward the trees on the edge of the road. For two small women lugging a really big man, they moved with amazing speed and strength. Made her proud.

Riah didn't move from her spot. Head high, hands on hips, she stood and stared into the distance. They were on her ground and her time. The night wasn't a hindrance; it was her ally. Little did they know they were up against a creature of the darkness. Their loss.

The trees were thick, the cover heavy. The air held a light but steady breeze, bringing with it the ever-stronger evidence of their approach. Unwashed, sweating men. She could almost hear them coming in excited gasps.

The thick forest was perfect hunting ground for someone wanting to stay hidden. Camouflaged in the wilderness waiting for the chance to overcome the small traveling party, they probably thought they'd hit the jackpot. Two noblewomen traveling with only one man and a slight-framed boy? Easy pickings, or so the fools believed. They were undoubtedly congratulating themselves on being in the right place at the right time. She had every intention of showing them exactly how wrong they were. Their first mistake was hurting her friend. Their second, underestimating their prey.

With Colin safe in the shelter of the trees, she left Ivy and Adriana to tend to him as she raced across the road and into the deep forest.

The worst part wasn't being dragged from her chambers to be taken to the Prince. No, the worst part was seeing the look on Lura's face as the guards took her from the room. Nicoletta knew what it meant and what he wanted from her. It was not the first night he and his goons had entered her chamber in such a way. The memories distressed her, and she still did not understand why she of all the women in the castle captured his fancy.

She was far from the prettiest woman in his court. Her brown hair was not special, her face plain. Rather than the rounded curves and full breasts of most of the women he seemed to favor, she was painfully thin and her breasts small. In her mind, she should have faded into the background like the tapestries that hung from the castle walls. Everyone knew they were there, but few ever really looked at them. That is how she thought of herself, though she was wrong, at least when it came to the Prince.

Instead, her life in the last few months had become a series of hide-and-seek games. She would hide and the Prince's guards would seek her out. No matter where she tried to conceal herself, they would find her and take her to his chambers. Like now.

Prince Vlad's private chambers were opulent and beautiful. The bed frame was made of a massive, rich wood, with four posters holding up a wooden canopy. The intricate carvings were beautiful, and under any other circumstances she would have been in awe. The mattress was down-filled and softer than anything she could ever imagine. It would be like sleeping on a cloud.

Except she never closed her eyes, not even for a breath. The beauty and comfort of the bed mattered not when she could do little but submit to his desires. He wanted her and made no excuses for his lust. He was, after all, the Prince of Wallachia. He had saved them all from a horrible fate at the hands of the Turks, and how she really felt about him was of no consequence. She, like all in Wallachia, owed him a debt for her life.

That she hated him and despised his touch was her cross to bear. She would do what she must to save herself and what was left of her family. To deny him would mean death to her, to Alexandru, to anyone she loved. Protecting their lives was worth any sacrifice she had to make.

She understood. She did not think Lura did. Her lovely face had mirrored the distress she did not give voice to. Nicoletta wanted to reassure her and tell her not to worry. The bastards following the Prince like pet dogs did not allow her even a moment to reassure Lura.

"Not at your prettiest tonight, are we, Nicoletta?"

At the sound of his voice she jumped and then just as quickly recovered. She had learned early in this odd relationship not to show fear. Respect, yes. Fear, never. He fed on fear.

"It has been a long, hard day, my Prince." And no time for sleep the night before, though she would not tell him of that nocturnal journey. She was so exhausted she could almost weep, unshed tears stinging at the back of her eyes. Her weariness was her cross to bear, and she would not allow him to see any weakness in her.

He came up behind her and leaned close. His breath was hot on her ear. "And we have all night."

She suppressed the shudder that threatened to topple her body. It was just such a reaction that he would find intoxicating. "Whatever you wish, my Prince."

He grabbed her shoulder roughly and turned her to face him. His piercing eyes were narrowed to slits, his thin lips tight. His skin was deathly pale, and she wondered why she had not noticed this until now. "You do not please me tonight, Nicoletta."

Her stomach dropped. She had heard this tone of voice before, and it did not come before anything good. "I am sorry, my Prince. What can I do to earn your pleasure?" She dipped her head and held her hands together to try to calm the trembling. This was easier to do when she did not gaze into his eyes.

He thrust her away roughly, and she nearly tripped on the edge of the thick carpet. She felt both hope and dread. His lack of contentment would keep her out of his bed. It might also be the thing that would spill her blood.

His silence brought chills to her arms despite the deep heat in the room. It was heavy with disapproval. His whims were quicksilver and often deadly. He had not been so back when he had married for the first time. She had been just a child, but she remembered the man he had been. He had smiled often and, though still strong and decisive, was not so quick to draw blood. She had not feared him then as she did now every moment she was awake. That all changed when his bride jumped from the parapet of the castle after learning of the Turks bragging of his death on the battlefield. It was a lie his love would never know.

As her life had drained away on the rocks below, so did any shred of compassion he had for the world. Knowing him as he was now, she could not find in him the heart needed to love, and yet she believed he had loved his wife deeply. When her lifeblood drained away on the cold, hard rocks at the mountain base, it was as if his had as well. Hardness edged everything he did from that day forward. He married once more, and they all hoped for the return of the man they had known before. The smiles did not return. Neither did the man. It seemed that when his true love died, so did a part of him.

In these times, she was not the only one summoned to the spacious chambers. Many women passed through the doors and into the well-appointed chambers. Many lay upon the magnificent bed. The best she could hope for was to fall out of favor without upsetting him. If he grew bored with her or turned his eye to another lovelier woman, she would be free. The thought brought both hope and dread. She wanted to be free of him, but at what cost?

His preoccupation with her slipped away like a stone falling beneath the waters of the lake, and he began to pace the large chamber. Tilting her head, she watched him move back and forth. Something unspoken drew him away from the needs of his body and into the silence of his head. She had never seen him like this before.

"You may go," he said abruptly, not looking at her.

Shocked by his command, she did not move. "My Prince?" Not once in the many times she had been brought here had he ended their night together in this way. She did not understand. Should she be joyful that she was being released from this luxurious prison? Or should she be cowering in fear?

He whirled. "I said *leave*." He tore the doors open and shoved her into the corridor. She stumbled and nearly lost her footing. Righted, she gave one puzzled look at the closed door, then picked up her skirt and all but ran.

The two guards outside sneered as she rushed away. Their snickers and graphic, unpleasant words were loud enough to reach her ears. She did not care. God had smiled on her this night and she was grateful. As fast as she could, she returned to her own chambers.

CHAPTER FIFTEEN

Riah was breathing hard by the time she made it back to the secluded spot in the forest where Ivy and Adriana were tending to Colin. Even with their limited supplies, Ivy had been able to remove the arrow and dress the wound. Once a doctor, always a doctor, alive or undead.

Still, it made Riah nervous. She retained vivid memories of infections going rampant and lives being lost in a matter of days. Something as insignificant as a scratch in the twenty-first century could end a life in these times. She'd seen it firsthand and didn't want to see it with Colin. The former vampire hunter had unknowingly wormed his way into her heart.

Bottom line, the sooner they retrieved Lura and returned to their own time, the better for everyone involved. She almost laughed out loud at the phrase "their own time." This time and place was far closer to her own time than where they'd come from. By all rights, this is where she should die once and for all. It would be poetic justice.

Then she glanced at Adriana, and all morbid thoughts of ending her long, long life faded. She wished for as much time with Adriana as she could have. She didn't want to die. Not anymore.

"Did you get them?" Colin asked as he sat with his back to a tree. Blood stained the front of his ragged shirt, and even in the darkness, she could see how pale his face had become. He was a tough man, but even tough guys were no match for a well-aimed arrow.

She gave him a curt nod. *Get them* was not quite how it'd gone down. It was a bit more like a well-played sucker punch. She'd zeroed in on the two hunters, who obviously thought they were about to make a big score, and then sauntered in with her head held high. An arrogant royal through and through.

The two men didn't flinch, and they bought her act hook, line, and sinker. They were accustomed to the mannerisms of the wealthy, and they hated them. She'd counted on that intensity of emotion to blur their vision. All they saw was a haughty noblewoman and had completely missed the danger that lurked beneath the façade. Her plan. Their bad luck.

Pissed her off though. She didn't like killing humans, even when it was a matter of survival. When she took the physician's oath all those years ago, it meant something very different to her than to her fellow graduates. It was more than just "do no harm." It was also to make amends. She'd hurt people throughout the time she'd spent at Rodolphe's side, many people, and even if she lived a thousand years she doubted she'd ever feel like she'd made reparations.

Yes, she still killed, but those she destroyed in this life weren't simply thieves or men so poor that robbing travelers would feed their families for a year. Those she'd dispatched over the last two centuries were killers who'd chosen the evil side over what was good and right. Her conscience was clear in that respect.

Tonight, she'd had to make a choice. Kill or be killed. It didn't matter that these men were not of the vast eternity she had been relegated to, but rather of a time and place where sometimes survival meant random harm. At the same time, she understood the dynamics because once upon a time, this had been her world. She'd always known of the dangers of highway robbers. While she felt for their families and the harshness of their existence driving them to their actions, she had to protect her friends.

If simply incapacitating them had been an option, she'd have gladly taken it. The whole scenario was far more complicated than that. Upon reviving, they would tell their townsfolk, and soon, a tale of the four strangers on the rutted dirt road would reach the ears of the one in power. Never a good thing. They were too close to the city to risk exposure now.

And so she'd killed them. Regrettable? Very much so. Necessary? Absolutely. Her unease now went beyond the mere act of destruction of life. She worried that what she'd just done would send ripples out into the universe that would have disastrous effects. When they made the return trip through the stones what would her actions have altered? The ramifications were staggering.

She pushed the troubling thoughts aside and studied Colin. At this point she couldn't do anything to change a single thing. They had to press on. "How's your shoulder?"

He winced as he tried to push up. "Hurts like a motherfucker."

She smiled. He was going to be all right. Funny how things worked out. Once not that long ago, she'd have been running from Colin, and now here she was worried about him. Quite a turn of events. She liked it.

"Can you travel?"

Though his face was tight he didn't hesitate. "Damn straight."

"Come on, Ivy. Let's get him up on the horse and have him ride as long as we can. Once we get close to the city, he'll have to walk. No choice there, but let's give him a chance to rest as much as he can."

Ivy was helping Colin mount the horse, trying to keep the pressure to his shoulder minimal yet still stop the bleeding. "How close do you think we are?"

She shook her head. "My days of horse travel are so far in the past, it's hard to judge. If I was to give it a guess, though, I'd say we have two more hours, tops." Glancing up at the night sky, she winced. "I'm hoping we get there before daylight."

"You think we'll still be able to walk in the light?" Ivy asked, a note of hope in her voice.

She wanted to say yes, only the truth was, she had no flipping idea. "Maybe. Just in case, I don't want to risk being caught in open space with nowhere to hide. If we don't reach the city before daylight, we better plan on finding shelter. Better to err on the side of caution."

"Then let's not keep standing around here talking about it." Adriana was pulling herself up on the horse she and Riah shared. "Let's get to the city before dawn, then haul ass to find Ivy's cousin. I don't know about the rest of you, but the sooner we get out of here and back home, the better. I gotta say I'm not finding this place all that cozy."

"Second that," Colin said as he shifted on his mount, a wince of pain crossing his pale face at the jostle to the injured shoulder. Ivy turned to look at him, careful not to bump him.

"You sure you're going to be all right?" Riah would hate to leave him behind. Colin was an incredible asset to the Spiritus Group, and in this violent world, they could use all the help they could get. Their odds of getting in, nabbing Lura, and getting out were much, much better with Colin in the mix.

On the other hand, if he wasn't able to function somewhere close to full capacity, they'd be better off if he stayed here. An injured, incapacitated man Colin's size would be a problem, and they didn't need two people to rescue. One was plenty.

He winked at Ivy and told Riah, a bit of color coming back into his face, "Flesh wound. Let's hit the road."

❖

This was killing her. Lura was worried sick about what was happening to Nicoletta somewhere in the dark regions of this castle. If she had any idea at all where to find Alexandru, she'd go haul his ass back up here and make him help her hunt his sister before something terrible happened. The look on her face when they dragged her from the room cut at Lura's heart. It wasn't terror; it was something worse.

She needed Alexandru to help her, and she didn't understand why all of a sudden he was MIA. Now that she thought about it, she hadn't seen him all day. Granted, she didn't know him well and had no idea what was or wasn't normal behavior for him. Still, last night when he left them, she'd had the sense that he and Nicoletta had a great deal to discuss. So, why the disappearing act today?

A horrible thought occurred to her. What if something had happened to him? What if he'd left Tirgoviste? How was she going to get home?

That thought made her stop pacing the spacious room and stare outside. Good God. If she was stuck here, she didn't know what she'd do. She inhaled deeply and almost choked. Foreign odors assailed her nose, and a cold wind blew through what passed for a window. Outside, the ground was ankle-deep, blackened mud, the result of snow and dirt that people and animals had trampled.

Where was the big beautiful bathroom with the jetted tub? Where were the central heat and air that switched effortlessly when it became too hot or too cold? Where was the cable television, the Internet, the shiny new smart phone? These were the comforts of her world, and she really didn't want to give them up.

He better still be here, and as soon as Alexandru showed his face, she'd drag him through every hall in this stone prison until they found Nicoletta. Once she was safe, Lura would demand they take her back to those stones and have them do their magic in reverse. Her trip to wonderland was way past the point of being interesting or intriguing. She wanted to go home. Now.

A creak made her whirl away from the window. The heavy door was opening slowly, its hinges groaning with the effort. Her breath caught in her throat. Were they were coming for her now just as they'd come for Nicoletta? She didn't have anywhere to run and, as far as she could tell, no way to escape. They'd both be lost.

The burly, sour-faced guards didn't barge through the door this time, their arms at the ready to drag her off into the nether regions of the castle.

It was Nicoletta.

The sight of her made Lura's heart beat like thunder, and relief turned her legs to rubber. It was all she could do not to crumple to her knees and sob. She rushed to Nicoletta, taking hold of her hands. Hard to tell whose hands were shaking the worst.

Training took hold and she began to run her hands over Nicoletta. Around her head, down her neck, across her shoulders, down her arms. "Are you all right? Did he hurt you?"

Nicoletta shook her head. "I do not understand what happened or why. The Prince was in a strange mood this night, and he sent me away."

Something in her face pulled at Lura's heart. So lovely and so haunted. She totally understood and for the first time refused to ignore all the feelings that rolled through her. She was tired of being what everyone else thought she should be.

Finding no wounds, no blood, no bruises, she wanted to pull this woman into her arms and kiss away her inner pain, along with a little of her own. Nicoletta's eyes were mysterious and full of secrets. She wanted to kiss her until they no longer had any secrets between them.

Before she could talk herself out of it, she wrapped her arms around Nicoletta and pulled her close. Slowly, she tilted her head and tenderly pressed her lips to Nicoletta's. Her lips were soft, yielding, and so wonderfully sweet. The thrill that raced through Lura at the touch was what she'd always dreamed of feeling with Vic and never did. More than that, it was the feeling of absolute rightness that made her want to hold this woman forever.

She'd intended to simply reassure Nicoletta by giving her a quick, compassionate hug, and yet the gentle kiss deepened into something much more. It wasn't just her either. Nicoletta returned the kiss and pressed her body close to Lura's. The feel of her breasts against her own was intoxicating. She wanted it to go on forever.

Sliding her hands up Nicoletta's back, she pressed her closer. She wished the thick, beautiful gowns were gone. To feel Nicoletta's flesh against her own was what she wanted more than anything. To feel the heat that set her skin and her soul on fire.

When Nicoletta broke away, something akin to despair poured over her. She wanted her so badly, she shook from head to toe. What she couldn't do was take what Nicoletta wasn't willing to give. Lura was left standing alone when she pulled away from her. She'd pushed too hard, let her desire carry her away. The woman had experienced enough without her piling on more.

Except that what she first took for reluctance was anything but. Instead of getting as far away from her as possible, Nicoletta walked to the door and latched it from the inside. They were together and alone. No one would come in without one of them opening the door. Privacy.

Spellbound, she watched as Nicoletta reached around behind her back and loosened the ties of her dress. The lovely embroidered wool gown slipped to the floor in a puddle at her feet. Her undergarments followed one by one until she stood before Lura completely naked.

Her breath caught, and the only thing that let her know she was still alive was the hammering of her heart. Nicoletta was so incredibly beautiful, with pale skin so smooth it was like looking at fine porcelain. Her breasts, while small, were firm and perfect, with rosy round nipples that grew hard from the cool air and Lura's hungry gaze.

A moment ago she'd have jumped her like a lovesick teenager, but faced with such perfect beauty she suddenly found herself shy and hesitant. Nicoletta was offering the very thing she'd desired since laying eyes on her, and now she was afraid that by taking it, she'd somehow let this precious woman down. She was, when it came to affairs with women, a virgin. What if she did something wrong? What if she was such a terrible lover Nicoletta would regret making love? How could she put herself out there and not disappoint?

Something of what she was feeling must have shown through in her eyes, for Nicoletta stepped forward, took her face in her hands, and said against her lips, "You are all that I want. For so long I was waiting for something, but until you came through the magical stones with Alexandru I did not know what it was. The moment I saw your face, my heart began to sing and nothing else mattered."

Nicoletta kissed her again with such incredible tenderness she thought her legs would finally give way. Nothing had ever felt like this before and she wanted much, much more.

She began to push at the dress that all of a sudden felt so confining it was as if she were suffocating. Nicoletta laughed softly and turned Lura around to begin unlacing the gown for her. It took longer than she would have liked, but finally free of the heavy fabric, she stood naked and trembling before flames roaring in the massive stone fireplace and the woman who made her feel alive for the first time in years.

CHAPTER SIXTEEN

R iah had become accustomed to the changes in the world. Certainly she had memories of the past, fairly vivid ones at that. Seeing the past before her eyes, however, was disconcerting. Living forever was one thing; reliving it was something altogether different. Not entirely pleasant either, for she'd long outgrown this century.

The closer they rode to the city, the more familiar things became in a déjà vu sort of way. So far, the night was holding, which was good for a host of reasons. If memory served her right, they could find shelter once they were inside the city. The first time Rodolphe had brought her to what he always referred to as the homeland, he'd introduced her to a "friend" named Antoine. He'd given them shelter, protecting them from the light and prying eyes. Antoine had been an old man then, both pleasant and understanding of their needs. While pleasant to Rodolphe, he'd been very solicitous to Riah. She'd liked him a great deal. If she guessed right on the timeframe now, he'd be much younger and, she hoped, as trustworthy as a young man as he was in later years.

If they kept the pace going, they'd reach Tirgoviste well before the sun was fully up in the sky. Plenty of time to make it to Antoine's home and the precautionary safety of shelter.

Adriana shifted behind her. "Are you all right?"

"Seriously," Adriana grumbled. "How in the fuck did anyone survive horse travel? Everything aches. I feel like I was on the losing end of a bar fight, and I'm pretty sure a bar fight would have been infinitely more fun."

"You've been in a lot of bar fights?" Riah was smiling to herself.

"Ha ha. You know what I mean."

Not to worry, love. You're going to get the chance to stretch out the kinks real soon."

Adriana groaned. "It's almost hoof time for me and broken boy, isn't it?"

"Afraid so."

"I don't know what's worse, the riding or the walking. Either way I'm going to feel like crap. At least it's still dark so we don't have to worry about you and Ivy going up in smoke."

She glanced over at the other horse. "Colin?"

He'd been awfully quiet the last hour or so. The wound had to be painful, particularly considering the constant movement of the horse. He was a tough man though, and injury wasn't a new reality for him. In his former life as a hunter, it was routine. In his new life with the Spiritus Group, pretty much a guarantee. Of course, an arrow through the shoulder wasn't exactly the kind of wound he came up against in the battle they waged in their century.

"Yeah," he sort of grunted.

From the sound of his voice, he'd felt better than he did right now. Unfortunately, they didn't have much in terms of choices, not if they wanted to travel without garnering unwanted attention. He wasn't going to be able to ride much farther. "You up to a walk into the city?"

"Sure. I've just been riding along here thinking to myself how much my shoulder feels like shit and what could possibly make it feel even worse? Oh yeah, tromping along a dirt road in the wee hours twisting ankles and stumbling on rocks."

"Anybody ever tell you you're a smart-ass?"

"Oh, oh, can I answer that?" Ivy jumped in. "He's regularly reminded of that particular character trait!"

"Hush, woman," he said on a small laugh.

"Hush yourself, big man. I might be small, but remember, I'm the one in charge. You're going to have to do everything I tell you." Her laugh was like golden bells on the night air.

"God, she's loving this," he said as he slid to the ground with a grunt.

"I hope we don't have to stay here too long. She's going to be even more impossible to live with than she already is."

"Me?" Ivy feigned indignation. "Why, I'm a joy to live with. Just ask me."

He reached up to pull her head down for a kiss before starting to walk alongside her horse. As she watched him, Riah decided that despite his size and out-of-place footwear, he'd be able to blend in somewhat. It was more about his carriage in the face of injury. People in this time and place didn't stop because of an injury. Stopping meant death. It was a hard environment, creating tough people. Survival of the fittest in the flesh. Colin was a strong guy, and that was going to serve him well for as long as they had to be here.

She hoped it wouldn't be long. Despite her relegation to the night, she rather liked cars, hot showers, and comfortable homes. Even the most opulent home in this world didn't hold a candle to her house in Spokane with its modern conveniences and fun extras. Refrigeration…well, it held its own very definite advantages, though she didn't care to think about that right now. For whatever reason, she and Ivy weren't needing or craving blood. She wasn't going to question that one, just be grateful.

With Colin and Adriana now walking, the reins of the horses held in their hands, their trek began to slow down. Riah cast nervous looks toward the sky, always watchful for the telltale rays of light. They were doing well so far. She hoped their luck would hold.

They made it to the outskirts of the city far quicker than she anticipated. She reined in her horse and sat upright, studying the buildings and open areas as best she could in the dim light. It was familiar and different all at the same time. It took her quite a while to get her bearings, but finally everything began to click into place.

Riah gave quiet instructions to Adriana, who silently guided the horses as she directed. One of the great things about living and working together was the unspoken communication. It served a very useful purpose on days like today.

At last they came to a modest home on a narrow street. Adriana helped Riah down even though she didn't need it. It would, however, be highly noticeable if she hopped off the horse by herself when her groom was standing right next to her. Ladies didn't do such a thing in this place. Of course, the fact that she didn't at all mind the touch of Adriana's hand had nothing to do with it. No matter the situation, it always gave her strength and comfort. Besides, that cute-boy persona hadn't gotten old yet.

She knocked on the door and waited. As long as it took him to answer, he must have been in bed asleep. Finally, Antoine came to the door, and the sight of his familiar face almost made her weak. His expression registered no recognition of her, further cementing her theory of time and place. Well, that and the fact that he was far younger than when she'd met him originally. Still, she'd have recognized him in an instant. He looked the same, with kind eyes and a gentle voice. Hopefully the attitude of assistance was still there too.

"May I help you?" he asked, his words hushed. His hair was tousled, his eyes still showing the lingering effects of slumber.

She bowed her head slightly. "I hope you can. I am Princess Catherine Tudor and we need your assistance."

Nicoletta was shocked by her own boldness, though not enough to make her stop. She had submitted to the Prince because that is what a woman did when summoned by Vlad the Impaler. To her, he was neither violent nor hurtful. He simply took what he desired and, when he was done, sent her on her way.

She was ashamed to be used that way and wished she could simply stand up to him and say no. But it was not to be for her or any woman he summoned. His power was too great and hers too small. She believed deep in her heart that he had made a pact with the devil, for how else could he do the things he did and still sleep?

Tonight when he sent her away, her prayers were at last answered. She could not undo what he had done to her. Could not change what would be in the seasons to come. But, if he now tired of her, at least her life would belong to her once more. She could leave this place and live far away in solitude and peace. It would be a lonely existence, but she would no longer have to be afraid of heavy footsteps that ripped her away from slumber.

For this night, this single night, she deserved the touch of the woman she longed for. Lura was the chosen one, the beautiful one, and if only for a moment, she could drown in her loveliness. It would be enough, and she could hold onto the memory of it for the rest of her life.

She took Lura's face between her hands and marveled at how soft and smooth her skin was. Her beauty took her breath away. She kissed her lips slowly, tasting, savoring. It amazed her how wonderful she tasted. When her tongue touched Lura's a delicious shock raced through her body.

Lura reached up and grabbed her hands, dragging her toward the bed. In the fireplace, the wood snapped and the flames roared while the room filled with the scent of the fragrant wood. She was only vaguely aware of these things, for all her attention was centered on Lura.

The room, already warmed by the fire, grew even warmer as they stretched out on the bed. Lura's hand stroked her cheek, dropping to her neck and then her breast. The feel of fingers touching her nipple made it spring hard and ache even more for the pressure of her hands and lips. A warm sensation unlike any she had ever experienced pooled in her stomach.

"You are so beautiful," Lura said against her lips. "You can't begin to know how much I want you."

"I give myself freely," she said in return. Something she had not said to anyone before, man or woman. The words came from her heart.

"As do I," Lura responded. The sincerity in those three words made her soul sing. For so long she'd felt alone, unloved. Not tonight.

Her kiss turned hard and deep, the need inside her booming to life. Her hands roamed over Lura's curves, her full breasts firm against her palms. She dipped her head and took a nipple into her mouth. Lura's moan was quiet but deep, and it made her own body quiver. As she sucked, she let her hand drop to the patch of hair at the "V" of Lura's thighs. Her fingers raked through the fine mass, and she loved the way it curled around her fingertips.

Lura's hips rose to meet her hand, and she took the invitation to part her lips and slide her finger between them. She was hot and wet. Nicoletta's own breathing grew rapid at the feel of her flesh. Her need was too great to wait and so she did not. She slid a finger inside Lura's waiting center.

"Oh God." Lura moaned. "That feels wonderful."

Her own body was on fire and wanted, no, needed, Lura's touch. Encouraged by her hot response, she slid another finger inside, moving in rhythm to Lura's thrusting hips. The sensations of heat and wetness and desire were so intense, Nicoletta wanted to cry. She kissed Lura as her hand continued to stroke. Suddenly, Lura's body arched and a stifled sob tore from her throat.

For a moment, Nicoletta thought something was wrong and started to pull away. Lura stopped her, holding her hand so that her fingers remained inside her.

"Don't leave me," Lura whispered. "Oh God, don't leave me."

Nicoletta's heart ached at the soft plea. Inside those words was something deep and full of longing. She understood completely. Without another word, she lay next to her and nuzzled her neck.

"I am here forever," she said as she kissed Lura's damp hair.

CHAPTER SEVENTEEN

Adriana's intake of breath was audible only to Riah. Truthfully, she'd never really been comfortable with the name or the title. After all, she was an adult before she even discovered she was King Henry VII's blood daughter. By that time, she'd lived her entire life as the daughter of a titled lord and his wife.

A childless couple, her "father" had won her in a card game with the King, who, when presented with another daughter only hours earlier, was not pleased. The solution was to shuttle her off to the lord, a man who really wasn't interested in a child at all, but who bowed to the desires of his wife. For the loyal English subjects, a proclamation went out that she'd died at birth. Many years later, she actually found that proclamation in a history book. Odd to read about one's own death.

After learning the truth, she'd hated her father and her brother, who succeeded him and who was responsible for the way of her life now. Henry VIII was, like his father, displeased to have another sibling who might lay claim to his throne. His solution wasn't to give her away but to set her up for something much worse. All it took was one vampire acquaintance to attack her carriage on a terrible stormy night, and Henry's problem disappeared.

In a manner of speaking. She was still here. Her brother was not. She wondered what he would think about that.

Tonight, she introduced herself by the one name she knew would open doors regardless of whether they were savvy of those like Riah. When a Tudor comes knocking, most, if not all doors open. Some in hospitality. Some to further their own perverted desires for power and position.

"Please, please, come in." He stepped aside and opened the door wide.

While the other three couldn't understand the language he spoke, they did grasp the hospitable invitation. Of course, Antoine would think it very odd when Adriana and Colin came in as well, but she would explain that one when they were all within the safety of the home. Right now the important thing was to get everyone inside.

Once the door was closed and latched, Colin all but crumpled on the floor. He didn't try to make it to one of the cushion-covered chairs. Ivy raced to his side and began to examine the wound, a frown on her normally pretty face.

"Do you have any clean water? Any salt?" She didn't look up from Colin.

Antoine's brow crinkled as he stared at the noblewoman who spoke with such authority but who was showing an inappropriate amount of concern for a servant. He didn't move, just stood and stared at her. Riah put a hand on his arm.

"Antoine, please. I will explain as we go, but we need water and salt, if you have it."

He studied her for a long moment, and she got the feeling he had no intention of moving. Then he nodded. "Please follow me."

She did as he asked, winding through a short hallway until they reached a doorway leading into a cluttered cooking area. He rummaged around on a shelf filled with bottles, bowls, and wooden boxes before coming up with a bowl holding about a quarter cup of salt. On the table, he picked up a pitcher of water.

"Now, if you have a pot?"

He pivoted and from another shelf snagged a cast-iron pot with a curved handle made to hang on a hook over the fire. Handing it to her, he watched in silence as she poured about a quarter of the water into the pot and then added some salt. On the edge of the table, several clean rags were folded, and she grabbed those as well. Taking the rags and the pot of water back to the front room where Colin, Ivy, and Adriana waited, she placed the pot over the flames in the fireplace. It took only a few minutes over the open flame for the water to boil.

"This is the best I can do for saline," she told Ivy as she set the pot on the floor next to Colin. Not quite a nice bottle of Betadine, but as an alternative, the homemade saline solution would work as a decent cleaner for his wound.

As they began to tend to Colin, Antoine watched without saying a word. Once Ivy and Adriana were cleaning Colin's wound as best they could, she once more took Antoine's arm and ushered him toward the hallway. She could almost see the wheels turning in his head.

"Who are you really? How do you know my name?" he asked once they were seated at the table in the cooking room. His intelligent eyes studied her face as though he was trying to see deep inside.

"I am Princess Catherine Tudor, just as I told you."

"Yes," he said slowly as he nodded. "Who else are you?" His shrewd eyes missed nothing. This was the Antoine she remembered well. She was glad of it.

She tilted her head and told him, "In the life I lead now, they call me Doctor Riah Preston. When you were first introduced to me—"

His head snapped up. "I do not—"

She stopped him. "It is true, in this time and place, you do not know me, have never laid eyes on me before this moment. I am to meet you many years from now. You are much older then."

Riah looked down at her hands and paused. This was the moment of truth. "You are much older then," she repeated, and then brought her gaze up to meet his. "I am not."

For at least a minute, there was silence. His eyes narrowed but didn't move from her. "What are you?" This time he asked the right question.

She didn't pull any punches. No point in it. "I am a vampire."

This time, he closed his eyes for a moment and breathed deeply. "Vampire."

"Yes." His calmness in the face of her explanation was surprising. Or maybe he just didn't believe her.

Slowly he nodded. "I knew you would come someday. I have always felt it in my bones. A destiny I could not escape. The old ones talk of vampires and creatures of the night. I did not believe them, and yet I did not misbelieve them. There are many things in this world we do not see and that exist just the same. It does not bode well to ignore the words of our elders."

He did believe her and yet his words shocked her. "You never told me of this night when I met you as an old man." She remembered him as engaging and free with conversation. Her sense back then was they were strangers meeting for the first time.

He shook his head and shrugged. "Much happens in life that we cannot explain, and still there are reasons for all things."

Not news to her. It wasn't like she was free with the truths of her life. She tended to keep them close to the vest. There were people along the way she should have shared more with and didn't, so she had no right to cast stones. "We need your help."

He nodded slowly. "This I understand. Your friends are not of this land, are they?"

"They're from a time many years distant." She wouldn't even try to explain what that meant. It would have to suffice for him to know they came from the future. "We came to find a relation who has been taken or has gotten lost in her walk through time."

"Ah." His eyebrows lifted. "Gossip in the square is that a beautiful woman arrived with Alexandru Vizulea. He has been away for many years and suddenly appears out of nowhere with the strange woman. She is said to have bewitched the Prince. Is she too a vampire?"

"Vlad Dracula?" She'd suspected as much since their arrival but had to make sure.

"Yes, Prince Dracul. Is the woman like you?"

It was as she suspected and feared. "No, Lura is not a vampire. Do you believe she is safe?"

He sadly shook his head. "One can never be certain. The Prince's favor changes from day to day. Favor is a fickle thing in this land we live in. One day you are his trusted confidant, the next day, a bloody puppet hanging from a spike. He has done much good. He has done much harm. To know where the woman you seek falls is measured in moments."

She suppressed a shudder at the thought of what could happen to Lura. Impalement was an incredibly cruel way to die. "Can we get to her?"

He studied her, really studied her for the first time. "Perhaps, but you will need to be very careful. You, like the woman who came out of the night with Alexandru, are very beautiful. Our Prince is drawn to beauty. He uses it and, often, he destroys it."

Shit. Shit. Shit. How in the world were they going to get Lura out of this place...alive?

❖

How crazy was this? Lura kept waiting to wake up and discover it was all a dream of fantastic proportions. Only it was real—as amazing as that was. She was wrapped in the arms of a woman who set her body on fire and made her feel complete. Never before had she felt like this, and she didn't want it to end.

Except it had to…didn't it? She didn't belong here, even though in Nicoletta's arms it was as though she'd finally come home. She was out of her time, out of her world, and had never been as content and happy as she was at this moment. Giving it up was going to be pure torture.

She closed her eyes and gloried in the softness of Nicoletta's body, the lovely scent of the fire, the sounds outside the shuttered window. She would take each memory with her when she left this place and hope it would be enough. At least the ache in her heart was filled, even if only for one night.

"What are you thinking of?" Nicoletta asked. "You seem quite far away."

She smiled and stroked Nicoletta's cheek. "I was thinking how wonderful it is to lie here with you. Being with you like this is the most breathtaking thing that's ever happened to me, and the most unbelievable too."

"Not so to me. That you are in my bed, yes. That you are here, no. I have known you would be coming since Alexandru went on his journey to bring you to this land."

They'd explained it to her and she still didn't get it. Alexandru, it appeared, was some kind of seer who had prophesied her coming. As he'd told it, she was to be the one to save the people of Wallachia from continued bloodshed at the hand of Dracula.

Now…what exactly was she going to do to make that happen? She was a doctor, a psychiatrist to be precise, and while in a sense she did in fact save lives, that was all in the twenty-first century. This was so out of her comfort zone and skill level it defied logic. What exactly could a shrink from her century do to save the medieval Wallachian people? Group therapy? Intensive counseling? Not likely.

"None of this makes sense, you know." Her mind was still spinning and coming up with precisely nothing.

"Oh, but it does," Nicoletta said with conviction. "It has been foretold. What Alexandru sees always comes to pass. He is a man blessed by God with vision. He has never been wrong. "

In her world seers were crackpots who had 1-800 lines. They were the lost and the scammers. People who didn't give a damn who they hurt as long as they made a buck. Their victims were often her patients.

She was a woman of science, which conflicted greatly with those who claimed to have the skills of sight. Then again, what did she really know, considering where she was right this moment? If it was possible to walk through time, maybe it was just as possible that Alexandru could see the future.

Made her wonder if maybe at least some of those folks on the other end of a 1-800 line might actually be able to see beyond the veil of the physical world. The last twenty-four hours had so far managed to shake up her perception of what was and wasn't. She'd be pissed off if she didn't feel so awesome right now.

She closed her eyes and sighed. "I don't want to think about any of it at the moment. It makes my head hurt."

Nicoletta took her head in her hands and kissed Lura very gently. The sweetness of the kiss took her breath away. None of the *hows* or the *whys* mattered when she kissed her like that. Passion raged in her body the moment they touched.

Lura deepened the kiss and began to run her hands over Nicoletta's warm skin. Her earlier trepidation about her lack of experience fled. She felt alive, confident, and sexy. Her tongue met Nicoletta's in a fiery dance that quickened her breath. It seemed to her that since Nicoletta had rocked her world, not to mention her body, it was only fair she return the favor, which is precisely what she proceeded to do.

CHAPTER EIGHTEEN

D awn started to flow into the sky, and outside, the sounds of life stirring filtered through the closed door. With Antoine's help they got Colin patched up fairly well. After a goblet of tuica, a wonderful plum brandy she recalled well from her time here, they were all feeling much better. Colin certainly didn't put up any fight when they placed the goblet in his hand, and he managed drink it all without spilling so much as a drop. His cheeks flushed and a smile pulled up the corners of his mouth. The second glass turned out to be a great sleeping aid, and now he was resting comfortably in a small bedroom in the back of the home, with Ivy keeping vigil at his side.

"You know, staring out the window isn't going to answer the burning question in your pretty little head."

Adriana stroked Riah's hair and she tilted her head against her touch. She had an almost uncanny ability to read her. No one else in her many years of existence had ever been as in tune with her as Adriana. No one.

And every day, she worried it would all end.

Especially today. Since they'd walked through the stones and through the open wormhole that moved them from one time to another, she'd had the feeling things were going to change. For the first time in centuries, she liked her life and hoped it could stay just the way it was. For hundreds of years she'd been alone, and at the time, she had been fine with her existence that way. Since Adriana had opened her heart, everything around her had taken on color, texture, and dimension. She liked it and wanted to make the most of every moment they had together. The gray neutrality she'd been living in before finding love just wasn't going to cut it anymore.

Certainly she understood that Adriana was human and a day would come when she'd once more be alone. It was unavoidable, and she'd deal with that day when it came. She only hoped it would turn out to be many, many years in the future.

What bothered her right now was the feeling that whatever change was on the way was going to happen soon. She feared what it might be and was far from ready to return to her isolated existence. Losing Adriana would crush her as nothing else had ever done.

Shaking off the dire thoughts, she smiled a little and turned to look into Adriana's deep-brown eyes. "A burning question, eh?"

Adriana rolled her eyes. "Don't pretend you don't know what I'm talking about. You got a little taste of acting like a regular old human-type person again, and you want to take your skinny white ass right back into the sunshine."

Leave it to Adriana to put into words exactly what she was feeling. On the one day they'd moved through the countryside she'd remembered how it had been before Rodolphe stole her life. Adriana was right, she did want to know. Could she do it again? Could she walk outside and pretend for a little while longer that she was once again a woman made of flesh and blood? Could she turn her face to the sun and feel its warmth as long as she wanted?

"Yes." She didn't have to explain. Adriana would know.

"I think, girlfriend, that it's gonna be. This place has your number, and whatever you were, whatever you are in our time, the rules have changed since we got here. In your favor, no less."

Always the devil's advocate, she said, "One day doesn't mean we're changed."

"Oh, I don't think you're changed. Pretty sure you're still my sexy vamp. I just think, for whatever reason, the sunshine doesn't hurt you while we're in this dimension, and I'm gonna find out why. I want to know what the mojo is that makes this place different."

"No microscopes here, A."

"Yeah, yeah, yeah. Details, girlfriend, just details. You know my mother used to tell me that where there's a will, there's a way. Besides, have you forgotten what a kick-ass sorceress I am? I can make wine out of water, baby."

"You know I believe you. If anyone can figure it out, you can." Riah kissed her and smiled.

Adriana wiggled her eyebrows. "Abso-damn-lutely." She held out her hand. "Now, come on, gorgeous. Let's take a little walk and see if you go up in a puff of smoke."

Riah took her outstretched hand in hers. "Easy for you to say, when you're not the one who'll get smoked."

Adriana tugged a little on her hand. "Come on, Riah, have a little trust. Have I ever led you astray yet?"

That was a loaded question. "Oh, you've led me astray all right. Remember the silk scarves, or how about…"

Adriana's smile grew huge. "Yeah, good times, good times."

Nicoletta hated the thought of leaving the bed. Lura was so warm, and the feel of her body throughout the night was the most wonderful thing she'd ever experienced. If Lura were in her bed forever, she would never want to leave her chambers.

Alas, staying beneath the covers was not to be. Soon, others would be up and about in the castle. If she was not among them, it would be noticed, and the last thing she wanted was to come to the Prince's attention. Her hope was that his disinterest in her of last night would endure and that he would ignore her from this day on.

As long as she was out of his sight and word did not reach the Prince that she had done something to displease him, her life could go on. Not that she could stay here much longer. She dared not take the risk. Whatever it was that made him turn away from her might not last, and she did not want to stay long enough to find out.

The only way to have any hope of freedom was to leave the castle. She would get as far away as possible and make the best of her life as she could, given what was to happen.

She dressed quietly after building up the fire until it crackled and popped. It quickly took the chill off the room. While they had taken turns keeping it stoked during the night, it had finally died down to embers, and the cold winter air had chased away the warmth.

Standing, she stared at Lura as she slept peacefully. Her hair fanned out around her face, and sleep softened her features. She was so beautiful. Nicoletta's heart beat faster, and her stomach fluttered as though filled with moths. The feeling was not unpleasant and made her smile. She had not had many occasions to smile in a long time.

A soft knock came at the door, startling Nicoletta and making Lura stir. Rubbing her eyes, Lura sat up and looked as though she was not certain where she was. After a moment, her expression cleared and, like Nicoletta, she smiled.

Nicoletta's breath caught in her throat at the sight of Lura's naked breasts. She wanted nothing more than to remove her own dress and return to the bed. She did not dare, for she feared who might be at their door.

She moved toward the door and motioned for Lura to pull the covers up and over her exposed breasts. Before she opened the door, she glanced back, and as Lura was properly covered up, she pulled on the ring, bringing the passageway into view. Outside the door, her friend Mia stood wringing her hands. Her cheeks were flushed and her lips pressed into a thin line. Dread pooled in her stomach.

"Oh, Nicoletta," she said with tears in her eyes. "It is terrible."

The look on Mia's face was frightening, the somber tone of her words dreadful. She was afraid to know what made such a cheerful woman look as though death had come knocking on her door. "What is it? What has happened?"

The tears could no longer be contained, and they spilled down her pale cheeks. "It is Alexandru…" His name was a sob on her lips.

Her body stilled and a glacial cold descended over her. "Dear God, tell me."

"He…he…I cannot…" Mia clamped a hand over her mouth, whirled around, and ran down the corridor.

Sickness rose in her throat as Nicoletta turned again to Lura. She choked out, "I must go. Something has happened to my brother."

Out of the corner of her eye she saw Lura scramble naked out of the bed and reach for her gown. She did not wait for her. Instead, she raced down the corridor in the same direction as Mia's fleeing form. Silent prayers went up to God that she would not run into the Prince or any of his trusted confidants. She had to get to her brother.

Catching sight of Mia's yellow gown exiting outside, she hurried on. A little faster and she would reach her. She flung herself out the door and into the cold morning air. Outside, the early day sun was chasing off the icy grip of the morning, and her fleeting thought was that the day was going to be a lovely one. No snow, no blowing wind, just a soft winter sunshine to warm their weary bones.

Then she noticed the quiet outside the castle. Normally the sounds of people going about their daily tasks would fill the air. Not now. Instead of the sounds of people's voices, the whinny of anxious horses, the clattering of wagon wheels, an eerie silence met her. As did the smell—a stench she recognized instantly: blood. No matter how many times she came outside only to be greeted by this same odor, she could never make peace with it. She despaired that her beautiful homeland was becoming all too often the setting for violence and death. She hated that the rich soil that grew their food and made the floors for their homes was turned crimson with blood.

Slowly her head came up and her eyes settled on the gory sight that in her heart she knew would be there. No one was spared from the horror of the Prince's fatal justice. Not the poor, the rich, the young, or the sick. All were to see and to take to heart the price of wrongdoing, whether it actually happened or not.

That was the hurtful part. While the Prince might perceive a sin, that did not mean the person was evil. She was too aware of the innocents whose bodies had been impaled and on display for the stares of friends, neighbors, and worst of all, family. Left to rot as though they were nothing more than food for vultures. It made her stomach roll.

Three men were impaled upon the tall, sharp spikes on this day. The first two were strangers, and their bodies sagged bloodless and devoid of life, their unfamiliar faces slack in death. As her gaze fell on the third man, a scream rose in her throat and her legs trembled, her knees buckling. The ground rose up to meet her as her sobs shattered the morning silence.

CHAPTER NINETEEN

The sun came up and Riah stayed at the window despite Adriana's coaxing her to take a risk and step outside. Rays of light crept through the opening of the heavy drapes, creating a growing pool of light around her feet. Hope began to build as the circle of light grew bigger and bigger.

Nothing happened.

She brought her gaze up to meet Adriana's, and seeing the smile on her face made Riah smile too.

Putting both hands on her hips, Adriana said calmly, "I told you so."

Riah nodded. "Indeed you did. No puff of smoke."

This was going to make getting around easier, though easier didn't necessarily mean easy. During the nighttime hours, while Colin rested and Ivy worried, Antoine had filled in the blanks.

She'd been fairly certain they were in Wallachia during the reign of Vlad Dracula, better known as Vlad the Impaler. What she hadn't been sure of was during exactly which reign they had arrived. He'd been the ruler of Wallachia during three separate time frames, although his last stint on the throne was relatively brief.

She'd been able to feel him the moment they'd stepped through the rocks. It was as if his life force permeated the very air. That in this time he'd been both a savior and a curse to this place was a conviction she agreed with. She'd seen firsthand how he'd saved the land from domination by the Ottoman Turks. At the same time, she'd also seen the devastation to families his bloodlust had caused. Did the good outweigh the bad? She didn't have an answer for that one.

Being here with him in the flesh was disconcerting. His spirit touched her for reasons she didn't want to explore too deeply. No other human had ever affected her like that. She didn't like it. Being on the soil where he'd been born and destroyed always made her feel dirty and unhappy. It really didn't make sense, but then again, it didn't have to. It just was.

The details Antoine filled in made a great deal of sense, given what she'd seen so far. It was the year 1476, and Dracula, aided by Stephen Báthory, great-uncle of the Blood Countess, Elizabeth Báthory, had once again gained control of Wallachia. Riah had met the bitch, Elizabeth Báthory, too, an encounter she'd never forget. Say what they would about vampires, that all-too-human psycho made even Rodolphe look like a not-so-bad guy. Whether or not Elizabeth's tendencies were a family trait she inherited from, say, an uncle, remained to be seen.

Riah's real plan? To find Lura and get of here as quickly as possible. The trick would be to make their way through the city, discreetly inquiring as to her whereabouts without raising the attention of Dracula. The fictional vampire was a pussycat compared to the real deal, and she didn't intend to find herself, or any of them for that matter, summoned to an audience before the flesh-and-blood man.

As she watched out the window, the morning sunlight began to turn to a cloudy gray. Soon snowflakes started to flutter again, only this time it wasn't the light dusting of the day before. So far the weather hadn't impeded their journey, but it appeared their luck was about to run out. November and December in this land could be harsh and bitterly cold. She remembered that clearly, and once again it made her all the more determined to get back to their century with all its comforts. She didn't plan to be here any longer than absolutely necessary.

It also reminded her that they'd have to find appropriate outerwear, something they hadn't come across at the manor house. Finding warm, fur-lined cloaks for herself and Ivy wasn't a problem. Paying for them was. She didn't exactly have fifteenth-century currency in her pockets. The only choice she could see was to appeal to Antoine, and the gold necklace she wore at her neck would more than likely ease any reluctance he might have.

Finding something to keep their *servants* warm and dry would be far more problematic. The roles Adriana and Colin were playing didn't lend themselves to expensive furs, even if that's exactly what she'd wrap her beloved Adriana in. If she was to keep them safe, they had to stay in character, and that meant winter attire that was in keeping with their station.

If she could get her hands on a couple of shepherd's cloaks and hats, the sheepskin outer wear would go a long way toward protecting Adriana and Colin from the incoming storm. Not the luxurious furs she and Ivy could enjoy, but sturdy nonetheless. She'd ask Antoine to help her, and then they could continue their quest.

Antoine must have possessed his own form of magic, because several hours later, the four of them stepped outside into the bright, white snow. Antoine had his man bring his carriage to the front, and Colin helped Ivy and Riah, heavy with the thick fur cloaks, into the coach. Colin and Adriana, dressed in the unbleached sheepskin wraps and black sheepskin hats Antoine had called cǎciulǎs, seated themselves behind the two horses. From all appearances, two grand ladies out for a winter ride.

Ideally, both Adriana and Colin should be inside the carriage and protected from the elements. Adriana was such a small woman, without any meat on her bones to fight the inclement weather. And Colin? He was much more alert this morning, but it was clear yesterday's injury was still taking its toll. That they were stuck in the falling snow pretending to be subservient to Riah and Ivy grated on her.

Unfortunately, they really didn't have a better choice. Laying low meant blending in. Blending in meant Colin and Ivy doing exactly what servants in this society would do…sit outside in the cold and cater to the needs of their *betters*. She was going to pay for this when they got home, no doubt about it.

Doing a passable job of pretending he knew what he was doing, Colin guided the horses through the city in the general direction of Vlad's castle. For a man more accustomed to driving cars, he was negotiating the world of horse-drawn carriages quite well. Pretty good for a guy who'd had an arrow pulled out of his shoulder less than twenty-four hours ago.

Pulling back the heavy brown curtain that covered the carriage window, she peered out at the city passing by. It suddenly struck her how quiet things were. Certainly the sudden snowstorm had something to do with that. Those who could stay indoors, out of the snow, would. Only those who had to ventured out. Even so, it seemed unusually quiet, and she had the impression it was much more than a storm.

As they neared Vlad's stronghold, the reason for the somber and quiet city became all too clear. Ahead, high on stakes rising at least fifteen feet in the air, hung the still forms of three men. They'd been staked through the trunk of their bodies, their arms and legs dangling, their heads drooping to their chests. Blood had flowed from their broken bodies down the stakes until it pooled on the ground beneath them. Instead of a pristine blanket of white snow at their feet, they were surrounded by the vermilion justice of Vlad the Impaler.

It took every ounce of strength Lura possessed to pull Nicoletta from the filth-covered ground and drag her back into the castle. Whispering into her ear the whole time, she hoped her words would soothe the distraught woman. They must have helped at least a little, because her screams had quieted into breathless sobs by the time she had her inside the stone walls.

If she lived to be a hundred years old Lura didn't think she could ever erase from her memory the sight of Alexandru's lifeless, blood-soaked body staked and on display for every eye in the city. If she thought the sight of the stranger being staked yesterday was the most terrible thing she'd ever seen. It wasn't. This was so much worse.

All she could think of was the handsome and gentle man who'd driven her around the streets of Bucharest and through the beautiful countryside. She remembered how he'd rowed across the water until they reached the grassy banks of Snagov Island. How he'd tried to make her feel at home and gave her heartfelt words of comfort about Vic. He was…had been…a good man.

She hated Dracula for changing all that. Hated that a good man had died because of her, and she was absolutely convinced that his life had been stolen in such a vicious way because of her. How was she going to live with that, on top of the guilt she felt over Vic? She'd believed Vic's death was the worst thing she'd ever experienced. She was wrong.

Feeling sorry for herself wouldn't accomplish anything useful. Some things were way more important. Nicoletta was on the verge of collapsing, and if she did, she could very easily meet the same fate as her brother. No way was Lura going to let that happen. Out of her element to be sure. Up to meeting the challenge, without question.

With much coaxing and whispered words of comfort, her arms around her for support, she managed to get Nicoletta back into their chamber. Funny how all of a sudden she thought of it as theirs, but she did. No doubt would always think of it that way when years from now she sat in her own home, alone with nothing except her memories for comfort.

Inside the chamber, she convinced Nicoletta to sit on the bed while she took a cloth and dipped it in a bowl of cool water. As Nicoletta had tended to her on their arrival, she now returned the kindness. Gently, she wiped away the tears that poured down her face. Only a little better. Her sad eyes still brimmed, and her face was an alarming shade of pasty white.

"We have to leave," Lura told her as she held her face between her hands. "We aren't safe here."

"What does it matter?" Her words sounded hollow and lifeless. Defeat radiated from her like the rays of the sun. It broke Lura's heart.

She stroked Nicoletta's cheeks. The coolness of her skin concerned her. She softened her voice. "I don't have a good feeling about staying here. I'm worried the Prince will come for you next, and not for the same reason he did last night."

Still she didn't look at her and didn't move. "Let him come."

"Nicoletta!" Lura almost yelled. She didn't know how else to snap her out of the funk that, while she was entitled to, was dangerous.

It worked. For the first time since they'd returned, life sparked in her eyes. She'd been around enough apathetic patients to know when it was time to put on her doctor hat and demand attention. For a lot of reasons, she wasn't about to let Nicoletta drop into a depression so deep she couldn't crawl out.

"We're leaving here right now. I'm not going to let him hurt you."

Nicoletta sighed and shook her head sadly. "He controls nearly all of the land. There is nowhere we can go and be safe. He will kill us just as he killed my brother. It is over."

Lura stepped back and began to pace. Think. Think. Think. Yes, she was way out of her element, but some things didn't change, including human nature. She'd spent her entire professional career with people fighting mental issues. Understanding their basic thought processes was what she did.

That's why she knew this guy wasn't done, and she'd put good money—a lot of it—on him coming for Alexandru's sister. He had some kind of point to make by killing Alexandru and was of the driven variety that wouldn't quit until he tied up all of what he considered loose ends. Both she and Nicoletta more than likely fell into that category. They might never know what their perceived sins were, but she knew exactly what the penalty would be.

Staring out the window at the unusually quiet courtyard, briefly she thought Nicoletta's remark was dead-on. He had power in every corner of the land, which meant nowhere would be safe for them. Then another thought occurred to her, and she realized how wrong that was. She knew exactly where they could go to be safe and, most important, out of his reach.

In the wardrobe chest she located two cloaks. One was beautifully embroidered, with a thick fur lining. Heavy as it was, it would be perfect. She wrapped it around Nicoletta. She didn't protest, though she didn't exactly help either. It didn't matter. It would keep her warm and safe from the snow.

The second cloak was plain black wool without the fur lining. It was obviously a day-to-day garment, not intended for severe weather or important events. With the snow continuing to fall outside, she wished it was a little more stout. But it would have to do. Her dress was a thick wool, which, combined with the cloak, would keep her warm for the most part. Hopefully, the snowstorm would lose its strength and their journey would be relatively precipitation free.

Nicoletta sat still as Lura covered her hair with a scarf, and then she did the same for her own head. Unfortunately she only uncovered one set of gloves, and those she slid onto Nicoletta's small hands. She doubted she'd have been able to wear them anyway. Her hands just weren't that delicate.

Finally, she decided they were as ready as they could be. Besides, they'd spent ample time here already. Too much, really, and departing was more than a good idea. She opened the passageway door enough to scan both directions. Thankfully, it was clear. Taking Nicoletta's hand in hers, she led her, unresisting, out of the chamber.

Her mind raced as they moved cautiously through the castle. Getting out with little to no notice wasn't her main concern. The more pressing problem would be the horses. Finding the stables wasn't exactly easy for a stranger. They all looked the same to her, and frankly, she hadn't been paying that much attention to begin with when the three of them came skulking in during the middle of the night. Still, she had to try; it was critical to the success of her plan.

They needed to cover ground as fast as they could. Walking wouldn't cut it. Not in these heavy long dresses and cloaks. Not if the snow continued to fall. She pulled her cloak tighter around her body. Her earlier optimism about her dress and cloak might have been foolish. Truthfully, she'd be lucky not to get hypothermia dressed like this, even with a horse to shorten their trek.

Keeping close to the walls as much as possible, she began her search, pulling Nicoletta unresisting along behind her. She managed to keep on the other side of the castle from Vlad's gruesome stakes. Nicoletta didn't need to see that again. For that matter, neither did she. As it was, she figured she'd have to practice a lot of what she preached in order to avoid the inevitable nightmares.

Outside, she scanned the area, looking for anything that jogged her memory. It seemed to her that the horses had been handed off on the outskirts of the city, so if she could get them off the main drag without attracting attention, she just might be able to find the right place. She hoped so anyway, or they had no hope at all. Without the horses they'd freeze before they made it back to Snagov Island.

Fortunately for them, a lovely coach, piloted by a large man and a thin black boy, was garnering the attention of those who ventured out into the snow-covered morning. A stroke of luck for her and Nicoletta, particularly when she looked up to see the Prince step out onto one of the castle's many balconies, his interest directed toward the carriage. He wasn't looking their way at all. As she hurried Nicoletta along, she wondered who was inside the carriage, though only briefly. Didn't have time. Didn't really care.

Once, as they neared the city's edge, Nicoletta stopped. Lura turned to see her facing back the way they'd come, her face pale and sad.

Her words shook as she told Lura, "I cannot leave him."

With cold fingers, she turned Nicoletta's face to hers. "You can't help him now. We have to leave this place before something horrible happens." She understood Nicoletta's reluctance and wished she could do something. She couldn't, and staying would bring nothing but trouble their way.

Nicoletta shook off Lura's hands. "Something evil has already happened." Her voice was hard.

True enough. Alexandru had been a good man, and why Dracula would condemn him to such a horrible death was beyond her. Like Nicoletta, she wanted to know why, but she certainly didn't want to stick around long enough to hear. The man gave her the creeps all the way down to her toes. She'd never be able to read *Dracula* again and not see a river of crimson in her mind.

She focused on Nicoletta again. "Yes, it has. Staying here and letting him do the same to you won't help Alexandru. If we have any hope of avenging your brother, we have to get to safety first. That isn't here in Tirgoviste. We have to leave now."

She thought Nicoletta would fight her. She didn't. Instead, she took a deep breath and, for the first time since they'd laid eyes on Alexandru's dead body, seemed to pull herself together. A light came back into her eyes, and it gave Lura hope.

The hardness of only a moment ago vanished. "You are right. Alexandru would want me to be safe. I am not sure how I can avenge him against the Prince, but I will find a way. You will help?"

"Of course I will." How? Lura didn't have a clue, especially considering her not-so-developed plan at the moment. Her hunch about getting out of the city was just that: a hunch. She didn't know this place even in her own time, and she sure didn't know it in Nicoletta's time. All she really knew was that she'd stepped through an outcropping of rocks and into Nicoletta's world.

Yet, despite her disorientation, the dots were beginning to connect in a way that sent a glimmer of optimism into her heart. In order to make Vlad and his violence fade and, more important, to keep Nicoletta safe, all they had to do was take a return journey through the rocks.

"Come on." She tugged Nicoletta's hand. "It would be a really good thing if we could get to Snagov Island before nightfall."

CHAPTER TWENTY

F"uck."
Ivy turned and looked at Riah. "What's wrong?"
She wanted to say *everything*. They were out of their own time, crippled by injury, with their chance of finding Lura fading by the second. Worst of all, her hope to get through the city unnoticed had just gone up in flames. Not only was everyone paying attention to them, but the one person she'd prayed would be otherwise engaged was standing on a balcony staring down at their little party.

Riah had realized from the outset that her plan was riddled with holes. Still, it had been the best she could come up with, given the circumstances. What she failed to take into account was the novelty of their group. Strange people simply didn't saunter through the city unnoticed. It wasn't the way of things in this world. Maybe back in the century they'd come from, but not here.

Vlad Dracula was most certain to get wind of them; she'd just hoped for a little more time than they'd been able to grab. Wasn't to be. Outside the coach window, two men approached, their boots kicking up fresh snow as they marched in their direction. She groaned and steadied herself for the certain confrontation on its way.

Before they had an opportunity to even speak to Colin or Adriana, Riah threw open the coach door and haughtily stepped down. She kept her back straight and her head high. "What is the meaning of this?" she barked, hoping to keep her accent to a minimum.

The larger of the two, an ugly man with deep scars on his face, not quite as big as Colin, stepped quickly to her. "Who are you?" he barked right back. He smelled of smoke, stale wine, and roasted meat, the stench making her back up a bit.

Despite her revulsion to his offensive odor, she narrowed her eyes and kept her gaze steady on his face. Show no fear was the first lesson Rodolphe had taught her. Strange how a man she held responsible for so many awful things about her life had actually given her some valuable skills.

"I asked you why you are stopping my carriage?" She kept the bite in her voice.

"I do not answer to you. Now tell me who you are." He motioned the other man to come in closer. Like this one, he was less than handsome, with big arms and a round, ruddy face. Not exactly an inviting countenance, and he certainly didn't smell any better than his buddy.

Above her, Vlad Dracula still watched. She could feel his eyes on her back, which made her skin crawl. How was she going to extricate them from this situation? Retreat wasn't an option, and she readied herself for more. Before she could say anything else, from above them Dracula bellowed out two words. Roughly translated: "Bring them."

"You," the first big man yelled at Colin.

Thank God, his tone of voice made an impression, because Colin certainly didn't understand the man's actual words. He did get the pitch and tone, and that's all he needed to respond appropriately. He turned to look while keeping his gaze down and unthreatening.

"You follow us."

Colin cut his eyes to Riah, and with a sinking heart, she nodded slightly. Colin understood.

She didn't say anything else, just retreated into the carriage and sat next to Ivy.

"What's happening?" Ivy whispered.

"Not sure exactly, but I'm guessing we're about to get an audience with Dracula himself." She didn't add how sick that made her feel.

"No way," Ivy breathed out. "That can't be good."

Riah was slowly shaking her head. "I'd say we have a better-than-average chance of being fucked."

Once at the castle, the two ugly men escorted Riah and Ivy through drafty corridors until they were ushered into a large chamber with flagstone floors covered in thick rugs. The furniture was bulky, made of heavy wood frames and padded with velvet upholstery. They were not invited to sit.

Colin and Adriana were left with the horses and carriage, several stable hands keeping an eye on them. She worried about the two alone and with strangers while having no way to communicate. Without her to translate, they were floating unaided. She didn't even want to think about how dangerous that was for them. If anything happened to Adriana, or to Colin for that matter, she'd never forgive herself for letting them come here.

She had no one to blame save herself. She was the one who'd led them to the stones. She was the one who'd taken the initiative and gone through. They'd only followed her lead. This was precisely why she'd chosen solitude for so many years. It was safer that way. Lonelier too.

Focus, she had to focus. Keep her wits about her and, for God's sake, keep calm. No, she'd never met this man, but she'd heard stories from those who had. She remembered them with alarming clarity, and they didn't leave her feeling particularly confident.

Dracula sauntered into the room and the air changed the moment he entered. The charge was so thick it could have powered a hybrid car. Seeing his face, she immediately thought the portraits hadn't done him justice. He was much more handsome than the representations revealed. His long black hair was shiny, his deep-set eyes intelligent and probing. The thick mustache suited his face, taking away some of the sharpness of his aquiline nose. It was easy to see how people were drawn to him.

She had a strong urge to reach out and touch him, the pull was so powerful. Wasn't hard to understand how such a man could maintain rule not just once or twice but three times. According to what Antoine had told them last night, they'd arrived here near the end of his final reign.

She knew that. He didn't. Perhaps it was the one thing that might play to their advantage.

God, she hoped so.

"You." He pointed a long slender finger at her. "Come." A giant ruby ring glittered on his finger.

She wanted to say "fuck you" and didn't dare. She hated the tone of voice men in power used when addressing women. Truthfully, she could rip him apart, and it galled her that she had to play the submissive. The lives of her friends were at the core of her decisions right now, and if that meant pretending to be a lady with all the proper manners, so be it. She'd swallow her distaste and play his game. Going vampire commando on Dracula's ass wasn't an option.

For now.

❖

Nicoletta wanted to scream and run back to confront Prince Dracula head-on. She wanted to hit him, to scratch out his eyes. He had no right to kill Alexandru. No right.

Except that he did. In their world, the Prince had every right to do whatever he wanted, justified or not. It was the reward for sitting on the throne. Despite how she or anyone else felt about it, that was the way of things and always had been. The Draculs had been in power in one way or another her entire life. That this particular one was bloodier than the others mattered little. Her life was tied to his, as was Alexandru's, and when he deemed that life unworthy, he had the privilege and the power to take it away.

She would probably never know what Alexandru's supposed sin was. The Prince perceived that her brother had somehow wronged him. By his unexplained absence, by his refusal to explain himself, by his simply being alive, whatever it was, the Prince took offense.

Alexandru's power to see the way of things was what had sent him on his quest to find Lura and bring her back. Nicoletta had never questioned it because it was who he was. To beg him to deny his own destiny was to deny his very existence. She did not have that right. He had always known what must be. Had he foreseen his own death as well?

Even without Alexandru's gift of sight, she should have realized the peril they were in. Each person in Wallachia noticed a change in the Prince when he came back this time. One of the glaring differences in the man was that he had failed to bring his wife and children with him to the castle. Though it was clear he did not hold his second wife in the same esteem he had his first one, she was still always with him. If he now deemed it unsafe for his family, what did that say for the rest of them?

A former ally who disappeared without a word and then reappeared the same way, only now in the company of a beautiful stranger? The Prince would want answers. Quickly. Completely.

She doubted very much that Alexandru had given him what he demanded. They all had sympathy for the Prince and his brother for their many troubling years held captive by the Ottoman Turks. The horror they must have been forced to endure was not something Nicoletta cared to think about. Any child ripped from its bed and kept as a prisoner in a foreign land for years was certain to return scarred. She did not wish such a fate for any child.

Her heartache had intensified as his reign grew. Not for the Prince, because he had begun to change in a way that brought evil to her home. The tragedy of his wife taking her own life changed him from a compassionate soul into a hardened man. His rule over Wallachia continued to change him, and it showed in his face as well as in everything he did. He kept them safe from the Turks, but at what cost?

Her brother was now one of the many whose lives drained away on the pointed end of a stake by command of the Prince, and it made her want to scream. Back for barely a day and now he was gone again. This time he would not return. He was the last of her family. She was alone and, very soon, she suspected, homeless. Lura was right; the Prince would be after her next. She had nothing more to give him or, rather, nothing more she would give him. Nothing left to protect. He would never touch her again.

The knowledge she possessed was dangerous. Seers were not held in high esteem, and if the Prince had discovered Alexandru's secret, that could be why he was suspended on the stake. It could also be what would bring him to her door.

She dared not tell the Prince what she knew. He would not believe her, though she felt in her heart that all Alexandru had shared with her and Lura was true. It would come to pass with or without Alexandru.

Nonetheless, if she were to tell the Prince of his fate, he would put her on a stake right next to her brother. Her life would pool at her feet just as it had done for him. Vaguely she wondered if that would be bad. What did she really have to live for now that Alexandru was gone?

Then her gaze fell on Lura at the same time her hand went to her belly. Despair had no place in her heart today. Misfortune had befallen her and her family. First her parents and then her beloved brother. She deserved to wallow, and she would not because Lura's presence here would save them all. She would do whatever she could to see that it happened.

"Come," she said quietly as she took Lura's hand. "The horses are this way."

Even in the dimness the relief that crossed Lura's face was easy to see. Bless her heart, she had been trying without much success to find the stable where Nicoletta's horses were boarded. She could easily find the right one, even in the deep black of night. But it was not night; it was the light of morning, which on any other day would be a welcome sight.

Lura had guided them unknowingly in the right direction. Nicoletta shook off her despair and pointed them toward the familiar stable where the horses waited. Soon, they slipped inside. Her horses, rested and fed, seemed pleased to see her. As always, she was terribly glad to see them. The two beautiful animals to her represented freedom, and tonight that was what they needed more than anything.

Slipping harnesses on, they each took a set of reins and led the horses from the stables. Still they kept to the shadows as much as possible. The less attention they drew, the safer they would be. Whatever else they did, they dared not attract the interest of the Prince's henchmen.

At last they reached the edge of the city, and before them stretched an endless landscape of thick trees and rough terrain, all blanketed with a beautiful white dusting of snow. The snow had at last stopped falling and the sun was beginning to shine. For that she was grateful, although they would need to keep to the trees so they could stay clear of other travelers.

Lura, on the back of the smaller horse, paused and studied the land ahead of them. "Do you know what direction that is?" She pointed straight ahead.

Nicoletta studied the sky, clearing now of the clouds that had earlier created a curtain of white. "That road will take us to Brasov. I have friends there who will keep up safe."

Lura eyes narrowed as if she was pondering something. Then she shook her head and turned her horse in the opposite direction. "We need to go that way."

Nicoletta frowned. If they were to do that, it would take them back into the city. But that was crazy. They would surely die just like Alexandru. "We cannot return."

Lura's nod was vigorous. "Not on your life. We're going to have to skirt the city—"

"Skirt the city? We have no skirt save for what we wear." She had never heard such a strange phrase. Why would they put a skirt on the city?

Lura's tiny smile was strange, considering the danger they were in. Comforting at the same time. "No, I mean we'll have to ride around the city without going into it until we're heading back in the direction of Snagov Island. We want to steer clear of Dracula and his men."

That she would have understood if only Lura had said it to begin with. Going back to the island did not seem like the best plan to her. If Dracula's men caught them there, they would have no way to escape. She thought it better to go in the direction of Brasnov, where there were many mountains and people who would give their lives to protect them. Perfect for keeping out of sight of the Prince. She told Lura as much.

She just shook her head and coaxed her horse into a trot. "We have to go back, Nicoletta. It's important."

Reluctantly, she followed, though not without misgiving. "I worry we will not make it."

The smile from a moment ago fled, Lura's face somber. "It worries me too, but I'm more scared of staying here after what Dracula did to Alexandru."

Shivers slipped down her spine as the vision of Alexandru's sightless eyes flashed through her mind. It seemed impossible that a man with a life of promise ahead of him was gone. He had followed the prophecy and fulfilled his part in saving their people. It was not fair that after all of his sacrifice, he then would lose his life. It was wrong, and no matter how long she lived, she would always feel cheated.

She had prayed for his safe return and that prayer had been answered. If she had really been thinking, she would have prayed for him to stay away. Here safety was fleeting. In the faraway place Alexandru had gone to find Lura, he had been well. He should have stayed there. Except, he never would have done that. Honor was but one of his finest qualities. He had said he was bringing back their savior, and that is exactly what he did, regardless of what it cost him. Like his life.

Nothing was as she thought it would be when she saw him step through the stones. Instead, her brother was on his way to the hereafter, and she was on the run for her life. Strangely, even though her family was now all gone, she did not feel alone.

Lura sat tall on her horse, her blond hair rippling in the breeze. She rode now as though she had been on a horse all her life. A stranger here and yet she moved like she had been born on the very soil. Nicoletta's heart fluttered. Fate was not smiling on her. First, she caught the fancy of the Prince, whose touch would leave her marked forever. Then she met a woman who taught her what love really means. She wished for forever, knowing it could never be. Finally, her brother died at the hands of the man who had taken away her hopes and dreams. The moment Lura returned to her own time, Nicoletta would be on her own for the rest of her days.

Her hand strayed once more to her stomach and she closed her eyes. The thought of Lura's leaving made tears spring to her eyes. If only they could stay together, she might find the strength to weather the coming months. Alone, she dared not think what might become of her. She worried that she would not find the strength to carry on.

Lura's shift into the cover the woods provided took Nicoletta away from her melancholy and back to the moment. As she became more aware, she heard what had made Lura embrace the shadows. Here the woods were thick enough to block out much of the morning sunlight. The air was cool and filled with the distinctive scent of the forest. The city was her home, and though she had traveled throughout the country and often rode her horse through the fields and meadows, she did not feel most comfortable in the wilderness.

Lura did not seem to share her unease. She moved deeper and deeper into the woods, one with her horse. The sight made Nicoletta's throat tighten. She was going to miss her with an intensity she hardly believed possible given their short acquaintance. Her heart did not listen to the voice of reason.

"This way," Lura said softly as she slipped from the horse and began to lead her toward the hillside.

How Lura had seen the cave, Nicoletta could not imagine, and yet there it was. From here it appeared big enough for the two of them and the horses. A perfect place to hide from those passing through the forest. Or was it people searching the forest? The sudden thought scared her.

Little light made its way inside the cave, although after a few moments, her eyes adjusted and she could make out both Lura and the horses.

"Do you think they saw us?" She had heard the sounds of approaching travelers just before they found their place in the shadows of the cave.

Lura shook her head. "I heard them when they were still quite a distance behind, and I'm sure I got us under the cover of the trees before they got close enough to spot us."

"It is the Prince's men." She had hoped it was simple travelers like themselves, but after catching sight of them, she knew better. She would recognize them anywhere.

This time Lura nodded. "I hate to say it, but I'm pretty sure you're right. That guy seems to have a hard-on for you and your family. What did you do to him to get him so pissed off?"

"A hard-on?" She had never heard such a term. Lura had such a strange way of speaking.

Lura's laugh was soft, and just the sound helped soothe her unsettled nerves. That she could find levity in such a dark time made Nicoletta feel better. "It's an American saying—oh, oops, you have no idea what America means either, do you?"

Nicoletta did not. Most of the time she understood Lura, though not always. She seemed to understand their language for the most part, and that was nice. Sometimes her words were not quite right, and her accent meant Nicoletta had to listen closely. Now, it was not either of those things. She simply did not understand what Lura spoke of.

"Skip the part about America. It's where I live, and I can explain more about that to you later. The hard-on part, I think you'll understand. It means a man's..." She made a motion near her lady parts.

A bit of a flush spread through her cheeks. Nicoletta immediately understood and could not stop the small laugh. "A man's horn."

Lura pursed her lips and nodded. "Sure, yeah, a horn. So hard-on, where I come from, means he's got it for you bad."

A frown creasing her forehead, she tried to put together what Lura meant, but still was not quite sure. All her strange sayings were so confusing, and then it hit her. "Oh," she breathed out. The image in her head made sense. "Yes, I believe the Prince does have, as you say, a hard-on for me."

"Why, Nicoletta? What is it that he hates about you so much that he would kill your brother and chase you down like a dog? Why does he want you dead?"

Her earlier amusement at Lura's funny way of speech disappeared. Sinking to the cold earth, a sharp rock poking her leg, she wanted to cry. The Prince did not want her dead. Far from it. He intended to keep her very much alive.

At least until the baby was born.

CHAPTER TWENTY-ONE

Y our name."
No please, thank you, or don't let the door hit your butt on the way out from this guy. Just a demand. There was no menace in his voice, his words clear and even. The threat was there though, just below the calm mandate. Riah felt the chill of him all the way into her bones.

"Lady Riah Preston." Though she'd revealed her true identity to Antoine, she dared not do the same with Vlad Dracula. Yes, she was of royal blood, and that made her special, but here in this time, she had not yet been conceived. Her father, her birth father, was a mere nineteen years old and not yet a king. How exactly could she explain that to another who was a member of the elite yet small society of royals?

"Lady? Your family is?"

She inclined her head. "My family…" She began to weave a fictitious family history based on those wealthy and titled friends of both her birth father and her adoptive father. To her ears it sounded pretty plausible. Whether or not this man would buy it remained to be seen.

At the conclusion of her tale, the room fell silent. His intense gaze stayed on her face, and she met his with a steady one of her own. She refused to be the first to look away, and if that was rude or improper, and it probably was, tough shit. Again, the mantra played in her head: show no fear.

He seemed not to take offense. Instead, his gaze moved first. With a slight shift, he turned his sharp eyes on Ivy. "And you?"

While he might have looked away first, she wasn't going to give up yet. Riah jumped in to cover for Ivy. "Your highness, this is Lady Ivy Hernandez, my dear friend from Spain. She, unfortunately, does not speak your language, but I am happy to translate for you."

His eyes narrowed and he looked from Riah to Ivy and back again. "What are you doing here? Why have you come to my Wallachia?"

Question one, easy. "We come to spend time with a friend and to enjoy your beautiful country. We have heard many wonderful things about Wallachia and you as well, Prince Dracula."

Standing behind Dracula was another man, shorter and with straight black hair. He'd been silently watching the exchange and now leaned forward to whisper into Dracula's ear. His eyes stayed on her face the whole time.

"Who is this friend you come to stay with?"

"Lura Tappe."

Dracula nodded with a knowing look on his face. Then he glanced behind at the man wearing an indolent smile. "Your advice is well taken, Stephen."

Riah hoped that wasn't the Stephen she thought it might be. That man could spell big trouble for them.

With a wave of his hand, four men stepped out of the shadows and directly behind Riah and Ivy. They were so close she could smell the odor of unwashed body and smoke. It was so strong it made her want to whirl around and toss them outside. She kept her eyes on Dracula.

"You lie," Dracula said in the same calm even voice. "Take them below."

Riah stomach dropped. When she and Rodolphe had come to this land so many years ago, she'd seen the rooms *below*.

And they scared the shit out of her.

Lura couldn't help it. Hot tears pricked at the back of her eyes until she could contain them no longer. She started to cry as Nicoletta told her what had happened to her at the hands of Vlad Dracula. The thought of how powerless she'd been made Lura want to run back and kick the crap out of the guy. No woman, no one period, should be put in that position. It wasn't right on so many levels.

It was hard for a woman of her culture and background to understand how different things were for a woman in the fifteenth century. The rights Lura took for granted didn't exist here. If the Prince wanted her, he had her. That plain. That simple. God, how she hated it.

The worst part was how Nicoletta would never be able to escape Dracula. She now carried his child, and no matter how far they ran, he would always be with her. She hated him even more for that.

Truthfully, it made her all the more determined to get back to the stones on Snagov Island. If she accomplished nothing else, she had to get Nicoletta through the opening and into her time. Only there could she shelter and protect her. In this place, her medical skills were limited at best. Back home, she could give her the best of everything, and if she couldn't, she sure knew the folks who could.

The child? She wanted to hate it because it was his. But she couldn't. That his or her father was Vlad the Impaler didn't make the child any less of an innocent, and Nicoletta would always be the mother. That by itself made this baby very special in her heart. The child was not responsible for the sins of the father. He alone would be accountable for those on the day he stood before the pearly gates.

Nicoletta put her arms around Lura and held her tight. "Do not cry for me. I am here. I am alive."

Once again her thoughts turned to Vic, and guilt washed over her. She'd spent so much time feeling sorry for herself because she'd been such a bitch to him. Here Nicoletta was grateful simply to be alive after every horrible thing that had happened to her. To say it was humbling was putting it mildly. She needed to suck it up and put on her big-girl panties.

With the back of her hand, she wiped away her tears. "Sorry. I just feel so bad for what he did to you."

Nicoletta kissed her cheek. "I was lucky. He was pleased with me. In his chambers with no prying eyes or braggart men full of wine, he did not harm me, only took what he wanted and then let me go."

She shivered at the thought. "I'm still sorry. You never should have been put in that situation."

Nicoletta shrugged, her expression somber. "It is the way of our world. The Prince takes what he wants and we must give what we have."

She squeezed Nicoletta's hand. "I tell you what. Let's you and I get back on the road. When we get to my place, I'll introduce you to a world where people like the Prince go to jail for doing what he did to you."

Nicoletta shook her head and a small laugh escaped her lips. "Imagine…the Prince in jail. This I would like to see."

Lura got up and peered out the cave entrance. Outside, the forest was calm, an occasional plop of melting snow falling from the branches of the trees. The men who'd been behind them were gone. No sounds of horses' hooves, no gruff voices talking of willing wenches and dinners of roasted deer.

She turned and nodded at Nicoletta. "I think we're all right. Let's get going. The sooner we get to Snagov Island, the sooner we get home." Clean clothes, a hot meal, and a nice comfy bed all sounded like heaven. Hopefully these horses were nice and fast.

They led them back outside and remounted. Alongside Nicoletta she leaned across and kissed her hard on the lips. "We will get through this and I will help you with the baby. It's going to be a new life for you, I promise."

Nicoletta smiled and returned the kiss with one of her own. "You have a good heart, Lura Tappe. Your family must be very proud of the woman you are."

That remark made her thoughts turn grim once more. Her family was proud of her, and that compounded the guilt she already felt. What were any of them going to think of her once they learned the truth? Would they still love her when they understood how she'd turned her back on the love Vic offered so freely? Would they still love her when they learned she was in love with another woman?

Screw it. It was time to stop worrying about all that crap. All of it was in another world. Here the important thing was Nicoletta. Vic, of all people, would understand that and even urge her to take extra care with the expectant mother. That was the kind of man he was. She might have turned her back on his love, but she would honor his memory in any way she could. Taking care of Nicoletta would do just that.

"Come on," she told Nicoletta. "We're burning daylight." She laughed at the expression on her face. "Sorry. Another of those things we say where I come from."

Nicoletta was shaking her head. "You come from a most strange place."

"Yeah, I suppose I do."

She nudged her horse and it began an easy trot through the forest. With any luck they'd make the village of Snagov before nightfall and be on the island long before the moon rose.

CHAPTER TWENTY-TWO

The dungeon was as bad as she remembered and probably smelled even worse. But that wasn't what worried Riah. After all, locking up two vampires wasn't the end of the world. Between her and Ivy, they'd got themselves out of this house of horrors. They were strong, skilled, and preternatural.

What she was concerned about was Adriana and Colin. Both human, one injured, and one a tiny woman. Mostly she worried about Adriana. Yes, she was a sorceress and had powers. Still, she didn't quite have control of those powers yet. They were relatively new to her and, with no mentor to teach her how to use them, a bit of a wild card. Someday she'd be incredible, but it just wasn't that day yet.

With no grasp of the language, both Adriana and Colin were also operating without a clue. In this place, it was not only dangerous; it was potentially fatal. She wanted to kick down the door, get out of this rancid, claustrophobic cell, and find her woman. The impediment at the moment was the iron door. She could kick the crap out of wood—iron, not so much. Even a vampire could shatter a foot on something like that. There had to be another way and she would find it.

She didn't trust Dracula as far she could throw him, and Stephen Báthory flat-out made her nervous. He might not be his bloodthirsty relative Elizabeth, but that didn't make him any less dangerous. After all, he was the one who was whispering in Dracula's ear right before the bastard tossed them into the dank regions of the castle. She'd kill to know exactly what he'd said to land them here.

Leaning a shoulder against one damp wall, Ivy asked, "So what's the plan, oh wise one?"

"Has anyone ever told you you're a wise-ass?"

Ivy laughed softly. "Every day. But seriously, how are we going to get out of this shit hole?"

Riah tried to take herself back in time and recall how things were done in the day. A long-remembered hierarchy formed in her mind. Not far from them, she was certain a guard stood sentry. All they had to do was figure out what would grab his attention. Down here, he wasn't going to be the best or the brightest. A plus.

Dull and uneducated as he might be, these men were different from those of the world they lived in now. On the other hand, she decided they weren't different in one very fundamental way. That could very definitely work in their favor.

She told Ivy her idea and her smile was mischievous. "Gotta love men," Ivy said as she lay down on the stone floor as close as she could get to the iron fence that served as the cell door. "They sure as shit don't change much in five hundred years."

Riah knelt beside her with one hand on the stone floor beside her head and the other as close as she could get it to the bottom of the gate. "Let's hope not and hope this works. If that man outside takes the bait, we have a slim chance of getting out of here without a bloodbath and, hopefully, without drawing attention."

Ivy winked at her. "Oh, sister, I can make this sound real good. He'll come looking all right. What guy do you know will pass up a chance to watch a little girl-on-girl action?"

Shaking her head, Riah smiled too. "So predictable."

"Yeah, ain't it beautiful? There are at least some constants in this crazy world. Now come on, lay some sugar on me." She pursed her lips with a broad smile.

"You sound amazingly like Adriana."

"That's what I'm going for. Figure it's more believable if you feel like you're making out with your sweetie. I mean, I'm hot and all. What I'm not is Adriana."

"You're so thoughtful."

"Why yes, I am. Now come on, show me what you got. Let's make it look real good for our audience."

And they did. With moans and sighs, they sent a seductive message to the man in the hall. At first Riah didn't think their plan was working and was just about to tell Ivy they should give it up, when a pair of boots came into her peripheral vision. At first the boots paused, and she thought for a moment he was going to turn around and leave. All he needed to do was come a little closer.

"Turn it up a little," she whispered into Ivy's ear. "We've almost hooked our fish."

She did and, as Riah hoped, instead of retreating, the boots inched nearer to the cell door. Oh, he came closer all right. He wanted to see firsthand the lovemaking of the two elegant women Vlad Dracula had thrown into the dungeon. The chance to see any two women making love was lure enough, but two noblewomen? As they hoped, he wasn't going to pass that up.

As the toes of his boots nearly touched the gate, Riah whipped her hand between the bars of the cell door and grasped his ankle, pulling it hard. He lost his footing, and his head smacked against the far wall with a loud crunch. Her plan had worked. The blow stunned him, and since the space they were in was so small, he crumpled to the dirty floor, his ankle still in Riah's grasp. She yanked him forward until she had his head in her hands. Then she snapped his neck. As the stakes rose, her reluctance to alter this world faded. Things were just going to have to shake out as they would.

On the belt at his waist, a single key hung from a leather cord. It was exactly what they needed and what she'd hoped she'd find on him. A moment later, they were free. Stepping over the body, she and Ivy moved on silent feet into the passageway. At least the uncomfortable hard leather shoes they were forced to wear were good for one thing, silence.

It was dusky in the dungeon and the odor rank. The air hung heavy with the scent of feces, urine, and death. Whatever and whoever hadn't died already was creeping ever closer. She wondered if Dracula planned the same fate for the unfortunate men and women who crouched in fetid corners. No way did she intend to hang around long enough to find out. This place was as horrible as she remembered. Maybe even worse, considering last time she wasn't an actual guest.

Self-preservation was kicking in, and as much as it might hurt Ivy, Riah thought their best course of action was to get back to the stones. Plainly, this world was too dangerous for them right now. They'd gotten lucky this time. If they stayed much longer, their luck was bound to run out.

It was more than just the volatility of Dracula. They'd come through those rocks at an incredibly dangerous time. Wallachia was going to be awash in blood, and not just those whose lives were drained away on the point of Dracula's spikes. His blood was going to spill as well, and she didn't intend to be anywhere close by when that happened. She planned to be in her own home in Spokane, Washington, some half a millennia in the future.

She didn't say that to Ivy. First, she'd enlist Colin's help. Ivy was far more inclined to listen to good sense from the man she loved, even though the two of them had been friends for a long time. Colin had a way with Ivy no one had ever had before, and Riah was pretty sure she was going to need his help to get Ivy through those rocks without her cousin.

They were good hunters, and since they'd come together as the Spiritus Group, they'd done a great deal of good. Their silent work had saved untold number of lives. Even given how well they all worked together, at times they simply couldn't win the fight. This was one of those times. They'd all lose if they stayed here.

Riah didn't plan to lose.

❖

"I must stop." Nicoletta reined in her horse and slid quickly from its back. She did not have time to think and hit the ground hard. Her ankle twisted as she landed, and a sharp pain shot up her leg.

Crumpling to the earth, she let out a strangled cry only a moment before she began to retch. For many, many days now, this had been her life. One moment she was fine, and the next, a horrible twisting in her gut. It was as if some evil thing was trying to tear her apart.

She knew what the elders would say. Her body was telling her of its displeasure. She carried the child of Vlad Dracula in her womb, and now it ruled her body. If it was to be, this would pass. If it was not to be, if the child was somehow wrong, her body would continue to twist in pain and sickness until one day, the child would be no more. She prayed the old women were right and the child would not be.

Fate so far had not been that kind to her. She had witnessed other women doubled over with sickness day after day, only to birth a healthy boy or girl child. She hated to think she would be such a woman and knew deep in her heart it would be so. This child was not going to leave her. But what would she do on the day it came?

She did not want to be different, wanted to be like the other girls she had grown to womanhood with. They married, had children, loved, and laughed. They held their babies in their arms, and their faces showed tenderness and love. How would she hold this child to her breast and gaze down on it with love when it was *his*?

Worst of all, she was going to be alone. Soon, Lura would leave her. Without Alexandru, she would have no one. She could not go back to the castle. Not with the Prince still in power. This was her one and only chance to escape.

Tears pricked at her eyes as the hot, putrid scent of her sickness rose on the air. With nothing left to expel, she rose unsteadily on her feet. Her empty stomach clenched, but it was the fire in her ankle that caused the tears to spill down her face. She was a strong woman. Always had been. Except right now she wanted to scream and cry like a small child. It was not fair. How much did God expect her to endure?

Lura's hand was on her arm, the feel of it reassuring. "Are you any better?" She helped her to a large rock where she sank gratefully to sit. With the weight off her ankle, the pain pushed back to a hot throb.

"I am sorry," she said through her tears. "You should leave me and be on your way. I only hold you back."

Lura took her face between her hands, her thumbs wiping away her tears. "Don't you dare apologize to me. You have absolutely nothing to be sorry for. None of this is your fault. If I could go back there and kick that man's ass, I would do it in a heartbeat. And I am not, repeat, AM NOT leaving you anywhere."

Her passionate words warmed Nicoletta's heart. If only they could have come together differently. If only Lura was from her world, it might all turn out well. As it was, there was no hope for them, and that truth made her sad.

"You sound like a warrior when you talk so."

Lura gave her a crooked smile. "In a way I am a warrior. I became a doctor because I hated disease, injury, and those events that hurt people to their soul. I wanted to fight what damaged people. To help fix them and guide them to a place of hope."

"You are a treasure."

This time she laughed. "I don't know about being a treasure. I'd sure be a tarnished one if I was, but I do know how to fight. This is going to be all right, Nicoletta, I promise. I'm here now and I will take care of you."

Yes, she was here in this moment. One thing Nicoletta had learned the hard way was that moments do not last. Sometimes that was a very good thing, especially when it involved the Prince. Other times, it was like a sword to the chest. Deep, lancing pain. Exactly what she was going to feel the moment Lura went away from her.

"Let me look at your foot." Lura knelt in front of her and pulled up the hem of her gown. A frown turned down the corners of her mouth as her fingers gently probed.

Nicoletta managed not to cry out, though it was hard. Lura's touch was soft, and yet pain radiated up her leg as she pressed feather soft against her flesh. The pain was almost welcome as it took her mind off the impending moment of their final separation.

"I don't think you broke any bones, but you twisted it badly enough that it's going to hurt a great deal. You need to have it iced and up."

"Iced?" She had never heard of such a thing.

"Yes." Lura smiled again, all traces of a frown gone. "Trust me, ice is the key to getting it to feel better quickly."

"We have no ice." She looked around. Snow was on the ground, though the storm itself had passed. She did not know how close they were to a lake or a stream that might have frozen enough to chip away a chunk of ice. The season was growing deep and ice would be forming.

"Yeah, I see that. Do you think you can ride a little longer? I hate the idea of your leg hanging down. It's going to make the swelling worse, but we've got to find some kind of shelter, and then I can get your leg up."

Nicoletta nodded. Of course she could ride. "I will be fine now." She believed it too, until she stood and her leg gave way. Lura was there to catch her with strong arms that wrapped around her body. Tears welled in her eyes again from both pain and pleasure. She loved the feel of this woman's body so close to hers.

"Come on," Lura said against her ear. "I'll help you up. The sooner we find shelter, the better."

Though her horse's gait was as smooth as could be, given the forest floor, the jarring of each step roared through her body. Sweat popped out on her forehead, even in the coolness of the day. She wanted nothing more than to get off the horse and lie down. It did not matter if she got cold or wet. Anything to stop the burning pain.

Finally, Lura brought the horses to a stop. Her gaze was fixed on a hillside. Nicoletta saw nothing but trees and mountains, not that she looked closely. It took everything she possessed just to stay upright on her horse.

"Come," Lura said as she took the reins away from Nicoletta. "I see somewhere we can stop."

Lura's vision was much keener than hers, for just as she said, there was an outcropping of rocks that provided shelter. Beneath the stone, the ground was cold but clear of snow. Nicoletta gratefully sank to the hard earth. The lack of motion was a gift from God.

With her back against the hard stone, she closed her eyes, listening as Lura tied up the horses. She moved without stopping, and if Nicoletta were not so tired, she would have looked to see what she was about. She did not, though, and was surprised when Lura took hold of her foot and set it upon one of the horse's blankets folded over many times.

"What is this?"

"Trust me, it'll help. Now I just have to figure out how to ice it."

The ice again. A doctor from the future, she certainly had strange ideas. Ice...

Nicoletta screamed and jumped when something bitter cold was laid against her ankle. For how long, she did not know, she had fallen asleep and only awoke to the frigid touch. Lura knelt in front of her again, holding a cloth packed with snow.

Nicoletta started to pull her leg away, but Lura stopped her with a hand on her foot. "It's going to help, I promise."

She stared into Lura's deep, expressive eyes and saw honesty. Whatever else might happen here, this woman would never hurt her. Ice was an odd thing to do, but in her heart, she felt the truth. Lura was her one and only.

And she was going to lose her.

CHAPTER TWENTY-THREE

The sound of footsteps made Riah stop. She grabbed Ivy's hand and they slipped behind an unlocked door. Outside voices carried.

"What are they saying?" Ivy whispered into her ear.

Riah was listening hard. She recognized only one voice. "It's Dracula. He's telling someone to keep us locked up until he returns."

"Returns from where?"

Riah shook her head. "Trying to get that, but he's talking so fast, I can't quite catch everything. This dialect is hard for me to understand. Everything's so different than what we hear in modern times."

Another man was also speaking, and that made it even more difficult for her to understand. As they drew close to the door they huddled behind, she shoved Ivy even farther into the empty room.

The men continued to talk as they tromped by, their boots heavy and loud on the stone floor. As their footsteps faded, Riah let out a breath. Tough as she generally was, she was still nervous to have him so close.

"They're heading into battle, from the sounds of things. But if memory serves me, he's off to conquer the rest of Wallachia again to secure his rule."

"Doesn't work out so well for him, does it?"

That was an understatement. The problem as she saw it wasn't that Dracula's enemies were going to kick his ass. It was that they were right smack in the middle of the mess. Taking him down was one thing; risking their own necks was something altogether different.

They needed to get out of here, and now. This was a disaster. In the time they'd all been together they'd been involved in some tricky situations. Her former lover turned vicious, vengeful vampire, a werewolf killing innocent hikers in a beautiful state park, and a self-involved preacher turned vampire were just a few. This, however, was a completely different beast. They were in a whole lot of trouble.

Not only were they up against a man who embraced violence at terrifying levels, but they also were in a strange land, in a time not their own, and she was the only one with even a passable grasp of the language. That wasn't saying much either. As an old friend used to say, they were up a creek without a paddle.

They needed to get back to Snagov Island.

Silence fell outside in the corridor. Finally she decided they could risk leaving the safety of the small chamber. Riah went out first, Ivy close on her heels. She moved quickly, silently. A door at the end of the corridor would hopefully lead them outside. Maybe then she could get a sense of where they were and beat a path to the stables where their horses were being housed.

She had to find Adriana.

The door opened easily and Riah pulled Ivy through. Sunlight made her squint after being cooped up inside for hours. The cold air was like a slap in the face. The castle had seemed drafty and cool until the winter weather confronted them.

"What's up, pussycat?"

Riah screamed, then clamped a hand over her mouth. Behind her, Adriana chuckled softly. "You're so easy."

Whirling around, she dropped the hand from her mouth and grabbed Adriana. Pulling her close, she hugged her tight. "You're here? How are you here? Why are you here? I'm so relieved to see you."

"Luck of the Irish."

An uncharacteristic giggle rose in her throat. "You're not Irish."

"Details, my lovely doctor. Details. Actually it was dumb luck. We were skulking about trying to find you guys while not attracting too much attention."

"Yeah, and all of sudden we see a couple of gorgeous women pop their pretty little heads out a door. There you two were, as if we'd ordered you up. Prime example of right place, right time," Colin said.

Riah turned her head to see him hugging Ivy as close as she was holding Adriana.

"You know," Adriana said loud enough for Colin and Ivy to hear. "The more I think about it, it probably was my wizardly powers that took us to the right door. I mean, really, with all the ins and outs of this place, what are the odds we'd be right here when you two creep out like a couple of burglars? Yeah, it was definitely me and my mad skills."

"I'm not going to touch that one, I'll just give it to you. That said, we have to get out of here." Riah didn't even try to tamp down the panic in her voice. Maybe it was Adriana's growing powers or maybe it was just plain luck. Truthfully, it didn't make a damn bit of difference. All that did was the sheer miracle that the four of them were reunited.

"Ahead of you there, girlfriend. We've got the horses waiting not far from here."

That was a welcome piece of news, though she was still astounded by the fact that they were even here. They'd left them fully in servant character with some of Dracula's people. They wouldn't have been allowed to simply walk out. "But how did were you able to slip away? Didn't the guards notice?"

"Ah, baby, you think a few puny guards are gonna be able to stop me and my boy here when we're on a mission to save our women? I thought you knew us better than that."

She kissed Adriana. "Now, why ever would I think that? Maybe because your boy is wounded and those guys were twice your size?"

"Such little faith you have in us. Girlfriend, we kicked their asses, didn't we, hunter boy?"

Colin nodded, his arm still firmly around Ivy's shoulders. "Absolutely. I might be wounded, but when it comes to rescuing my woman, I'm a man of steel. Now come on, ladies. The sooner we get out of here the better. I don't care what they say about Dracula in the history books; the real thing isn't the kind of guy I'd invite over for a beer. I know you keep saying he's just a regular human, but it sure doesn't feel that way. Something about him is very preternatural, and not in a way that bodes well for anyone. I'd like to put some serious distance between him and us."

Colin was right. They shouldn't stand here talking, let alone embracing. Given the roles they were playing, the whole thing would be blown to kingdom come if someone discovered them hugging and kissing their *servants*. And he wasn't wrong about Dracula either. He gave her the creeps too, and that was saying a lot, given everything she'd seen during her time on earth.

"A really good idea, Colin. Come on, you heard what the man said. Let's get moving."

Colin took the lead and, keeping a low profile—not a small feat for him—got them to the grove of trees where the horses waited. As they did when they first entered the city, Ivy and Riah rode astride the horses while Colin and Adriana walked beside with heads down and eyes properly cast to the ground. Once they were off the main road and surrounded by thick trees, Colin and Adriana joined them on horseback. They made much better time as soon as all four of them were mounted.

Though she would have preferred to take the horses at a run and get back to Snagov Island more quickly, given Colin's injury, it wasn't a good idea. Instead, as they trotted along at an easy, steady pace, Riah filled them in on what had happened during their audience with Vlad Dracula. She didn't pull any punches, not that she ever did with her fellow hunters.

Adriana shivered as Riah finished her story, and Riah asked her, "Are you cold?"

"A little, but really, it's more thinking about what he could have done to you both. Seriously, Riah, the guy's a psycho, and we're lucky he just decided to toss you in his morbid jail. I'd have died if I'd have seen your body on one of those god-awful stakes."

She too shivered, thinking of the bodies in various stages of decomposition currently suspended from sharp-pointed stakes. People in the world she came from wouldn't even be able to fathom it. She hoped they never had to. But, for Dracula, it was just another day. He didn't come by the name Vlad the Impaler by chance. He'd earned it.

"Can't say I'd have liked that option any better myself. I've always had to look behind me, worried about who might put a wooden stake in my heart or lop off my head. But this is the first time I've ever worried about a wooden stake going somewhere else in my body. Honestly though, I'm not sure why he decided to spare us. He's got some kind of agenda. You can see it in his face. The wheels are turning in that man's head. I just have no idea what his secret plan is or why he didn't kill us."

"Shhh," Colin suddenly hissed. His hand up, he motioned for them to stop. Riah immediately reined in her horse.

The sound of pounding hooves cut through the air. The Prince and his men? It was more than possible, except she'd have expected them to be ahead of them, not coming up from the rear. Their approach was most decidedly from behind them.

A flash of color crashed by on the road. Horses and riders raced along again and again. From their hiding place inside the thick trees, they couldn't see exactly who it was, but she had a pretty good idea, and it wasn't the Prince. All she could think of as she watched the riders gallop by was that Dracula better watch his ass. The Turks were on the move again, even without his brother.

Radu the Handsome might be out of the picture, but others just as dangerous were on the road this day and out for his head...literally.

❖

What Lura wouldn't give for an ice pack and a couple of hydrocodones right now. Nicoletta's sprain was severe, and if she had her at home, she'd be in a comfortable chair, her foot up on a couple of pillows with an ice pack on the ankle. Toss a hydrocodone down her along with a cup of nice tea, and she'd have Nicoletta healed up in no time.

Instead, they were in the midst of a forest in the Middle Ages with irrational royals and eager soldiers racing around the primitive roads looking for anyone who might offer resistance. In other words, they were in crazyland...and that wasn't a term used by people in her profession. It was, however, the only one that fit the bill right now.

The best she could do for Nicoletta at the moment was rip off a section of her dress at the hemline, fill it with snow, and wrap the icy cold, wet cloth around her swollen ankle. The horse's blanket became a makeshift pillow, and that allowed her to get the foot elevated. It wasn't great. It was certainly better than nothing.

Before she'd tended to Nicoletta, she'd tied the horses to a couple of trees ten or so feet away. She wished she could do something for them as well, except she had no grain to give them, and the snow had covered any grass that might still be edible. All she could do before she sank down next to Nicoletta was heartily pat them both.

Leaning back against the rock face she asked Nicoletta, "Feel any better?" She was pleased to see some color had returned to her cheeks and the lines of pain eased.

"A bit better. The sickness seems to have passed."

"Your leg?"

She wiggled her foot a little and then gasped. "Like a blacksmith is using his poker on it."

That's what she was afraid of. Even though she'd tried to cut their time on horseback as short as possible, it had still taken longer than she'd hoped to find a spot that could provide them at least a little shelter. By the time she did, the swelling in Nicoletta's foot and ankle had blossomed.

"We'll need to stay here for a bit. Let your foot rest."

"It will be too dangerous. The Prince will send his men to find us once he discovers we have left the castle." Fear wavered in Nicoletta's words.

True. Danger was so near she could almost taste it. Didn't matter. She wasn't going to let Nicoletta get back on that horse until at least some of the swelling went down. They had some measure of cover here, and the snow, thank goodness, had stopped. For at least a little while they could rest, dry and safe. It worked for her, and whether or not Nicoletta liked it, it was going to work for her too. The rocks weren't going anywhere, so they could wait.

"We'll be all right. You need to have this leg up for a bit before we go any farther."

Nicoletta leaned into Lura at the same time she gazed down at her wrapped foot propped up on the blanket. A tiny smile graced her lips. "It does feel better."

Lura kissed the side of her head as she put her arms around her to pull her close. "Of course it does. You just have to trust me. I'm a doctor, after all."

Nicoletta shook her head slowly. "A healer. When we were told you were coming, I did not think you would be so much as you are. I expected someone wonderful, and you are far more than I ever dreamed."

"I'm nobody special." Wasn't that the truth! She was a healer of sorts, for the mind, not the body. She couldn't banish illness and injury to make a person whole like Vic had done. She didn't give of her own time and resources to go to places where care didn't exist. No, she'd hidden away in her own little office pretending to be someone she wasn't. He was the true healer and he was gone. Nicoletta was wrong; she was definitely not special.

"You do yourself dishonor," Nicoletta said sternly. "You look too closely at your own heart and decide it is not good. We are not fit to judge ourselves, for that belongs to one much higher than we."

Like she'd ever pass through anything even close to the beautiful gates of heaven. Pretty sure those would stay locked up tight when she showed up. Saint Peter would be foolish to give her a pass after what she'd done to Vic.

"Judging is easy when I look in the mirror."

"It is the man you were promised to, yes?"

She had to stop and think about that for a moment. "Not exactly. In my time, we are not promised to a man, and that's the real problem. I made the promise to him, no one else. Me, standing before God and family, promising to love, honor, and cherish. I broke that promise. He never did."

It got quiet, with neither of them saying a word. A breeze ruffled the trees and the horses whinnied softly. For at least a little while it felt like they were the only two people in the universe and her broken promise hadn't sent a man halfway around the world to die alone.

Only it did, and she didn't think she'd ever be able to reconcile to it. Even if she couldn't, she would at least own up to it. It was too late to save Vic. It wasn't too late to honor him with honesty. With Nicoletta's head resting on her shoulder, her arm around her tiny waist, Lura began to speak.

She told Nicoletta the story of growing up with Vic, of meeting him again in college. Explained how they rekindled their friendship and embarked on a marriage full of promise. With careful words she told of how she tried to love him and tried to be the wife he deserved. She'd wanted to be and had tried to be the proper wife to Vic and daughter to her parents.

And then she explained how she'd failed at all of it.

CHAPTER TWENTY-FOUR

They rode in silence for a long time. Riah's thoughts were a jumble of anxious need and regret. She didn't doubt that they were in the wrong place at the wrong time. It was a classic Greek tragedy that Ivy's cousin Lura had stumbled into this world, but none of them could do much about it.

Yes, the Spiritus Group had come into being as a way to help innocents in a war against evil that most didn't even realize existed. It was also true this was exactly that kind of situation they dedicated their lives to battling.

Well, not exactly. More like sort of. If it was just a case of preternatural evil, they were on board. The problem, as she saw it, was none of them were equipped for the Jules Verne type of scenario they were currently experiencing. No Captain Nemo would appear to help them escape. Out of their element in a big way.

It equated to their being in a whole heap of trouble with time running out. It didn't matter that she'd actually been in this world once upon a time. She'd moved on with the times and was now a woman— vampire—of the twenty-first century, leaving her ill-equipped to deal with fifteenth-century violence. Particularly violence of Vlad the Impaler variety.

As much as she hated leaving someone behind, she didn't see that they had a better choice. The Spiritus Group was on the road to an epic failure in this instance. If they stayed around, the crash would grow even larger as they were killed or destroyed.

Still, even given all those elements, the one thing that made her regret not staying was the sunlight. She hadn't enjoyed full-on daytime exposure since she was a young woman, before Rodolphe and the endless years that followed. This world, where she and Ivy could walk freely in the daytime, was a dream come true.

Ever since she'd joined forces with Ivy and Adriana, they'd searched for a cure that would let Riah once more walk as a human. When Ivy was turned, the mission became even more important. She desperately wanted to give her friend back the human existence she'd been robbed of. Ivy had lost it only because of her friendship with Riah. That wasn't right in any way, shape, or form, and she hoped that no matter what else happened, she could give Ivy what she deserved.

Going back to her own existence in the shadows was a small price to pay for saving her friends. She'd never forgive herself if anything happened to Ivy or Colin. She didn't think she could go on at all if Adriana was taken from her.

She urged her mount to move a little faster. The sun on her face, the wind in her hair, and the woman she loved holding tight to her waist was something she would keep in her memories long after the sunlight was gone. Once they returned, the sunlight would once more be denied to her. This moment would not. No matter what else happened, no one could take this from her.

A groan made her turn and look. Not Adriana, not Ivy. Damn, it was Colin, and his pallor had gone from mildly pale to downright pasty. When they'd met up outside the castle, she'd been encouraged by the color in his face. The rest at Antoine's as well as the wait in the stables seemed to have provided him with the break he needed to be steady on his feet.

A couple of hours on a horse in the cold Wallachian countryside, and what color had returned to him had drained away. He was as white as the snow being kicked up by the horses' hooves. She reined in her horse and brought it up next to Colin and Ivy. Ivy's eyes were full of the same concern that Riah felt. She noticed too.

"Colin, how are you feeling?"

"Does the term 'Mack truck' mean anything to you?" he said without much enthusiasm.

She nodded. Indeed it did, and more than once she'd had the same feeling of being run down by a speeding semi. "Why don't we stop for a little while?"

He shook his head with more force than she would have believed possible, given his pale complexion and drooping body. "No, we can't stay here. I have to believe those men we saw earlier were just the beginning. Between those guys and the action we saw while we waited in the stables, Dracula is getting ready for a fight. We don't want to be anywhere near him when that happens. I'm pretty sure the guy embraces the take-no-prisoners philosophy."

Her thoughts exactly, although she hadn't wanted to put them into words and frighten the group. Colin, always the pragmatist, didn't share her reluctance. "I'm afraid you're right. He as much said so when we heard him speak to the guards outside our cell. He's on a charge to retake control of the entire country. I doubt he plans to stop until he's cleared any and all obstacles out of his way."

"Yeah, and we sure don't want to be in his path when he comes through. This," Colin waved a hand out toward their surroundings, "is dangerous. Too wide open. I wouldn't mind getting off this horse for a bit, just not here. Let's ride on and see if we can find something a little more secluded."

"We have to return tonight," Riah said as she stared off into the distance. She didn't dare look at Ivy's face. The feeling of letting her down was so great, she simply couldn't meet her gaze. It was a hard truth, though, and it had to be voiced.

Ivy reached across and took her hand. "I understand," she said simply. "I hate it but I do understand. We're at the point where we can't risk the many to save the one."

Riah raised her gaze to meet Ivy's. It was in her eyes. She did understand. Without another word, she began once more to head south. Again they moved into the trees, and their journey was slowed by the need to travel under the cover of the forest. She wished they could make their way back to the road. Rough as it was by modern standards, the speed it would afford them would cut their time significantly. Dodging branches and fallen trees flat-out slowed them down. She hated the delay.

The risk was too great to do any different. They had to stay off the road and far from easy view. It didn't matter which group encountered them—Dracula's men or his enemies—they would be screwed either way. On the open road, it was a given that her half a millennia of existence would come to a halt at the bloody end of one those swords all the riders carried. They weren't for decoration. Each and every one of the men who passed them by on horseback knew exactly how to wield those weapons. And though they carried their own small arsenal retrieved from their car before stepping through the stones, they were no match for the forged long swords.

They pushed on, pleased that at least some of the sunshine pierced the canopy of thick trees. The air was cool but not frigid, and for that she was grateful. Sometimes all it took was a little thing to keep spirits raised. Despite the cold winter weather, she was plenty warm in her cloak, and Adriana assured her that she was as well.

Warm or not, she wanted to get somewhere safe, let Colin rest, and then make one final push to those stones and hope against hope they could get back to their own time. Turning to make sure Colin and Ivy were close, she opened her mouth to ask how he was doing. But before a single word could pass her lips, Colin rolled from the horse and hit the ground at a dead run.

Nicoletta awoke slowly. Rays of light, red and gold, spread across her skirt. She was surprised, for that meant she had slept longer than she believed possible. Gingerly, she stretched her toes out, and the simple movement made her gasp. The pain was still sharp as knives, though the cool cloth did seem to help. Odd as it seemed to her at the time, Lura's snow-soaked rag did a bit of magic on her ankle.

Lura was asleep, her head tilted back against the rock. In slumber, her features were relaxed and she looked much younger, much softer. Nicoletta recognized the pain in her eyes and understood that which weighed heavy on her shoulders. Many times, she had felt the same. Her family, her society, her God expected so much of her. The burden was at times too great.

For Lura, even living in a world so many years in the future, it seemed that little had changed. Husbands were expected, even if the marriages were no longer arranged. Appearances were everything. And, like her, Lura tried to be all that was demanded of her as a woman.

Like her, Lura failed.

How was it that two women born centuries apart could share so much? She did not understand how it could be so, but she did know how it made her feel. Pulling her cloak tight against the breeze and leaning her head against Lura's shoulder, she stilled, her gaze steady on the setting sun.

This was a moment she wanted to remember when it came time for their paths to part. The thought of Lura leaving brought heaviness to bear on her heart. She did not want to dwell on that because she would have the rest of her life to do so. It was hard not to let the sorrow wash through her, yet with effort she pushed it away. For now, just being close to her, touching her, sharing the sunset with her was enough.

"What are you thinking about?"

Lura's voice made her jump. "I did not know you had awakened."

Her laugh was gentle. "I was enjoying being here with you."

Nicoletta let a small smile turn up the corners of her mouth. "I too was enjoying our closeness."

"How's your ankle?"

Her smile turned to a frown. "It is not right."

"I was afraid of that. I wish I had you in the office. You'd be patched up and ready to go in no time. Here? I'm worried everything we have to do will make it worse."

"It is better now because of your ministrations."

Lura shook her head. "I need to do more. I've got to get you to safety and to proper medical facilities."

The calmness that slumber had given Lura was fading. Now, her eyes looked troubled and her face tight once more. Nicoletta wanted to make it go away and to restore the peace of only moments before. It was not to be. No matter what she said, it would not give her comfort. Of that she was most certain.

"We keep on with our journey." If it were possible, staying here tucked into their own little shelter would be heaven. No one to bother them and no one to fear. It was like one of the beautiful stories her mother used to tell her at bedtime, only much sweeter.

"As much as I hate it, you're right. Snagov Island isn't getting any closer while we sit here. Do you think you can ride the rest of the way, or does the foot hurt too much?"

Using the rock face at her back, Nicoletta pushed her way up until she stood. With deep breaths, she put her foot down and flinched at the pain. The burning flowed up and made her frown.

"I can ride." Riding upon her horse would be better, she was sure. It was the standing that was not pleasant.

Lura studied her, and Nicoletta shifted uncomfortably under her probing gaze. She did not know what she searched for or what she hoped to find by staring at her so. Nicoletta touched Lura's face, her fingertips tingling when skin met skin.

"I can ride," she said again. "I give you my word. We must not tarry."

"I hate this," Lura whispered. "I just want to keep you safe. This is all so messed up."

It was a strange thing to be standing in a forest, snow all around, the Prince's men surely searching for them, and her body injured while all the while feeling a joy that compared to none other. "I am happy just to share this day with you."

Lura smiled, the shadows leaving her eyes. "I am thrilled to share the day with you too."

CHAPTER TWENTY-FIVE

S couts," Colin said, his chest heaving and his breath short. "The bastard sent out scouts." At his feet two men lay motionless, their open eyes staring sightless at the winter sky.

Riah's heart sank. She'd hoped for more time, but they were, as she'd feared all along, running out of it quickly. "It won't take them that all that long to come looking for these men, but we'll have at least a little time before they realize something's happened to them. It's not like our world with instant communication. Thank God for small favors." She was grateful this was a time of no cell phones, radios, or any other type of voice notification. They could use any advantage they could get, no matter or large or small.

"How long do you think we've got?" Ivy asked as she helped Colin move the bodies deeper into the forest and then cover them with frosty leaves and brush.

"A couple of hours." She hoped. Ivy and Colin did a good job of hiding the bodies, and it would take some serious tracking skills to see the evidence of tampering. She doubted anyone would be looking that close, thinking they'd be blundering through, leaving them a clear trail to follow.

"Well," Adriana said as she stood holding the reins of two new horses. "At least we have a couple of new cabs."

It was true that the men Colin intercepted had been riding beautiful horses. Adriana had deftly captured the animals, who seemed quite content in her hands. She had a way with horses, for sure. Who would ever have guessed? Might be a good skill to pursue once they returned to Spokane.

"We can travel faster with four mounts, and that's certainly going to play to our advantage. They're obviously on the hunt for us. Let's give ourselves as much distance as we can and as little for them to follow as possible."

"Have I mentioned what a pain in the ass this Dracula is?" Adriana screwed up her face in a mask of disgust. "He was a lot more palatable in Stoker's novel. The real guy is just nasty."

Leave it to her beautiful Adriana to paint a vivid picture with her words. She was a world-class researcher, a sorceress, and a call-it-like-she-sees-it beauty. Riah was proud of her every single day.

"Nasty is one word for it. I think he sees himself as a determined ruler who knows how to keep his people safe and his place on the throne intact…not necessarily in that order."

"Whatever!" Adriana mounted one of the horses. "You know it doesn't really matter. We just gotta haul ass out of here and get back to the Ponderosa, if you know what I mean. I'm pretty sure there's a hot shower with my name on it. Oh, and a latte," she said longingly. "Yeah, a latte…"

The latte, she could pass on. Not so with the shower. Adriana had the right idea. Riah turned to see if Ivy and Colin were ready to go. The fight seemed to have rattled Colin, even though he was the victor. He now carried one of the two swords appropriated from the fallen soldiers, and she carried the second. Even injured and half out of it, he was always thinking.

Still, despite the advantage of the newly acquired armaments, Colin's skin tone was getting paler by the minute. His color was alarming, but she couldn't do much about it for the time being. They were all going to have to toughen up and ride like they were born on horses if they hoped to have any chance at all of staying out of the path of Dracula and his men.

If Dracula tracked them down, they were dead. Her five-hundred-plus years would be done. She didn't mind so much for herself, but she was really worried about the other three. They didn't deserve to die, especially not here. While it might prove to be poetic justice in her case, it wasn't fair to them.

She was going to get them home if it was the last thing she ever did.

❖

This might be Nicoletta's world, but Lura was getting a pretty good feel for navigation in the thick woods. Probably because right now she was highly motivated. She'd had enough of this place. She wanted to get home, and she wanted to take Nicoletta with her. After everything the woman had endured, she'd earned a whole lot of pampering, and Lura wanted to be the one to pamper.

The snow began to fall once more, lightly, tiny specks floating down slowly and landing on her lashes like the beat of tiny butterfly wings. Out here, far from the city, the scent of smoke no longer filled the air. It was clear and cold. Quiet.

Every so often, she'd glance at Nicoletta, keeping an eye on how she was holding up. To her credit, she seemed strong and alert. The ankle had to be throbbing terribly. She didn't wince or whine or even let on that it was hurting her at all. She was a strong, beautiful woman, and that made Lura's heart race.

Now, though, she wanted to push harder to get back to Snagov Island. She wished Alexandru was with them. For the brief time they'd spent in each other's company, she'd felt comfortable, as if they'd been friends forever. Her BMF.

That they'd probably never know why Dracula had killed him pissed her off. She didn't like loose ends, and she wanted to know what Dracula felt was so terrible that he had to take Alexandru's life in such a brutal way. It was wrong on so many levels, and she'd miss him the rest of her life. Some people touch the heart deeply and forever.

Like Nicoletta.

Like Vic. What she'd done to him was wrong, and trying to rationalize it didn't change a thing. Wrong was wrong. She should have been honest with him from the moment she'd finally gotten honest with herself. An honorable person would have. She spent so much of her life counseling others to take the high road, to reconcile their actions, and to make amends when they had harmed others. When it came to the physician-heal-thyself situation she was currently in, she pretty much sucked. The high road appeared to be under construction. She wasn't anywhere close to reconciliation, and the chance to make amends with Vic was gone forever.

With Nicoletta, for the first time in ages, an opportunity to start over spread out before her. She wanted to be true to herself and to be a faithful, caring partner. In her head it was shaping up to be simple. Return to the twenty-first century, take Nicoletta with her, and start over. Nicoletta could get the care she needed, not just for the injury to her ankle, but for the baby coming as well. It didn't matter that the father was a brutal, vindictive man from the fifteenth century. That wasn't Nicoletta's fault, or the child's. What mattered was delivering a healthy child who would be given a happy, loving home. With happiness and love, anything was possible. She would make sure Nicoletta and the baby had both.

The more she thought about it, the more it worked in her head. Thoughts of Vic entered as well. She knew him, knew his heart, and could almost hear his words. He would have been an ally, and maybe, just maybe, she'd sold him short. It occurred to her now that when she'd been hesitant to take the trip to Romania with him, he hadn't protested very hard.

In fact, the more she thought about it, the more she realized he hadn't argued against her staying at all. He'd been happy, engaged, and excited to go: alone. Did he know? Had he been trying in his own way to let her go? Tears began to prick at the back of her eyes as the truth of her marriage began to settle at long last. How she did love that man, would always love him—as a friend.

She turned and looked at Nicoletta riding tall and proud on her horse. Fresh starts. That's what it was all about. For Vic, for her, for Nicoletta. A smile was spreading across her face as the first arrow whizzed by so close it left a bloody slash across her cheek. Her scream shattered the silence, and instinct kicked in. Ignoring the pain in her face, she whipped around to see if Nicoletta had been injured.

From all appearances, she was fine. For the moment. Lura opened her mouth to ask if she was hurt and didn't get the chance. The words died on her lips as she went flying through the air and then tumbled hard to the ground. Her horse, kicking wildly, was bleeding from the throwing axe buried in its chest.

"Damn it," she screamed as she scrambled to her feet, her legs tangling up in the yards of skirt fabric. These stupid dresses were a nightmare. Why didn't these women wear something more practical, like pants?

She managed to right herself just as Nicoletta brought her horse around to Lura's side. With power she didn't know she possessed, she managed to vault up, bulky gown and all, to mount the horse behind Nicoletta.

"Go, go, go," she whispered into Nicoletta's ear, her arms tight around her waist.

Nicoletta spurred the horse and it took off at a run, deftly maneuvering around trees and fallen logs, snow slapping their faces as they raced through the forest.

Behind them, hooves pounded. She risked a look behind and was dismayed to see half a dozen men on horses. They were big, they were angry, and worst of all, they were armed. One was pulling back on his bow and, as he released, Lura yelled, "Down."

They both drew themselves down as close as they could to the horse's back, and the arrow sailed over their heads before lodging in a tree twenty feet away. It was close, very very close.

"Son of a bitch," Lura muttered. Every nerve in her body was on fire. She hated this place.

"We must get far from the soldiers," Nicoletta said with an urgency in her voice Lura hadn't heard before.

She wanted to say *no shit*, but that was just rude and unnecessary. Besides, it wouldn't help anything. She'd done a turn in the ER of a Houston hospital during her residency, and even though she practiced a different kind of medicine, she'd learned a lot in that time that still stayed with her. Crisis and fast thinking were staples of each and every night in the emergency room of an inner-city hospital. She'd handled everything from massive heart attacks to motorcycle accidents to drug-fueled gunshot wounds. Panic wasn't an option then, and it wasn't an option now.

"We'll beat these bastards," she said as she hugged herself even tighter to Nicoletta's body. "We haven't gotten this far only to have them put an arrow in our hearts."

"I don't want to die," Nicoletta said very softly, her words nearly lost in the snowstorm growing stronger with each passing minute. "I don't want the child to die."

Lura understood. It didn't matter who the baby's father was; the child was a part of Nicoletta and important. She tightened her arms around Nicoletta. "And I won't let you."

CHAPTER TWENTY-SIX

*R*odolphe was beautiful in the black-velvet doublet with leather
sleeves and shiny brass buttons down the front. His breeches
fit him well, not hiding the strength in his buttocks and legs. Tall leather
boots rose past his knees, polished to a high shine. A black-wool
chaperone hat gave him a regal, almost royal appearance. All eyes
followed him the moment he stepped into a room.

Catherine studied him, knowing much of his secret lay in the
beautiful package he presented to the unsuspecting. He was a true
master at deception. Few would believe that beneath the pristine velvet
beat the heart of a monster.

She knew and hated him for it. In many ways, he'd created her in
his image. She'd been a beautiful young woman of means when he'd
taken her life away, and from that night forward he'd groomed her to be
the perfect companion always at his side. Always scheming.

Looking down at her burgundy wool tweed dress, the best money
could buy, she frowned. It was lovely, made to complement every curve
of her body. Only the finest fabrics, the most skilled seamstress, the
latest fashions. Like Rodolphe, her package was deceiving. Pretty on
the outside. Bleak and ugly on the inside.

Standing here in the monastery, a matching burgundy turret hat
covering her beautifully arranged hair, she was the proper maiden head
to toe. No one would question her; no one would think her anything but
a genteel lady. They were the picture of well-heeled society patrons with
enough money to command a private audience inside the monastery.

In this place, pretending to be human was a joker's game. Here they understood the darkness and those who came from it. They did not turn away in confusion, and they did not make-believe. Here they lived in a world very real and very bloody, and rather than run, they faced their fears and fought. It was not a land for the weak.

Rodolphe called it the motherland. She called it perdition.

He took her hand and laid it upon his arm. Into the monastery they walked as the moon shone high and bright outside. To look at them was to believe them little more than a handsome couple visiting a holy place to pray.

Only three of them knew why they were really here. She, Rodolphe, and the priest who walked before them down the long aisle. The click, click, click of Rodolphe's boots and her slippers was the only sound. Ahead, the priest stopped at the edge of the altar. A large stone with rounded edges was set into the floor, a cross carved deep into its smooth top. Years of footsteps crossing it had filled the indentations with dirt as thick as if it had been mortared into place.

The sight of the stone sent cold shivers up her spine. It took much effort not to pull her arm away, turn and flee outside to where fresh air awaited. She did not want to be here. Longed for the wind to blow through her hair and clothes, and to take with it the evil that clung to her like dirt. Rodolphe did not share her reticence. He seemed to literally quiver with excitement. He had been so since the moment they stepped foot on this island. She hated him all the more for it.

The priest waved his hand as if to encompass the stone. "He awaits you," he said with a small smile on his lips. The sight of that smile sent ice into her veins. A priest should not look so.

Rodolphe took her hand off his arm. "My maker," he whispered with a reverence she had never heard from his lips before. Somehow that seemed even worse than the sickening smile of the priest.

Rodolphe knelt at the edge of the stone. His fingers searched for purchase and, when at last found it, lifted the stone from its resting place as if it weighed no more than a pebble. She put a gloved hand to her nose as a horrifying stench rose from the earth beneath.

Catherine wanted to retch. Her eyes stung with the rancid odor that now filled the church. Resisting the urge to run, she was sickly gripped by the look of rapture on Rodolphe's face. Never had she seen such an expression cross his features, and it made her shudder. His *eyes glazed with something akin to love as he stared down into the murkiness of the hole beneath the stone.*

She followed his gaze, and bile rose even higher in her throat. Time had not destroyed what lay in the earth at their feet. A crimson-brocade Cotehardie, black breeches, tall black boots. The supine body rested with hands clasped at the waist, a large ruby ring on one finger of the left hand, the stone sparkling in the light of the priest's torch.

It was not the body inside the elegant clothing that turned her stomach, nor its almost pristine condition despite having been in the grave for many years. It was that the body had no head.

In the shadows, Riah was still as stone as she watched the Prince ride past accompanied by a league of men traveling close behind him. She wasn't shocked to find him so near them. No, what he wore as he traveled past made her want to scream. A crimson-brocade Cotehardie, black breeches, and tall black boots. If she'd been closer she'd have definitely seen a large ruby ring on his left hand.

Why today of all days? Their only hope of survival was to get to those damned rocks and pray that whatever let them walk between worlds was still open. After Rodolphe's meeting with his messiah that long-ago night, she'd never wanted to set foot here again. She'd done it now because Ivy had asked her to.

This, however, was far more than she'd bargained for. She should have known it'd all blow up in her face. Fighting evil was tough, especially when it involved always keeping low so humans didn't get wind of what was happening around them. The regular folks in society just didn't want to know about those who lived in the shadow lands. No vampires. No werewolves. No witches. No nothing but plain old human beings.

What people wanted and what was reality were two very different things, and that's what kept them busy. Even so, on occasion she seemed to be signing on for trouble to come knocking. An invitation for a bit of an adrenaline high that she honestly didn't need. This was one of those instances.

Riah should have known better than to come back here. Her instincts were usually so much better than this. In Adriana-speak, she'd just screwed the pooch. Her decision to walk through the stones could end up costing everyone their lives. From all indications, instead of going home, she was leading them right straight into the hornet's nest.

What she realized and no one else probably knew was that the final battle for Vlad the Impaler was on Snagov Island on a wintery December day...just like this one. He was buried after the battle inside the Snagov Monastery just as he had fallen, headless and wearing the clothing she'd seen in the grave that long-ago day with Rodolphe—the same clothes she'd just glimpsed riding by.

Sometimes, her life really sucked.

Nicoletta ignored the growing pain in her leg. When they first mounted their horses and set off at a brisk pace, she had been unconcerned. The magic Lura had done worked and her foot felt better. Before long, though, the pain began to creep back in. Now, with Lura behind her, their bodies low to the horse and arrows winging past them, the pain grew with each pound of the horse's hooves on the hard earth.

Snow flew at their faces so fast it was like a winter blizzard coming in to blanket the land. As a child, she had loved the storms. She would sit by the fire, listening to the wind howl and sing outside, while her mother told her stories of love and adventure.

This snowstorm did not have the ferocity of any from her remembered childhood, and yet this one felt more menacing than any of those she could recall. Perhaps in her heart she understood that this one could be the last she ever rode through and certainly the last she would be one with the woman whose arms encircled her body. She prayed they would make Snagov Island before the soldiers caught up with them or, worse, before one of their arrows found its mark in Lura's heart.

She spurred their mount forward, praying for God's help in getting them to their journey's end. All she wanted, all she prayed for, was Lura's safe return to her own world. What happened to her no longer mattered.

Nighttime dropped quickly in the worsening storm, and for once she was grateful. With their heavy cloaks and their black horse, they could blend more easily into the dusky light.

"Are you hurt?" she asked Lura when she heard her gasp.

"No. But my butt's getting so sore I won't be able to sit for days if and when we ever get out of this mess."

Despite the terrible events around them, this remark made Nicoletta smile. She had grown up riding the horses her father kept in their large stables. She had ridden many times with her brother, and it was there, on the back of a horse, that she always felt most free. After her move to the Prince's castle, she would occasionally take one of the horses out for a brief ride in the countryside. It was far from the freedom of her youth, and she longed for a return to those carefree days. Still, each and every time she rode tall on a horse's back, she felt alive and happy.

Even if she made it out of this, and even if the Prince saw fit to spare her life, this was the last time she would ever ride a racing horse through the countryside. Once he had her in his thrall again, he would never allow her freedom. Upon her return to his castle, she would be his prisoner. If she lived.

He would not call her a prisoner. Oh, no, he would call himself her protector. That is what he professed to everyone. He committed each evil, deadly, and gruesome act in the name of his people. To protect them. Yet each time she wondered what he protected them from.

Bringing her head up to let the wet snow slap at her face, she pushed her dark thoughts away. They would make it to Snagov Island. Lura would go back to her world, where she would be safe and far from the Prince's reach. Nicoletta would live the rest of her life with memories of the woman who had opened her heart. It was enough because it had to be so.

After a little bit she realized the only sounds she heard any longer were the snorts of their horse and their own rapid breathing. The pounding of the men charging behind them had faded until there was nothing left to hear.

"Are they gone?" Lura asked, sitting up for the first time in a great long while.

Nicoletta also straightened and peered into the distance. "Perhaps."

"What do you think they're up to?"

At first she thought they had probably tired of chasing them in the storm but, as she thought about it, decided that was not what they would do. The Prince would not tolerate retreat. He would not do so, and he would expect his men to be as courageous as he. If they failed to show courage, his punishment for such a crime would be harsh. No, they were using strategy to capture them; she was certain of it. That is what she would do, and that is what they would have to do if they had any hope of completing their journey to the island alive.

"They will try to capture us as we reach the boat."

"Sucks to be us," Lura muttered.

Nicoletta smiled as she wiped melting snow from her face. Her cheeks, icy to the touch, were wet, yet she did not feel cold. Determination to get Lura to safety warmed her despite the winter storm that was making the sky deepen to a steely gray.

Much of what Lura said she did not understand, though listening to the sound of her voice and the strange words made her heart light. She wanted to remember every detail and every odd word for the long days and nights stretching ahead of her.

"I too have a plan. I do not wish for the soldiers to stop us."

She shivered at the thought of what could happen to them if they did. The men would return them to Dracula, but only after they had enjoyed the capture. What that meant sent dread into her heart. She would not permit that to happen. Men would fall before she would allow them to touch her beloved Lura.

Their race to evade the soldiers had helped them cover much ground. They were close now, but instead of heading to the spot where the boat waited to take them to the small island, she guided the horse much farther south. The trees were thick here and flowed nearly to the water's edge. Inside the trees, the snow cover was lighter and the wind barely moving at all. The protection they afforded was the cover Nicoletta wished for.

She winced as she dropped from the horse. A dull ache in her leg made it feel as heavy as stone, while her ankle throbbed as though someone was hitting it. She ignored it all. As long as she could still stand and walk, it was enough.

Reaching up she offered Lura her hand to help her down to the snow-covered ground. In the gloom they gazed out from the trees to the island beyond. The steeple of the monastery rose in the night as though it beckoned them. Perhaps it did.

She did not bother to tie the horse; she was not sure she would make it back. The horse should not be made to suffer if she was never to return. She patted its back end and it trotted off into the night, disappearing quickly from sight.

"Come." She put out her hand for Lura to take. "I do hope you can swim."

"Say what?" Lura stopped and stared at her. With the moon sending down shafts of golden light through the treetops, she could easily see the expression of confusion on Lura's face. It was only right. What Nicoletta proposed was madness, and yet it was the only way.

Nicoletta explained her idea, and while the confusion in Lura's face began to clear, concern took its place.

Shaking her head, Lura said, "We can't...it's far too cold to make that swim."

"We do not have another way. Here the island is the closest to land. It is our only chance to make it to the island without being seen."

Lura squinted and studied the water, still slowly shaking her head. "I don't know, Nicoletta. It seems like a suicide mission."

"Suicide?"

"Killing ourselves."

"Oh." She nodded, understanding Lura's concern. "Even if we perish, our souls will be safe. I do not ask this of you to end your life. I ask it to save you. They have our boat. They will be looking for any other boat that goes across the lake. If we are to survive, we must swim."

"You're a crazy woman, Nicoletta, though you do have a point. I just hope I can swim like a fish and get to shore before hypothermia sets in."

Once more Lura spoke words she did not know. All she did understand was the urgency, and of that she shared her concern. It did not slow her down. It could not. They had no more time. "Now, you must quickly disrobe."

Lura shrugged, apparently giving in to Nicoletta's arguments, and after fumbling with laces and yards of fabric, she discarded her gown much more quickly than Nicoletta. With creamy moonlight on her naked body, Nicoletta could almost forget they were in a race for their lives. She had never seen such a beautiful woman and never would again.

Once her gown was off, they bundled their garments up and laid them within a thicket of bushes so that unless one was hunting them, they wouldn't be found easily. Their footsteps were all over the ground, and anyone who put their head down to look would know they had been here. All she could hope for was that the falling snow would hide their movements before anyone riding by came to look.

Without waiting to think about what they needed to do, she took Lura's hand in hers and walked rapidly across the snow-covered ground. Sending up a prayer to God for their safe delivery on dry land, she stepped to the water. Silently they both slipped into the frigid lake and, after the initial shock of the icy water enveloping bare skin, began to swim.

CHAPTER TWENTY-SEVEN

They were running out of time. Once Dracula and his followers were gone, Riah kissed Adriana hard and then urged her horse to go faster. They couldn't hang around here a minute more than absolutely necessary. Fate wouldn't smile on them much longer.

"I don't have a good feeling about this," Ivy said, bringing her horse close to Riah.

Riah couldn't agree more. "This is too close to his death."

"Dracula?"

Riah nodded. "He's going to die soon, and trust me. It's not going to be pretty. I don't want to be anywhere close when blood begins to flow. We've got to get back to the stones and return to our own time."

"As sick as the thought of leaving without Lura makes me, I'm with you on this one. I don't like the feel of this place, and I sure as heck don't like the way Colin's looking. He's holding it together, bless his soul. I just don't know how much longer he can before he collapses. We've got to get back home."

"We better ride hard and beat them to the boat."

"Right behind you."

The relief she felt at hearing Ivy's words was immense. Under any other circumstances, she'd fight against leaving any relative of one of the Spiritus Group in a strange land and would be devastated by the resulting sense of failure. Despite that, if it meant saving the lives of others, she'd do it. If they stayed here, four of them would go down. As it was, their chance of making it back seemed to be getting slimmer by the second, and Colin was fading with each passing moment.

As they neared the lake, the sounds of their aggressors drifted to them on the wind. Deep night cloaked them, while the snow muffled the pounding of the horses' hooves. She didn't glance behind to see where Dracula and his soldiers converged. She kept her eyes locked on the lake and beyond to the island that offered their only chance at salvation.

It was a given, even without looking, that Dracula would have commandeered the small boat they'd used to cross the lake earlier. He might not know they were coming here, but it wouldn't matter. He would make certain no one could advance on his rear. God, she hoped they could find another boat somewhere on the shore.

Weaving in and around trees, they all scanned as they rode, searching for a boat that could take them across the lake. Surely they'd find one somewhere.

"What's this?" Ivy slipped from her horse and hurried over to some snow-covered bushes.

Riah's concentration was so intent on the shores of the lake she hadn't noticed whatever it was that caught Ivy's attention. Footprints, many of them, not quite covered up by new snow. Not just footprints, but women's, judging by their size.

"What on earth…" Ivy held up beautiful dresses, one in each hand. "This doesn't look right. They're not soaked through."

Meaning, of course, they'd been tucked into the bushes recently. She reined in her horse and stared at the clothing Ivy held. She'd lived in these times, and people did not, wealthy or poor, toss good clothing into the forest. Ivy was dead-on; something wasn't right here at all.

"Something's rotten in Denmark," Adriana said as she rode up next to Riah.

"No kidding," she whispered, a chill of foreboding washing through her entire body. "We've got to move and get to that island *now*."

Gazing over at Colin, her resolve strengthened. The fight to stay alert and involved was taking a toll on him. No more time. They had to get him back to their reality where he could receive proper medical attention. She couldn't do much more for him here than they already had. Once they were back and on the Learjet home, she'd be able to do so much more. He'd be himself soon…if they could escape from the nightmare they'd unwittingly stepped into.

For no reason Riah could figure, Adriana rolled up the dresses and took them with her. In her mind, the move was unnecessary, but then again, she wasn't going to second-guess her woman. Adriana had saved her ass more than once. Still, why bring them along? If everything came together, they'd be back home within hours.

A few hundred yards from where Adriana uncovered the clothing, Riah spied something bulky on the lakeshore. She spurred her horse and, risking exposure, burst out of the trees and onto the shoreline. Her heart was racing as fast as the horse's hooves. She sent up a quick prayer as she vaulted off her ride and ran over to a small boat tipped on its side and partially hidden by brush. It was intact and dry. Maybe God was on their side after all.

"Hurry," she told the other three as she grabbed hold of the side of the boat and righted it. Two oars clunked inside as it settled into the sandy beach. Plenty of room for the four of them. Her prayer had just been answered.

It took the three of them to get Colin down from the horse and into the boat. His pale face glowed in the gloom of night, reminding them how precious time was. Her nervousness increased tenfold the moment she touched his cool skin. He was a strong, strapping man, and this was so not like him. Tamping down worry was impossible, and, if she was concerned, Ivy had to be a wreck.

Once Ivy and Colin were in the boat, she and Adriana pushed it to the edge of the lake waters, trying to make as little noise as possible. Pulling her skirts up, she climbed inside right after Adriana. With one oar and a lot of strength, she freed the boat from the grip of the sand and they were on the water. Riah took both oars and quietly began to row the four hundred or so yards to the island…and the stones.

Hypothermia was the thought that roared through Lura's mind with each painful stroke of her arms. The water was so damn cold she could barely feel her fingertips. Her shoulder screamed in protest, the rotator-cuff injury she'd believed healed letting her know it wasn't. Knifing pain filled her chest every time she exhaled. She'd followed Nicoletta not because she thought it was a good idea, but because she didn't see a better option. Not to mention that Nicoletta wouldn't be deterred. She was clearly determined to go into the lake with or without Lura.

Frankly, Nicoletta was right. They were out of options. Good ones anyway. Dracula and his men seemed to be everywhere. They had their boat, they had weapons, and they were out for blood—specifically hers and Nicoletta's, judging by their determination to catch them. Two women, one of them injured, didn't stand much of a chance.

As painful as the swim was, she'd rather die from hypothermia than on one of Dracula's hideous stakes. So here she was, concentrating on making one stroke after another, pushing to cross a distance no longer than any one of the sprint triathlons she'd done over the last few years. The difference between those events and now was very clear: she'd never competed in a triathlon in a snowstorm in ice-cold water. What she wouldn't give for her wetsuit right now.

Hopefully God would be with them tonight and they'd make it without succumbing to the very real dangers of frigid water. So far so good. Of course, even if they made the swim, the island, like the mainland, was covered with snow, and both of them upon hitting land would still be naked as newborns. If the icy water didn't kill them, the snowstorm would.

Yes, they had a very good chance of dying tonight. Damn.

Something drew her attention away from the painful swim and toward what she thought could be a boat. She wasn't sure if hypothermia was beginning to set in because she thought she heard the *slap slap slap* of oars cutting through the water. If she wasn't hallucinating because of the cold, they might have just run out of luck.

More determined, she stroked faster. As easy as it would be to give up right now, she didn't have the heart to quit. She certainly didn't want Dracula or any of his men to discover them crossing the lake. The thought of what they would do to two naked women made her shudder.

Suddenly, her fingertips touched something. After a second, her mind sluggish from the cold and exertion, she registered what it was and wanted to scream. It was the bottom of the lake, and a shot of hope roared through her body, charging her with a last sudden burst of energy. Within a heartbeat she was standing, both feet on a rocky bottom, and beside her Nicoletta was struggling to her feet. Putting a hand under Nicoletta's elbow she steadied her as the two of them made it to shore.

She didn't stay standing for long, her relief at making the shore overshadowed by the realization they weren't alone. Lura dropped to a crouch and pulled Nicoletta down to her side. Both of them shivered so hard she wondered if they'd ever be able to stop.

Whispering shakily into Nicoletta's ear, she said, "A boat."

"Is it him?" Nicoletta's teeth were chattering and her body shook.

"I don't know, but if we can stay low and hold still maybe they won't see us."

In the murky light of the moon she could make out the shape of the boat nearing the shore. Despite her shivering, she was afraid to move, to give away their position. Their only hope was to stay invisible.

The boat thumped onto the shore fifty feet away, but rather than sounding like men looking for battle, the occupants slipped out of the boat in near silence. Only then did she notice something quite odd: it appeared that women powered the vessel to shore. Possibly she was hallucinating because she wanted so badly to be safe. Whatever it was, it still looked like women to her, except for the tall, slouched-over figure the smaller ones helped out of the boat. That one was definitely a man.

As she watched, one woman turned and moonlight caught her full-on, revealing her face. Shock rippled through Lura's quaking body. That face was one she'd known all her life: the small stature, the jet-black wavy hair, the full lips that she'd seen stretched into smiles so many times. Take away the period gown, throw on a pair of jeans and a sweatshirt, and it would be…

But it couldn't be. Impossible under any circumstances.

"Ivy?" The name rattled through her chattering lips in a cry full of trembling hope. Her mind might reject it, as hypothermia evoked vision. Her heart did not.

For a second she didn't think anyone heard her thready voice, and then the woman whose face she'd glimpsed in the moonlight turned and cocked her head. Again, louder this time, Lura managed to ask, "Ivy?"

Another voice floated across the night air, as if coming from far away. "Lura?"

Pushing to her feet, she still held onto Nicoletta's hand. Funny, it even sounded like her cousin. It had to be an hallucination. No way could Ivy be here. Only Mom knew she'd gone to Snagov Island. They certainly wouldn't know about the stones. Face it, she thought, the lake had won. She was succumbing to the cold and imagining the comforting arms of her favorite cousin.

The voice came again, stronger this time. "LURA!"

If she was going to die, this was a nice way to go—holding on to Nicoletta and with Ivy's voice in her head. Then everything happened as if in slow motion. The women who had stepped out of the boat turned and began to race down the beach in their direction. It wasn't a dream and she wasn't imagining it. She didn't know how and she certainly didn't know why, but Ivy was here. She wanted to jump up and down, wave for them to hurry, but her feet wouldn't move. Just standing took every ounce of her willpower.

Nicoletta, still crouched near the ground, gave a small sigh. Then her grasp on Lura's hand weakened and dropped. With a soft thud, she toppled to the sand, her body still as death. No, no, no, they were so close. Lura peered back toward the running figures, trying to see clearly, to make out the faces of the women racing their way. Like Nicoletta, her body failed her. Her eyes closed and her legs gave way. She crumpled to the sand next to Nicoletta, throwing one arm over her lover's body on the snow-covered beach.

CHAPTER TWENTY-EIGHT

O h my God," Ivy cried as she dropped beside the two women motionless on the shore, their naked bodies so white and cold they almost blended in with the snow. Her head turned up to Riah with a mixture of disbelief, relief, and fright all showing on her expressive face. "It's Lura."

Riah was busy ripping her cloak off and wrapping it around the smaller of the two women. Ivy followed suit and soon had her cousin enfolded inside her sheepskin cloak. The shaking began seconds after she had her covered up. Even through the thick wool, Lura's body shook uncontrollably. Not a good sign.

"What was she thinking?" Ivy muttered as she cradled Lura in her arms. "She had to know they couldn't survive a swim in waters this cold." She kissed the side of her head.

Riah wondered the same thing. They'd been lucky to make it through the swim in this weather and still be conscious when they got here. If they hadn't seen them, the two wouldn't have had any chance to survive. As it was, they had to get them warm before hypothermia did its worst and they lost them anyway.

"Let's carry them to the monastery," Riah said. It was the closest building and, while perhaps not warm, was certainly warmer than where they were now.

Colin leaned down and tried to pick up Lura's companion. A hiss escaped from between his lips, and he crumpled to one knee. In the moonlight, Riah could see the sweat that popped out on his forehead. Adriana stepped in and put a hand on his shoulder. "We've got this."

He shook his head, a frown creasing his forehead. "This is so fucked up," he muttered, but didn't stand in Adriana's way. Riah knew then how badly he was hurt.

Keeping to the shadows as best they could, they managed to get the two freezing women to a back door of the monastery. The difference in temperature was immediate, though to say it was warm inside would have been a stretch. Still, it was enough. At least there was no wind or snow, and, best of all, it was dry.

"We need to find some food," Riah told Adriana, who nodded and set off.

Riah wasn't hungry, none of them were, but the sooner calories entered the body and began to generate heat from the inside, the better chance the person had to survive hypothermia. It was time to jumpstart their internal furnaces.

Both began to come around as their bodies warmed inside the heavy cloaks. Lura and Ivy both cried, and when Lura's teeth stopped chattering so fiercely, she introduced them to Nicoletta.

By the time Adriana returned with a bottle of wine and some bread, Lura and Nicoletta were once more dressed, with Riah's help. It took some serious coaxing to get food down them. Neither one wanted to cooperate. Patience won the day and finally Riah got them to eat. A little wine and some bread brought a bit of color back into their pasty white faces. For the most part, the uncontrollable shaking subsided. Riah expelled a sigh of relief.

"We don't have long," she told them. As much as she hated the thought of Lura and Nicoletta moving after experiencing a near-fatal swim, they didn't have much choice. They were on borrowed time as it was. It was either make a run for the stones and hope for the best or stay here and die at Dracula's hand. He was on his way. They might have managed to slip by him this time, but they probably wouldn't get a second chance. The island wasn't that big.

She wasn't really up for a date with Dracula's sword. Her time with Adriana had been short so far, and she didn't intend to give up easily. She wanted decades more time with her and would fight for that right if she had to. She had to leave this century and return to her own. They didn't belong here, and that fact was made abundantly clear to her each and every second they remained.

Nobody else was arguing the point either. Not that she was terribly surprised. After all, what was there to argue? Colin had to feel like he'd been through a war already, and in many ways he had been. If Lura and Nicoletta were willing to risk a naked swim through frigid waters to reach the stones, she had to believe they were more than ready to dash for safety.

She just wanted to get home and see the faces of all of the Spiritus Group—Cam and Kara, Naomi and Tory. To all be together again. Right fucking now.

"Okay then," she said as she slipped her cloak back on. "We have to be careful. This is the night it all comes crashing down. We'll have to make one hard race for the stones, and rest assured, we won't get a second chance."

"The night?" Lura asked, a confused look on her face. "I don't understand what you mean."

There wasn't time to stop for a history lesson, even a short one. "Dracula isn't going to make it another day, and we want to be long gone when everything breaks loose here."

Nicoletta, who was putting her cloak back on, paused and looked at Riah. "The Prince is going to die this night?"

Riah nodded. "And it's not going to be pretty."

"If he dies then we have nothing to be afraid of." Her face turned hopeful. "We do not have to hurry. We can hide and wait for his death."

Riah shook her head. "He dies, but we don't belong here and it wouldn't be safe for us to stay. You can, if you'd like. We have to go."

"No!" Lura spit out the word with such force, they all turned to stare at her. She said in a calmer voice, "She has to go with us. Just trust me on this. I can't leave her behind. It's important."

Ivy put an arm around her shoulders and hugged her. "If you want her to come with us, she can do that, but we still have to make tracks or none of us will get there in time. I, for one, don't want that to happen. I'm all for going home."

Lura turned to Nicoletta and put her hands on her face. "You must come with me, please."

Riah knew that look and that tone of voice. She felt the same way about Adriana. Whether Lura or Nicoletta knew the significance yet was hard to say. Nobody else in their small group would misunderstand, however, since each of them had discovered love in their own way. Not a single one of them was willing to let it go. Nicoletta was coming home with them to the twenty-first century.

Nicoletta seemed to study Lura's face for a long time, her eyes deep and serious. Her indecision was clear, and yet after a moment, her expression cleared and she nodded. "I will go."

That was all Riah needed to hear. She started for the door. "Come on," she urged them. "Let's go. This place is making me very nervous."

Outside, the sound of movement through the storm hardened her resolve. It sounded like a hundred soldiers marched in the direction of the monastery, their pounding feet making the ground shake. Time was up, the clock had just struck midnight. It was now or never.

Colin took the lead. Though the injury had to hurt him with each step, he raced forward with a determination she'd come to admire. He'd had so many of his own challenges in life, and yet he'd survived them all. Like her, Riah didn't think he'd give in. When he did die, he'd do it kicking and screaming all the way. He would not, as poet Dylan Thomas wrote, "go gentle into that good night."

This wasn't his time to die because he wanted his life with Ivy and wasn't going to let some fifteenth-century monster take it away from him. Just another thing Riah found to admire about him.

Following each other closely, they trudged determinedly through the ever-thickening snow. The storm was picking up steam, as if feeding off the intensity of the coming battle. They paid it no mind. Instead, heads down, they powered through the storm, refusing to look back, refusing to let the encroaching soldiers keep them from their destination.

The rocks grew larger the closer they came, and Riah's heart began to beat with welcome anticipation. They were so close, so terribly close to going home. She started to allow room for a little relief that they were going to make it in one piece.

Except it occurred to her quite suddenly that something wasn't right. The roar she'd heard from between the stones when they'd come through the first time was silent on this side. The low rumble she expected to hear simply wasn't there. It should be growing louder and stronger as they edged closer, and yet with each advancing step, the silence became more frightening. *Oh God, please don't let it be closed.*

At the gap between the stones where not so long ago they'd walked from one time to into another, she stopped and stared. Nothing but bottomless black stillness. Panic had her hands trembling, and though she tried to make words come, nothing would pass her lips. Her throat was dry and her eyes stung.

So this was how it was all going to end.

"Step aside, sister." Adriana pushed her sideways with an unexpectedly powerful thrust. "The wizard is on deck."

"What…"

Adriana rolled her eyes. "You know, for a pretty smart chick, sometimes you're kinda dense. I mean, seriously, how quickly you forget. Tell you what, you just stand there and be beautiful. I'll do all the heavy lifting."

Riah was so astonished she did just that. Adriana held her hands out toward the gap in the rocks and her eyes narrowed in concentration. Her lips moved, but her words were too low to make out in the swirling snowstorm. For a moment nothing happened, and then slowly a tremor began to shake the earth at her feet. The thunder below grew, and as it did the stones began to sing. Soon the song became a cacophony and the world opened up to them.

That was her woman, so full of magic and always ready to embrace the impossible that she could open a doorway between dimensions. And, yes, Adriana was right-on as usual; she'd forgotten what the love of her very long life could do.

Colin stepped forward first and stood staring into the blackness at the entrance to the stones. Turning his head, he squared his shoulders and then held out his hand to Ivy. She took it and together they stepped through and disappeared. One moment they were there, the next swallowed by a blanket of infinite darkness. Adriana, Lura, and Nicoletta followed at her insistence. Only she now remained at the yawning opening where her friends had once been. She should rush through; after all, that's what they'd been pushing toward, and yet something held her back. Riah stood at the edge of the stones with a view of the meadow beyond, the roar of the dimensional doorway background music to the portrait of a world she didn't belong in.

"There you are, you bitch!"

Riah heard his voice just as she stepped to the edge of the rock formation, only an inch away from the portal that would take her home. She didn't move. As Dracula charged, his face a mask of fury, she stood her ground, feet apart and eyes wide open. How had he gotten so close to her in such a short amount of time? Was fate bringing them nose to nose?

Still, she didn't move. Her hand strayed to the sword Colin had taken from the soldier earlier that night, the finely forged metal cold and lethal. Her fingers stroked the hilt, her mind racing. Adriana was safe, her friends were safe. Nothing else mattered but making sure they survived…and ending this once and for all.

Dracula's scream made her turn once more. His arms were stretched toward her, his eyes black and filled with rage. She returned his gaze for one moment and then made a decision.

She jumped through the stones. The roar of the wormhole drowned out most sound…except for that of the man known as Vlad the Impaler. His scream didn't fade, and with a feeling of total synchronization with the universe, she understood why.

He'd followed her.

Nicoletta did not understand what had just happened. One moment she was standing at the rocks near the monastery at Snagov Island, and the next, she tumbled through some long, shadow-filled place only to once more stand upon the island's grounds. Except it was not right. It looked the same and yet was different.

"What has happened?" she asked as she took Lura's hand and held it tight. Her heart was beating very hard. She had heard the Prince and his men pounding after them and was certain they were going to die. They had been so close she could make out the voices of those loyal soldiers she knew, and now she heard nothing but the sounds of their own breathing.

After a moment, the woman called Riah came tumbling through the rocks screaming, "He's following me."

Nicoletta did not pause or even give thought to what she was about to do. Moving on pure instinct, she let go of Lura's hand and raced to the tall man's side. In one hand he carried a sword, and she ripped it from his fingers, not breaking from her run. At the edge of the stones where Riah had just tumbled through, she raised the sword high above her head with both hands.

Like something only magic could make happen, his head appeared first. She did not hesitate; with all the power she could summon, Nicoletta brought the sword down. His severed head hit the ground with a thump, rolling until it came to rest at her feet, his dull, lifeless eyes staring skyward. She waited for his body to follow. It never came.

Nicoletta peered between the now-silent rocks. Nothing. No body. No sound. No magic. Only the dead, staring eyes of the man they had called the son of the dragon.

"Son of a bitch," Colin muttered. "Way to shut that fucker down."

Nicoletta crumpled to the ground, her burst of strength leaving her as quickly as it had given her courage. What she had just done hit her with the force of a giant rock: she had killed the Prince. Now, they would come for her. She would join her brother on the pointed end of a stake.

Lura seemed to sense the turmoil filling her heart. She kneeled next to her and kissed her head. "You're safe here, I promise."

"I killed him." Her words were hollow, lifeless.

Lura laughed and Nicoletta's head snapped around. Was she daft? Did she not understand what happened to people like her? She had just signed her own death warrant. Though the Prince was dead, his supporters were not. They would come for her.

Lura's bright eyes never wavered. "You'll never see him or his people again. You're in my home now."

Slowly Lura's words started to settle and Nicoletta began to see, began to understand the whole of the prophecy. She thought of Alexandru's words and how he had spoken of the woman who would come from the future to save them from the madness of the Prince's actions. Never did the words of the prophecy say that Lura was the one who would kill the Prince. Only that she was the one who would bring to them salvation.

Now she understood.

She put her hand in Lura's and rose to her feet. Glancing back at the stones, she felt a pull to return. Then she recalled that she had nothing in her old life to go back to. No family, no home. No future.

The prophecy had been fulfilled. She had done her part, Alexandru had done his, including giving his life. All she had now was tomorrow in a new world and with a woman who made her heart sing.

Yes, she still carried the child of Dracula in her womb, and she could live with that for the child was also a part of her. In this world, in this place, both she and the child would have the liberty to love and to be loved. No one would know of the father. No one would know his sins. They were both free.

Kissing Lura deeply, she sighed and said, "I'm hungry."

CHAPTER TWENTY-NINE

Nicoletta was constantly amazed by the wonders of Lura's world. Even now as she lay naked on the big bed in the room so warm and comfortable without a fire, she was astounded. She liked it. Very much.

The door to the bathroom—another modern wonder—opened, and Lura came out. The light behind her highlighted her tall, slender figure. She was beautiful, and just the sight of her made Nicoletta's heart race.

Never in her wildest dreams did she see herself living out her life so incredibly happy. Yesterday, the most wondrous of things happened: she married Lura. She was married, to the person she loved, and that was something she had no way of believing possible for her.

So many exciting things in this place. Every day she learned of something new and wonderful. When Lura had asked her to marry, Nicoletta had not understood. How could it be? Lura had smiled and explained to her that the right for two women to marry was new, although it was perfectly fine. The laws in this place were made by the people, not a prince or other person of royal birth, and the people had decreed that two women could marry. She had been thrilled and readied herself for promising her love to Lura for the rest of her days. Everyone around them shared in their happiness, and she had never known such a perfect day.

And each day her love for Lura grew deeper and more true.

"Hey." Lura smiled from the doorway. "You look like you're thinking about something really hard. Got something on your mind, beautiful?"

Nicoletta smiled back, loving the way the sound of her voice warmed her from head to foot. "I am thinking of you and how happy I am. How much I love you." She smiled even more brightly. "I am thinking that loving you is the most wonderful thing ever."

Lura pushed away from the doorway and came over to the bed, where she lay down next to Nicoletta. Lura's hand stroked her leg and Nicoletta sighed. She would never tire of that gentle touch.

"You're not the only one," Lura told her, returning her smile. "I'm surprised every day how just being with you makes everything perfect. You're the best thing to ever come out of the fifteenth or twenty-first centuries."

Nicoletta rolled close and kissed Lura deeply. The beautiful words that came from her lover were like love songs that she never wearied of. She moved her hands to Lura's breasts and filled her palms with them. Her heart hammered and she pressed closer. Even if she lived a thousand years, it would not be enough.

EPILOGUE

Riah stood, along with Ivy, Colin, Tory, and Naomi, staring at Adriana as she sat at one of the long tables in her lab. She'd summoned them all with a "get your ass down here" command. Nobody dared to disregard that kind of directive. So here they all were waiting to hear her big news.

It had been two months since they'd returned from Romania with Lura and Nicoletta in tow. Colin had healed nicely once they'd gotten him the proper care, and they'd even had a wedding for Lura and Nicoletta.

It was an understatement to say that Lura's marriage shocked a lot of folks. First, because it hadn't been that long since she'd lost Vic, and some people took great offense at that. They were the minority, however, because more seemed genuinely shocked that she'd married a woman.

Lura had been exceptionally skilled at hiding her true feelings, and no one close to her, with the exception of Ivy, had any inkling of the inner self she kept buried from the world. When she finally let go of her fear and dared to stand for what was right for her, love opened the door to a new and wonderful relationship. Riah was very happy for both women.

Adriana, on the other hand, had gone directly downstairs and holed up in her lab the minute they got home. Before they'd left Romania, they'd made sure Dracula's head disappeared, easy enough to do with a cemetery on the island. One little hole on the edge of the place and *poof*...head gone. No one was the wiser, although she now understood why the body she and Rodolphe had seen on that long-ago night was headless. Made her smile to think of it now.

The only trace of him that remained was in a glass vial. Adriana had insisted she wasn't leaving Europe without a sample of the man's blood, and as usual, she was right. Her justification had to do with a theory about the phenomenon of the daylight Riah and Ivy had enjoyed while in the fifteenth century. It didn't carry through upon their return, and life had gotten back to what passed as their norm. The why and the how had made her tiny beauty start thinking, though, and they'd barely seen her out of the lab since.

After weeks of spending a zillion hours downstairs, Adriana looked like the cat that ate the mouse. To say she glowed wasn't much of an exaggeration. Still, when Riah looked deep into her eyes, she saw something unsettling. She wasn't sure what it was. Fear? Sadness?

Adriana finally got down to the purpose of the call to conference. "I've got some great news and some not-so-great news."

Riah stroked a hand across her head. "Tell us the good news first."

Adriana's expression brightened. "It was him all along. I had a hunch when we were back there, but it wasn't until I got home that I could prove it. It's all about the blood, baby. Specifically, Dracula's blood."

"I'm not following," Colin said, and the rest of them nodded.

"The blood," Adriana repeated, as if it should be obvious. When nobody nodded in agreement with her, she sighed. "Dracula, he was the godfather, so to speak. You know, Riah, that was why Rodolphe was so jacked up to go to Romania and find Dracula's final burial spot. It's why the sunlight couldn't hurt you when we were there. You were in the presence of the one."

Riah shook her head. "Rodolphe was my maker, not Dracula. None of us have anything to do with him. The blood argument doesn't hold up, at least where we're concerned."

"Nope, wrongo, girlo! On my mother's grave, he was the key."

"Pretty strong words. You don't usually swear on your mother."

"And for good reason. It's because I got it, baby. I fucking got it! I found it again."

The pride on Adriana's face made a believer out of Riah. She knew what her beautiful lover was capable of. Her mind was incredible, and she'd believed deeply ever since Adriana's house had blown up, along with the cure she'd discovered, that she'd find it again. A detailed explanation, she didn't need, because she knew exactly what Adriana had found.

She'd hoped and prayed for a chance at being human again. Now at last, here it was. Her chance. Yet something still lingered in Adriana's eyes that made her wonder if all was as it seemed.

"What's the catch?"

Adriana sighed, and the brightness faded from her face. "I only had enough to make the cure for two of you." She looked from face to face, her eyes incredibly sad and suddenly filling with tears that spilled down her cheeks. "I'm sorry," she whispered. "I'm so, so sorry."

Silence fell heavy over the room, where only moments before, hope and anticipation had been a bright light. Riah didn't hesitate and didn't stop to second-guess. She owed them, all of them, and she would do the only thing she could.

"Cure Ivy and Tory."

They all started talking at once, and Riah held up her hand, warding off their words. Her smile was real and from her heart. She let her gaze flow from one startled face to another. "You have all given me so much. I never thought I'd have a real life again, and you gifted it to me without reservation or condition. You didn't see me as a horrible creature but as a friend. You've been here for me as no one in my very long years has ever been, and for that I can never thank you enough. This is all I have to give back to you. Please understand that I have to do this."

She could see the struggle in the faces that stared back at her and understood it all too well. They were in this together and had been for long enough to become a family. No one had ever had her back before, and now they all did. She was so proud and so humbled she wanted to cry.

She turned and settled her gaze on the one who was the most important to her in all the world. It didn't matter what anyone else thought or said. It all came down to Adriana. As their eyes met, she saw a look that made her heart melt.

Adriana touched her face and gave her the tiniest of nods. "You're sure." It wasn't a question. She knew her too well.

She nodded in return. "I'm sure."

Giving Riah a big hug and a kiss, Adriana then turned around and faced Ivy and Tory, a big grin lighting up her face. "Okay, bitches, you heard my woman. Belly up to the bar and rejoin the human race."

About the Author

Sheri Lewis Wohl grew up in northeast Washington State, and though she always thought she'd move away, never has. Despite traveling throughout the United States, Sheri always finds her way back home. And so she lives, plays, and writes amidst mountains, evergreens, and abundant wildlife. When not working the day job in federal finance, she writes stories that typically include a bit of the strange and unusual and always a touch of romance. In addition to being a member of a local K9 Search & Rescue team, she works to carve out time to swim, bike, and run so she can participate in triathlons.

Books Available from Bold Strokes Books

Desire at Dawn by Fiona Zedde. For Kylie, love had always come armed with sharp teeth and claws. But with the human, Olivia, she bares her vampire heart for the very first time, sharing passion, lust, and a tenderness she'd never dared dreamed of before. (978-1-62639-064-5)

Visions by Larkin Rose. Sometimes the mysteries of love reveal themselves when you least expect it. Other times they hide behind a black satin mask. Can Paige unveil her masked stranger this time? (978-1-62639-065-2)

All In by Nell Stark. Internet poker champion Annie Navarro loses everything when the Feds shut down online gambling, and she turns to experienced casino host Vesper Blake for advice—but can Nova convince Vesper to take a gamble on romance? (978-1-62639-066-9)

Vermilion Justice by Sheri Lewis Wohl. What's a vampire to do when Dracula is no longer just a character in a novel? (978-1-62639-067-6)

Switchblade by Carsen Taite. Lines were meant to be crossed. Third in the Luca Bennett Bounty Hunter Series. (978-1-62639-058-4)

Nightingale by Andrea Bramhall. Culture, faith, and duty conspire to tear two young lovers apart, yet fate seems to have different plans for them both. (978-1-62639-059-1)

No Boundaries by Donna K. Ford. A chance meeting and a nightmare from the past threaten more than Andi Massey's solitude as she and Gwen Palmer struggle to understand the complexity of love without boundaries. (978-1-62639-060-7)

Sacred Fire by Tanai Walker. Tinsley Swann is cursed to change into a beast for seven days, every seven years. When she meets Leda, she comes face-to-face with her past. (978-1-62639-061-4)

Queerly Beloved: A Love Story Across Gender by Diane and Jacob Anderson-Minshall. How We Survived Four Weddings, One Gender Transition, and Twenty-Two Years of Marriage. (978-1-62639-062-1)

Frenemy of the People by Nora Olsen. Clarissa and Lexie have despised each other as long as they can remember, but when they both find themselves helping an unlikely contender for homecoming queen, they are catapulted into an unexpected romance. (978-1-62639-063-8)

Timeless by Rachel Spangler. When Stevie Geller returns to her hometown, will she do things differently the second time around or will she be in such a hurry to leave her past that she misses out on a better future? (978-1-62639-050-8)

Second to None by L.T. Marie. Can a physical therapist and a custom motorcycle designer conquer their pasts and build a future with one another? (978-1-62639-051-5)

Seneca Falls by Jesse Thoma. Together, two women discover love truly can conquer all evil. (978-1-62639-052-2)

A Kingdom Lost by Barbara Ann Wright. Without knowing each other's fate, Princess Katya and her consort Starbride seek to reclaim their kingdom from the magic-wielding madman who seized the throne and is murdering their people. (978-1-62639-053-9)

Uncommon Romance by Jove Belle. Sometimes sex is just sex, and sometimes it's the only way to say "I love you." (978-1-62639-057-7)

The Heat of Angels by Lisa Girolami. Fires burn in more than one place in Los Angeles. (978-1-62639-042-3)

Season of the Wolf by Robin Summers. Two women running from their pasts are thrust together by an unimaginable evil. Can they overcome the horrors that haunt them in time to save each other? (978-1-62639-043-0)

Desperate Measures by P. J. Trebelhorn. Homicide detective Kay Griffith and contractor Brenda Jansen meet amidst turmoil neither of them is aware of until murder suspect Tommy Rayne makes his move to exact revenge on Kay. (978-1-62639-044-7)

The Magic Hunt by L.L. Raand. With her Pack being hunted by human extremists and beset by enemies masquerading as friends, can Sylvan protect them and her mate, or will she succumb to the feral rage that threatens to turn her rogue, destroying them all? A Midnight Hunters novel. (978-1-62639-045-4)

Waiting for the Violins by Justine Saracen. After surviving Dunkirk, a scarred and embittered British nurse returns to Nazi-occupied Brussels to join the Resistance, and finds that nothing is fair in love and war (978-1-62639-046-1)

Because of Her by KE Payne. When Tabby Morton is forced to move to London, she's convinced her life will never be the same again. But the beautiful and intriguing Eden Palmer is about to show her that this time, change is most definitely for the better. (978-1-62639-049-2)

Wingspan by Karis Walsh. Wildlife biologist Bailey Chase is content to live at the wild bird sanctuary she has created on Washington's Olympic Peninsula until she is lured beyond the safety of isolation by architect Kendall Pearson. (978-1-60282-983-1)

Tumbledown by Cari Hunter. After surviving their ordeal in the North Cascades, Alex and Sarah have new identities and a new home, but a chance occurrence threatens everything: their freedom and their lives. (978-1-62639-085-0)

Night Bound by Winter Pennington. Kass struggles to keep her head, her heart, and her relationships in order. She's still having a difficult time accepting being an Alpha female. But her wolf is certain of what she wants and she's intent on securing her power. (978-1-60282-984-8)

Slash and Burn by Valerie Bronwen. The murder of a roundly despised author at an LGBT writer's conference in New Orleans turns Winter Lovelace's relaxing weekend hobnobbing with her peers into a nightmare of suspense—especially when her ex turns up. (978-1-60282-986-2)

The Blush Factor by Gun Brooke. Ice-cold business tycoon Eleanor Ashcroft only cares about the three P's—Power, Profit, and Prosperity—until young Addison Garr makes her doubt both that and the state of her frostbitten heart. (978-1-60282-985-5)

The Quickening: A Sisters of Spirits Novel by Yvonne Heidt. Ghosts, visions, and demons are all in a day's work for Tiffany. But when Kat asks for help on a serial killer case, life takes on another dimension altogether. (978-1-60282-975-6)

Windigo Thrall by Cate Culpepper. Six women trapped in a mountain cabin by a blizzard, stalked by an ancient cannibal demon bent on stealing their sanity—and their lives. (978-1-60282-950-3)

Smoke and Fire by Julie Cannon. Oil and water, passion and desire, a combustible combination. Can two women fight the fire that draws them together and threatens to keep them apart? (978-1-60282-977-0)

Asher's Fault by Elizabeth Wheeler. Fourteen-year-old Asher Price sees the world in black and white, much like the photos he takes, but when his little brother drowns at the same moment Asher experiences his first same-sex kiss, he can no longer hide behind the lens of his camera and eventually discovers he isn't the only one with a secret. (978-1-60282-982-4)

Love and Devotion by Jove Belle. KC Hall trips her way through life, stumbling into an affair with a married bombshell twice her age. Thankfully, her best friend, Emma Reynolds, is there to show her the true meaning of Love and Devotion. (978-1-60282-965-7)

Rush by Carsen Taite. Murder, secrets, and romance combine to create the ultimate rush. (978-1-60282-966-4)

The Shoal of Time by J.M. Redmann. It sounded too easy. Micky Knight is reluctant to take the case because the easy ones often turn into the hard ones, and the hard ones turn into the dangerous ones. In this one, easy turns hard without warning. (978-1-60282-967-1)

In Between by Jane Hoppen. At the age of 14, Sophie Schmidt discovers that she was born an intersexual baby and sets off on a journey to find her place in a world that denies her true existence. (978-1-60282-968-8)

Secret Lies by Amy Dunne. While fleeing from her abuser, Nicola Jackson bumps into Jenny O'Connor, and their unlikely friendship quickly develops into a blossoming romance—but when it comes down to a matter of life or death, are they both willing to face their fears? (978-1-60282-970-1)

Under Her Spell by Maggie Morton. The magic of love brought Terra and Athene together, but now a magical quest stands between them—a quest for Athene's hand in marriage. Will their passion keep them together, or will stronger magic tear them apart? (978-1-60282-973-2)

Homestead by Radclyffe. R. Clayton Sutter figures getting NorthAm Fuel's newest refinery operational on a rolling tract of land in Upstate New York should take a month or two, but then, she hadn't counted on local resistance in the form of vandalism, petitions, and one furious farmer named Tess Rogers. (978-1-60282-956-5)

Battle of Forces: Sera Toujours by Ali Vali. Kendal and Piper return to New Orleans to start the rest of eternity together, but the return of an old enemy makes their peaceful reunion short-lived, especially when they join forces with the new queen of the vampires. (978-1-60282-957-2)

How Sweet It Is by Melissa Brayden. Some things are better than chocolate. Molly O'Brien enjoys her quiet life running the bakeshop in a small town. When the beautiful Jordan Tuscana returns home, Molly can't deny the attraction—or the stirrings of something more. (978-1-60282-958-9)

The Missing Juliet: A Fisher Key Adventure by Sam Cameron. A teenage detective and her friends search for a kidnapped Hollywood star in the Florida Keys. (978-1-60282-959-6)

Amor and More: Love Everafter edited by Radclyffe and Stacia Seaman. Rediscover favorite couples as Bold Strokes Books authors reveal glimpses of life and love beyond the honeymoon in short stories featuring main characters from favorite BSB novels. (978-1-60282-963-3)

First Love by CJ Harte. Finding true love is hard enough, but for Jordan Thompson, daughter of a conservative president, it's challenging, especially when that love is a female rodeo cowgirl. (978-1-60282-949-7)

Pale Wings Protecting by Lesley Davis. Posing as a couple to investigate the abduction of infants, Special Agent Blythe Kent and Detective Daryl Chandler find themselves drawn into a battle over the innocents, with demons on one side and the unlikeliest of protectors on the other. (978-1-60282-964-0)

boldstrokesbooks.com

Bold Strokes Books

Quality and Diversity in LGBTQ Literature

victory
EDITIONS

Drama

MATINEE BOOKS

E-BOOKS

SCI-FI

MYSTERY

erotica

EROTICA

YOUNG
ADULT

BOLD
STROKES
BOOKS

LIBERTY

Romance

W·E·B·S·T·O·R·E

PRINT AND EBOOKS